Edward de Vere, 17th Earl of Oxford, born 1550.
For those who have studied the evidence, he is the true Shakespeare.

The
Which of
Shakespeare's
Why

The
Which of
Shakespeare's
Why

A NOVEL OF THE AUTHORSHIP MYSTERY
NEAR SOLUTION TODAY

LEIGH LIGHT

CITY POINT PRESS

Hardcover ISBN 978-1-947951-68-6

eBook ISBN 978-1-947951-69-3

Cover design by Barnaby Conrad III

Printed in the United States of America

Published by

City Point Press

PO Box 2063

Westport CT 06880

(203) 571-0781

www.citypointpress.com

To my dear wife Susan.

SHAKESPEARE SPEAKS TO POSTERITY

Horatio, I am dead; thou liv'st.
  Report me and my cause aright to the unsatisfied.

O God, Horatio, what a wounded name,
    Things standing thus unknown, shall live behind me!
If thou didst ever hold me in your heart,
Absent thee from felicity awhile,
    And in this harsh world draw thy breath in pain
To tell my story.

Hamlet, Mr. Trouble and Troubled,
The Tragedy of Hamlet

Guilty creatures sitting at a play
Have by the very cunning of the scene
Been struck so to the soul that presently
They have proclaim'd their malefactions.

Hamlet, at least it was a plan.

I have had a dream past the wit of man
to say what dream it was.

Bottom, not always a clown,
A Midsummer Night's Dream

William Shakespeare is the biggest and most successful
fraud ever practiced upon a patient world [meaning gullible].
                    Henry James, with whom his scientist
                    brother William for once agreed

Man is least himself when he talks in his own person.
Give him a mask and he will tell you the truth.
                    Oscar Wilde

A THRESHOLD NOTE TO THE READER

Leigh Light is not my name. For good reason. But if you are the sort I like you just Googled it anyway looking for a clue. And finding it.

In WW II the British Leigh light spotlighted incoming German night bombers to shoot at. The bombers' eyes were blinded, like their minds, and could not perceive the Leigh's surrounding. Where it was coming from, you could say.

In writing this funny novel ... funny, yet ... *The Which of Shakespeare's Why*, I had to consider the present contentious state of scholarship as to who actually wrote the works of Shakespeare. This argument involves some fiercely ideological bombing from above, you could say. Thus the pen name. I have a dog to walk along university streets.

The Which began in one moment, upon hearing familiar Shakespeare lines simply changed in key. The way a single bell coda tolling in major's carefree tone creates another perception when rung in minor key's somber profundity. A student encountered at a campus performance of *The Tempest* passingly remarked she believes Shakespeare was a mask name for the actual author. A subject not in my field and so not discussed, I just sought my seat. But then as *The Tempest* performance proceeded my heart grew more interested than my mind.

The Which's inspiration moment came in the dramatic turn of the concluding epilogue. Exhausted magician-king Prospero crosses the dark emptied stage, peering from the footlight edge into alerted faces of his audience. There in seat C43 suddenly I grasped this was indeed *The Tempest's* author. Speaking as such, the author of Shakespeare's whole canon.

The fake-bearded student Prospero actor must have been an old soul. He delivered that epilogue as a slow pained plea. Here quoted is the begging imprecation the author of Shakespeare wrote 400 years ago. Said to audiences who themselves knew much unwritten about their time's dangerous world. Which today is obscure.

Release me from my bands [means restriction]
With the help of your good hands!
Gentle breath of yours my sails
Must fill or else my project fails,
Which was to please. Now I want [means lack]
Spirits to enforce, art to enchant,
And my ending is despair,
Unless I be relieved by prayer,
Which pierces so that it assaults
Mercy itself and frees all fault.
And so from crimes would pardoned be.
Let your indulgence set me free.

Immediately a circa 1600 audience would have understood the magician author's prayer for "indulgence" as the Catholic idea of release from its Purgatory. As well as begging sympathetic mercy.

That is what this novel, *The Which of Shakespeare's Why*, offers. Set in modern New York and London speaking today's language, this laughing tale does grant indulgence to that troubled beseeching genius. Who is the author of Shakespeare and yet is not the man long called Shakespeare.

The Which casts aside the mask placed over him. Releases the Shakespeare author from the Elizabethan Crown's expedient political stratagem to hide his identity by force of its "bands," *The Which* offers that hidden author voice through a novel set today. And by a tale woven in form similar to works of Shakespeare himself, using some persistent thematic elements of his plays. So yes, *The Which* is alive in Shakespearean comedy. And yes too, twining in helix, alive also in Shakespearean anguish.

Thus you will find a kingly displaced noble beleaguered amidst hidden identities. There shall be comely young women with steel at their center. There shall be comely young women with steel at their center, and also outsized male ego and hot-headed behavior. A clever secret player or two or three. A truth-telling clown. Eerie personages. Laughter you did not see coming.

And as was always there in the plays' real time the author's underlying, biding, mocking anger. Complex as the brutally shifting Elizabethan Court. There shall be no simple male hero inside *The Which* since there are none in all the works of Shakespeare. Nor, as we shall understand soon, was the actual author other than a very complex man like so many of his unforgettable characters.

Regarding the Man Who Was Shakespeare

Here below is a painted portrait of the man who really was and is Shakespeare. All here following written in this prefatory letter to readers is simply fact stated from published books. Without using Internet ephemera. These documented facts are reported in this note without embellishment. Embellishment is a matter for the tale of our following novel, *The Which*.

This portrait of the 17th Earl of Oxford was created in Paris at his age 25 in 1575. That is when Edward de Vere began his

Edward De Vere, 17th Earl of Oxford

vitally seminal sojourn observing aristocratic courts of France and Italy. Which included reveling in the lively new *commedia dell'arte* theater spirit, which soon after his return to England innovatively animated several of the plays eventually included in today's Shakespeare canon.

The Which is soberly scholarly where it conveys to readers the Earl's historically documented biography. Where that textured arc of life experiences seems to closely merge into the works of Shakespeare is both the comedy and the tragedy of this novel.

The Earldom of Oxford, originally spelled Oxenford, was created in the 11th century by William the Conqueror to reward his general named Vere. When Edward inherited the Earldom in 1562 as a boy it was the most wealthy in England.

Yet he died in 1604 close to a pauper. Then living on saving sustenance granted for still mysterious reasons by both Queen Elizabeth and her successor King James. Both sovereigns were well documented Shakespeare play enthusiasts.

The Earl of Oxford had other ancient inherited designations, being principally Lord Great Chamberlain and Viscount Bolbec. In our 21st century day Edward would likely be given additional identifying tags. Such as manic-depressive bipolar. Suicidally profligate. Obsessive compulsive.

But, and by far most importantly as to the Earl's personal qualities, we must fairly call him the most well-rounded advanced scholar of the English Renaissance. Fluent in Greek, Latin, French, Italian, and Spanish. The Earl's boyhood tutors in history, science, botany, law and, above all, languages were the most erudite in Britain. They schooled him rigorously all through adolescence, drawing upon the most rare and sophisticated libraries of the realm.

Because he was a Prince the Earl did not matriculate at a university. But in respect for his achieved tutored advanced learning he was awarded honorary degrees by the universities of Cambridge and of Oxford, both ceremonies attended by Queen Elizabeth. He also studied at England's pre-eminent law school, Gray's Inn.

From his early 20s the Earl financially subsidized several writers. In gratitude about 30 books were dedicated to him, some mentioning his own contribution to content. And, notably, into his 30s the Earl employed two successful playwrights as personal secretarial assistants.

One of those seasoned theater writers continued to work with the Earl longer. He was made artistic director of a theater playhouse that the Earl bought but could not retain in his insolvency.

Some scholars conclude that while under age 20 and still a legal ward of the Crown, the Earl, Edward de Vere, was the first translator to English of the Latin works of Ovid. Ovid is by far Shakespeare's favorite source of tales and images. These detective scholars' theory is that the late teenage precocious scholar Edward used his uncle and Latin tutor's respected name as a mask to gain necessary approved registration of the book with the Crown's censor. That uncle's other publications were grim Puritan religious tracts and translations of nonfictional classics. And so that old man was an unlikely actual author of the lubriciously sexy first English translation of Ovid. Scholars trace tell-tale matching patterns in both the Earl's and Shakespeare's language; they report distinctive matching idiosyncrasies of grammar and spelling.

As to the Earl's publicly acknowledged youthful translations, they include the first into English of both classic Latin and Italian Renaissance books of advanced philosophy. Some scholars trace links from them to Shakespeare's thought and language. Links in the Shakespeare canon texts are also suggested from dozens of passages that the Earl marked or annotated in his personal bible. Which was long withheld from scholarly inspection but is now the thematic subject of a meticulous published Ph.D. thesis.

The scholarly Earl's personality is documented as unusually vivid. He was a much younger beau of the Queen. The Earl twice won the championship at major jousting festivals in her honor. And the boisterously lively Earl was Elizabeth's lauded performance dancer among her favored athletic courtiers. They bantered one another in Latin and French and shared irreverent humor.

However, after a flamboyant first decade of adulthood, profound existential change began to overtake the Earl. His downward spiral worsened through loss of vital royal favor. Amid Court rivals the Earl wandered into a sequence of embarrassing personal scandals. He temperamentally disobeyed Crown authority and made some dangerous enemies. From his 20s to mid-30s the Earl steadily sold for cash almost all his ancestral land holdings that still remained after aggressive seizures by Court individuals in power over him.

Those liquidations of his patrimony supported the Earl's lavish annual personal expenditures. Including generous subsidy of several writers and actors, and hopeless service on the huge debt gratuitously imposed by both the Crown and individual creditors. *The Which* views the Earl's idealism and, as well, considers relentless documented power manipulations of his dangerous Elizabethan contemporaries.

Our tale highlights resonant lines of *Hamlet* and *Lear*, probing beneath them to biographical underpinnings. There is no need for you to now read or reread any of the plays. Because all relevant text is set out here in *The Which*.

By his late 30s the Earl had become thoroughly ostracized from

Court. All his efforts to become a military leader in family tradition were quashed. As were his expectations as a senior noble to join elite political authority groups. As were his attempts to secure some economic patronage of the kind often bestowed upon Court favorites.

By age 38 the Earl was living close to indigency. But from then he was supported by a very unusually large and never explained pension from the famously parsimonious Queen. The last 14 years of the Earl's life were basically reclusive. He was wholly reliant for solvency upon the mysterious terms of the Queen's capriciously terminable quarterly pension on unexpressed terms.

So this man, who *The Which* flatly says wrote *The Tempest* line quoted above, indeed did live into his full maturity in such "bands," contemporaneously meaning imposed constraint. The Earl lived his long latter years quietly ensconced in a gracious house bought by his second wife and her family. Apparently chosen because it was a few minutes' walk from the Globe and another theater.

The Earl's three daughters each married a wealthy peer of England. One such, together with his brother who controlled authority over Crown permission to publish, were the sole payors of printing the extraordinarily expensive 900-page First Folio in 1623. It comprises 36 Shakespeare plays, a dozen of which mysteriously were not known previously to exist. Both these aristocratic publishers of the First Folio were longtime friends of their peer the Earl.

A second daughter of the Earl was married to another longstanding friend of the Earl. A wealthy lord, he like the Earl was an advanced scholar and also well experienced in Italian aristocratic courts. This son-in-law lord was rumored in a contemporaneous letter to be secretly writing plays for public performance.

Scholars supporting the case for the Earl posit thus: That dozen of the Earl's previously unknown plays in the First Folio surfaced due to his daughters' possession of them held private for 20 years after his sudden death in 1604 amid a severe plague outbreak. In Oxfordian theory those unknown draft plays were discreetly polished by his literary friend and son-in-law before submission for the Folio. With about 100 household servants, this intellectual son-in-law friend had abundant time to work for years editing the Earl's draft manuscripts.

Upon Queen Elizabeth's 1603 death her successor, King James, even before coronation, voluntarily continued the Earl's pension. At that time James's wife requested more Shakespeare plays because by then she had seen all known to exist. James also immediately voluntarily conveyed back to the Earl some valuable land previously seized by the grasping Tudor Crown. The incoming Scottish Stuart King seems to have been well briefed as to the dignity due to the Earl.

Susan de Vere's wedding to the imminent Earl of Montgomery in 1604, the year of her father the 17th Earl of Oxford's death, amounted to a Shakespeare plays festival. Five plays in the canon were performed sequentially and none by others. As signally noted above, Montgomery and his brother the Earl of Pembroke eventually became the sole funders of the enormous cost of the comprehensive 1623 First Folio of Shakespeare's plays.

Also in the Holiday Revels of 1604/1605 under King James, occurring between November 1 and February 12, 10 plays in the Shakespeare canon were performed. Oxfordians see this unusual gathering of Shakespeare works in a few months as in a spirit of tribute to their author who died that same year. Only Ben Jonson's *Every Man Out of His Humor* was also performed in that Revel season; the play savagely ridicules a rural uneducated character named Sogliardo who pretends to be a writer.

The Earl's grave is lost. The plays stand as cenotaph if you accept his authorship.

Perspective as to the time of these works' respective composition is quite difficult to reconstruct but of vital importance. Much of the perennial dispute as to the Earl's authorship, versus the now sole alternative claim for the Stratford native man William Shaksper, roots in chronology. In sum Oxfordian proponents see evidence that by 1585 about half the mature works in the Shakespeare canon already existed, as contemporaneously reported performed in some cognate title or form but most without script extant today. In 1585 the Stratford man was just 21 years of age and still living impoverished in rural Warwickshire far distant from London. There is a contemporaneous document reference to a *Titus Andronicus* private Court performance in London in 1574. Shaksper was then 10 years old.

Until after 1570 there was no public theater structure in England. Traveling actor troupes presented morality plays and miracle plays originated in medieval times, utilizing residence and inn spaces. The advent from 1574 of purpose-built theaters led to explosive demand from large new London audiences for a flow of entertainments. The resulting new generation of playwrights, due to rigid social hierarchy and cultural reasons, typically were not identified and the scripts seldom printed.

Thus dating early plays in the Shakespeare canon often involves inference only, not documented clarity. However, a central Oxfordian perception is that the Earl in his mid-20s (so from about 1573) to mid-30s produced much of the canon plays as juvenilia. And then throughout his increasingly reclusive long later years maturely rewrote them, refining quality for posterity.

Oxfordians assert that the Stratford man's longstanding ortho-dox chronology is strikingly factually unrealistic, because William Shaksper's birth date 14 years after the Earl compresses the Shake-speare canon's composition into a very doubtfully short period of finished work. Appearing only from 1592 and amounting to three dozen plays plus two long elaborately erudite poems. Mysteriously all this blizzard of theorized creative output by Shaksper left behind no trace of juvenilia or revision, for there exists literally not a single scrap of manuscript among the 900 pages of plays in the First Folio. There is absolutely no sign of correspondence to or from anyone regarding the 20 performed plays and two popularly selling con-troversial printed long poems. And the archival record now seems to confirm the man who was Shakespeare completely ceased writ-ing by 1604. A few academic claims of later co-authorship are not convincingly documented; they could be explained as theft by other writers of material after the Earl died in 1604.

Oxfordian scholars see the contemporaneously reported 1574 to 1585 proto-Shakespearean plays to be Oxford's own immature creations. Not as "sources" for Shakespeare. Thus not as "copied" plays written by mysteriously unknown earlier authors, who were never heard from again despite centuries of academic scholarship.

The circumstances of the Earl's internal exile for basically the last 14 years of his life are at play in the life portrait that *The Which* sketches. Both the key plays and Shakespeare's sonnets speak clearly of their author's despondent distress as to reputation and posterity. The sonnets' aging author knows his name is lost; see numbers 29, 37, 72, 81, 112, and 121. And recall Prospero's and Hamlet's expir-ing sadness, imprecating not to be forgotten.

A modern person naturally questions the Earl's motivation to write anonymously, as opposed to hiring a sharp marketing firm. But insight emerges from literal personal statements of the sonnets, and in those last utterances of Prospero and Hamlet quoted above. Shakespeare revealing himself as a lost soul does seem to hope for personal redemption in some future time. That writing is not the voice of a busy jobbing writer for cash pay. The Earl did not write for pay. He was too rich to need money payment .... until he went broke. And thereafter the Queen stepped in as his sole patron, financing him completely for those last 14 years of secluded writing.

These above are simple contemporaneously documented historical facts as to the life of the 17th Earl of Oxford, Edward de Vere. But as to that man's feelings, and as to the art welled up from them, that tale is written on the wind. *The Which* is itself a kind of wind.

The vision and voice of Shakespeare affects our culture. Most of us today walk the world with some conception of his works somewhere in mind. So comes *The Which* for you to consider. A tale lightly laughing and yet serious. For indeed it is fittingly woven much in the very patterns of Shakespeare's own dark comedies.

Regarding the Mask

But first in proper scholarly perspective you should have a purely factual overview of William Shaksper of Stratford-upon-Avon, whom tradition has long placed as author of the canon of Shakespeare, despite doubt expressed contemporaneously and over the past 150 years. By now that doubt has come to a focus, and *The Which* surveys it by a lively modern tale.

All factual statements in this prefatory letter to readers as to William Shaksper, the Stratford man, are drawn only from published books, not Internet content. These facts are reported here without embellishment, except a few factually unfounded popular assumptions are correctively addressed. Embellishment as to the William Shaksper figure, as with the Earl, is placed in the realm of our tale *The Which*.

But *The Which* is not much "banded" by the man Shaksper. This soberly considered novel believes Shaksper surely was not the great writer Shakespeare who the world sees and hears. But Shaksper actually was involved in the real life times of the works of Shakespeare in other ways. Curious, still mysterious, ways that *The Which* touches upon.

First Folio Portrait Engraving

This appearing on the cover of the First Folio of Shakespeare's collected plays is said there to be a portrait of the author. It was engraved in 1623 by someone who when William Shaxper died in 1616 was 15 years old living in London. Shaxper lived his final dozen years in far distant Stratford. So this 22-year-old artist had never seen the man. The 1623 Folio was the very first print to point to the Stratford man as being the writer William Shakespeare.

Over centuries scholars have questioned the portrait's peculiar crudeness. Not just the blank stare, with a line at right that looks like a mask edge and an ear like a pull tab. It is remarked that this man seems to have two right eyes and two left arms, with one of his jacket's shoulder sleeves reversed back to front. The hydrocephalic head seems a sacerdotal image served on a whitewashed platter. Floating disconnected from an improbably small body.

The early 17th century was an era fascinated by hidden message cryptograms, a popular European art form. To some Oxfordian scholars this sketch is one. Meaning "Here's a mask of a mask." As the exquisitely real portrait of the Earl above examples, artists of the period were quite capable of lifelike portraits.

This Stratford man's name cradle to grave was recorded officially as William Shaksper. Regionally pronounced Shaxper; it is spelled Shaxper here in *The Which* to avoid even more confusion of identity. On scripts the name Shake-speare or Shakespeare was printed 92 times before the 1623 First Folio bearing that author name; never was it spelled Shaksper in any printed document.

Of record the Stratford man never once anywhere spelled his name Shakespeare. And of record never once claimed to be a writer, much less the famous William Shakespeare. In period pronunciation his surname's "a" would have been soft like in hat; in contrast the "a" in shake would have been hard like in aim.

Actually a lot evidencing Shaxper has survived 400 years. There is a dossier of about 70 documents. But nothing, nothing at all, not one extant scrap of paper, shows he was a writer of any sort or even that he physically could write. As opposed to identity as an opportunistic Elizabethan businessman occasionally operating in its rumbustious new theater world.

Many books and ephemera have stumbled at Shaxper's troublingly scant yet factually inconvenient biography. The pro-Shaxper academic orthodoxy basically urges students to limit attention to those glowing literary works of Shakespeare. Urging readers to simply ignore Shaxper's incongruous biographical record as irrelevant to texts. Though a couple of professors, as well as Harvey Weinstein's perennially popular sex-crazed movie *Shakespeare in Love*, actually have jumped across the hard factual history border line to creatively envision a colorful, lovable Shakespeare basically detached from his own contemporaneous biographical records. These offer a Shakespeare image that pleasantly confirms to the general public their simple received assumption of unique intuitive genius.

But that assumption sits atop a steep staircase of assumptions. Shaxper's documented record is of a man with no formal education. Only just speculatively some years in a one-room school that reportedly taught rote Latin and not English. School ended for all students at age 13. The school's records in Shaxper's period were destroyed. No evidence has been found of any tutorial or formal school education of Shaxper anywhere, despite two centuries of determined search by scholars for that missing key puzzle piece to the erudite brilliance of Shakespeare.

It is known that this man with a wife and lifelong illiterate children remained poor in birthplace Stratford until into his twenties, reportedly apprenticed for some period to his illiterate bankrupt father by trade a glover. No evidence shows Shaxper came to London before 1592, when a tiny loan he made was written down by a debtor. He would have been age 28. Possibly he arrived before, in his mid-20s, after abandoning his destitute wife and three children to live on the kindness of neighbors and his impoverished aging parents.

Shaxper may have found some stage jobs. But no record exists of any payment to him for any role onstage. A surviving account book of a major London theater covers the decade 1592 to 1602 and is specifically detailed as to playwright and actor payee identity. Among thousands of surviving entries Shaxper's name never appears as actor, much less playwright. The names of 27 playwrights do appear. London's dominant theatrical producer and, also, the most famous actor of the 1590s, wrote several surviving letters about theater personnel matters; neither ever mentions Shaxper or Shakespeare.

However, it is clear that Shaxper once in London soon moved into diverse money-seeking efforts. He is evidenced as a money lender, as some sort of broker for plays written by others, and as acting troupe practical functionary. Also as an omnivorously opportunistic investor. The source of his funds used in these investments is a mystery that *The Which* entertains. He bought into (or perhaps was granted by Crown arrangement) a share ownership of a governmentally permitted acting troupe that later produced several Shakespeare plays. And then came to own a share of the newly constructed and governmentally permitted Globe Theater.

Even while a part-time resident in London, always in rented rooms for which he repeatedly defaulted on local taxes due, Shaxper stayed continuously active in his business dealings in three days travel distant Stratford. He is extensively documented there as an aggressive commodity speculator, real estate investor, and moneylender. He was fined by Stratford for hoarding grain in a famine and also was censured for illegal wool trading. A London man got a court protection order based upon threat of violence from Shaxper.

Shaxper filed various lawsuits over oddly tiny sums due to him in his loan shark line of business. However, although perennially litigious he never sued anyone over any literary property or related fee matter, despite the fact that ascribed and un-ascribed Shakespeare scripts were the most brazenly pirated by printers of all Elizabethan plays.

While Shaxper is evidenced in some relation to London's theater world, there is simply no record extant of any payment to him for writing or performing anything. No extant direct or indirect document shows that Shaxper was ever paid a penny for supposedly writing about 20 performed plays and also two popular printed long poems. There were about one hundred playwrights active in the Elizabethan 40 years. London theater production flourished and money matters were professional for writers; business records were kept.

Yet for supposedly the most prolific playwright of the age, who became very rapidly wealthy enough to buy a 24-room mansion with land, no record of payment at all for anything written exists throughout his dozen years as a part-time resident in London. Such record does survive for most professional Elizabethan writers. A recent book documents 25 of them, finding only the man Shaxper has no evidence of being a writer of any sort.

Nor is there any trace of a possible financial patron of Shaxper that would mitigate the absence of any recorded payment for literary work. Scholars of all stripes broadly concur that Shaxper never had a patron. The 3rd Earl of Southampton was the only named dedicatee of any works ascribed to Shakespeare, those being the two long poems *Venus* and *Lucrece*. However, two centuries of vigorous academic research failed to provide evidence that Shaxper ever even once met the Earl of Southampton.

Conversely, as *The Which* notes well, young Southampton and the Earl are contemporaneously documented as intimately well acquainted. The Earl for a year urged young Southampton to marry his daughter Elizabeth, among other specially intense connections between the two men.

A writer? There is no surviving letter from Shaxper to anyone on any subject. There is no extant writing delivered to him from anyone. When Shaxper died there was no eulogy at all anywhere in Britain in an epoch of frequent printed remembrances of writers; Ben Jonson had 33 and Francis Bacon 52. Not one person in all Britain wrote a surviving letter or other expression even mentioning Shaxper's or Shakespeare's death, though the plays of William Shakespeare were then in 1616 still in performance.

Shaxper's carefully detailed bequests of objects in his will do not include a single book, play script, or even any scrap of manuscript though a dozen Shakespeare plays had never been performed to that time (appearing mysteriously only in the 1623 First Folio). At some time in a different handwriting than the scribe's text a small money bequest for two actors was interlineated in the will.

This Stratford man's only surviving handwriting samples are six discordant signatures on legal documents. Even pro-Shaxper academics find them puzzlingly labored in their crude letters, and very discrepant between examples even as to spelling his own name. Illness or a stroke is gamely suggested by some Stratfordians though the signatures are spaced over some years. In stark contrast to this evidence, dozens of Elizabethan period playwrights and other professional writers were using smoothly stylized signatures that survive today. Common sense adds that any playwright would need legible handwriting for actor scripts and a printer.

A contemporaneous historian's published pamphlet list of prior deceased distinguished residents of Stratford does not include Shaxper post-mortem. Nor does a book of his region's notable natives written by a historian neighbor who knew Shaxper well, from involvement in his purchase by probable bribe of a bogus coat of arms. No resident of his birth and death hometown Stratford or its surrounding region wrote a surviving reference to him as any sort of writer, much less the then famous author William Shakespeare. Shaxper's Warwickshire contemporary who was a playwright and poet was buried in Westminster Abbey. Shaxper's Stratford grave is lost.

On the record of his business history Shaxper obviously was energetic. That competence does open theoretical possibility of being additionally a uniquely gifted literary genius. Able in some creative binary mode to very rapidly produce a massive encyclopedically erudite canon. While still simultaneously aggressively pursuing his various documented business enterprises.

So this uneducated untraveled rural man first in London from his late 20s would need be a very quick and adept playwright. But accepting that much, then how to explain the setting of most of his drama. Which is feudal in basic setting and sentiment. And why are the plays, other than histories, often populated almost entirely by European aristocrats? Shaxper was himself a working-class person grown up in an "early modern" England already evolving far from ancient feudalism. And the English population attending plays, for generations had been cut off from life exposure to Europe, by war, plague and Crown bars to travel to Catholic countries in fear of treason.

Thus the plays of Shakespeare in their own era were oddly anachronistic. Both in their feudal characters and their foreign settings. There is no scholarly suggestion that Shaxper ever left England. Yet in fact about 106 Shakespeare play scenes are set among about 15 named cities in Italy. By now most of his Italian local setting detail references have been confirmed as accurate by a cottage industry of fact checkers. Much of this foreign detail could not have been derived from books and some Shaxper academics' suggestion he spent time talking to travelers strains credulity due to the volume and accuracy of European setting facts. Thus the author of the plays seems to have been to Italy observationally, as most certainly was the Earl.

The man Shaksper seems by records to have lived his life only in Warwickshire and for a dozen years or so in London. There is no significant local Warwickshire dialect in the Shakespeare works. And no scene is identifiably set there; some scholars conclude Shakespeare's magical forest of Arden alludes to the famous Ardennes forest near Paris which the Earl toured in 1575, and not to the phonetically similar Warwickshire area.

In counterpoint, the Earl's boyhood was in Essexshire. Over 100 Essex dialect words have been marked in the plays.

Logic stumbles taking so many high steps of assumption. Consequently it seems academic consensus long ago basically simply leapt to accept Shaxper as England's unique working class hero. Meaning by hero a wholly instinctive genius of both absorption and abstraction. And it is just bad luck, in this pro-Shaxper view, that there is extant not one physical scrap of literary matter connected to Shaxper despite Shakespeare's massive canon of writings for public performance. Anyway, they insist, the plays are the thing.

A prolifically published professor cautions general readers that, because Shaxper/Shakespeare's lifetime period is known by specialized academics like him as "early modern," therefore his personal mentality must be considered too remote to perceive today. Because we today are classified by some such academics as "moderns." And so the Shakespeare author's underlying intentions are "invisible." These academic theoreticians insist that to even consider personal intent today would damagingly distort Shakespeare. The Stratfordian academics thus disdain the biographical curiosity of Oxfordians.

A *New Yorker* website article reports a leading professor stiffly dismissing by letter one of the six justices of the Supreme Court of America who have said they favor the Earl of Oxford as being actual author of Shakespeare. This teacher reports earnestly to *New Yorker* readers that he warned the Justice, who had published a law review essay, that fringe radical national politics might get out of hand if people thought about an author other than Shaxper.

Another well known Shaxper literary academic proponent has famously intoned that "the absence of evidence is not evidence of absence." But this also is fatuous. Since in simplest logic as well as ancient law, which certainly those six Justices of the Supreme Court all well knew, a circumstance of no evidence at all is indeed a kind of important evidence.

Thus it seems Shaxper's writing-free biographical facts can produce some contorted academic constructs. Scholars of the Middle Ages had similar difficulty parsing their elusive illiterate Christ's mythic divinity. And modern academic constructs bear some similarity to the regrettably bloody Protestant/Catholic liturgical disputes of Shakespeare's own second half of the 16th century. Now as then there is reasoning backward from conclusion, there is circular reasoning, there is assertion of inference as fact, there is suppression of fact. And in academia a strongly contemptuous cancel culture enforcement by Stratfordians of Oxfordian scholarship.

The prevalent profile of Shaxper thus has long insisted he was a uniquely effortless supernal genius. Harvey Weinstein's *Shakespeare in Love* went pretty far gilding this simple image. His popular movie's plot seems to me equally about the genius's overdue accounting and distraction over smoldering Gwyneth Paltrow. But even Weinstein probably would agree that through the centuries, "This guy Shaxper has had a lot of work done."

Here is a contemporaneous etching a historian made of the memorial bust that Shaxper himself commissioned. That sculpted bas relief portrait he paid for is plainly possessively holding a full commodity sack. Which was in keeping with local Warwickshire tradition to indicate profession on some monuments.

Shaxper's Historical Memorial

And here below is Shaxper's very same bas relief several decades later. Subsequent generations of Shakespeare fans decided in "repair" to plaster over reality to match their conception of what by then had become a cult figure.

Shaxper remodeled as Shakespeare

Yes, they made the sack into a fancy satin pillow and stuck an unrealistically big writing plume in his fist. Yes it would be goofy to write with a big sharp quill on a soft pillow as desk though this dreamy fellow looks capable of trying. And yes that silly moustache-goatee is anachronous to period style. So yes, a lot of work has been done on Shaxper over time.

The Two Stage Doors Ajar

This Shakespeare authorship binary choice matter still teeters uneasily. There really seems to be no conclusive contemporaneous tangible proof. Not even one extant brief scrap of real time written evidence that one man or the other, either the Earl or Shaxper, wrote the works of Shakespeare.

So stasis abides. But published output of the Earl's proponents, the Oxfordians, now catalogs to about 5,000 book, periodical, and blog entries archived on a comprehensive website. Over 3,000 scholars and laymen have signed a public declaration urging more genuinely open scholarly dialogue in the authorship dispute between Stratfordians and Oxfordians.

The established orthodox scholars' output about their man Shaxper is smaller since the 1920s, when the Earl was first proposed as the alternative Shakespeare. But is also dauntingly large for a reader.

I have been through a bookshelf but found no simple factual resolution. What I did find is a surprising amount of literature scholars' ad hominem insults, passive aggressive slights, and deep suspicion. On grounds ranging from labeling someone a pathetic fantasist to an intellectual fraudster to a reprehensible snob from one social extreme or another. Opponents bark books, chasing tales.

Well, Reader, let's not argue here. Let's be open minded. *The Which* gives the centuries-old religious cult of Will Shaxper of Stratford a rest for this while. Let's lighten up and now give that major piece of work the Earl a chance to explain himself a bit better. Waked out from behind that crude Shaxper mask. And from behind all the character masks of those cleverly coded plays about the Earl's own period of history, his own life, and his own feelings.

And since it is the due fate of even a comic novel to break boundaries of thought, let's watch *The Which* try to break a band of constricted perception. Just as Shakespeare himself clearly did soulfully ask us to do in the conclusions of both *The Tempest* and *Hamlet*. In his own words fitting for the end of a frustrated magnificent literary journey.

To luminance,
Leigh Light

Part One

"What's wrong with your ruff?" Then Lance focuses to my chin's overnight black whiskers.

"I slept on it. And some of the Nut Brown spilled. Naturally enough."

"Yeah . . . yeah." His eyes sunken in more shagbrow shadow than a usual morning. "Ah Harry *buzzitall*, *Buzz* Lester the moron."

I did write creatively, before that did not work out. You'll see why. I may as well say "Buzzem as he hath buzzed unto us."

Lance was thinking not listening. Then to my silence, "One clumsy click on WhatsApp and our world ends. Pathetic. All for some . . . who?"

"Some Veronica. Which is a nice name actually. But still." Lester's immensely rich wife Valerie has a nasty pre-nup, nasty from the viewpoint of a younger husband with impulse control issues. And a hot temper from the viewpoint of all her 3,000 employees. At letter "V" on his shaky phone screen Lester made a very wrong turn off a cliff.

"But still you say. Still hasn't even started yet, Harry."

We are sitting alone in the former convent mother superior's office, on chairs suitable for bad girls due a lecture. Amid tacked-up past Shakespeare production posters. The door is closed but our moment is growing more urgent as the Trenton Shakespeare Festival cast convene jolly-actor-style in the auditorium beside us. Lance now must go tell them we are all unemployed as of today. Lester underfunded us before he skipped the country. Our infant troupe is rent broke months in arrears, promised salaries defaulted too.

Lance is good at not speaking when he should. Sometimes troupe actors say he's not a helpful director. But it sharpens wit to guess what is in his mind. It does with this Hamlet anyway. Now Lance is not looking at me or anywhere. Women actors' lovely full voices penetrate the flimsy door, those are no uniformed unformed girls at sport out there in the gym hall. This mess is serious, play is not in it.

I wait to do as Lance tells me now. He was daring to hire me for Hamlet in the new company's debut. I only drifted into acting two years ago. In his way he did not tell me why my audition worked. But it's pretty obvious I am usually thinking of something else and cannot make up my mind. That's before the acting part. And too I bring onstage enough unseen baggage to fill a Fed Ex truck.

There is a double window beside the mother superior's desk, suited to close interrogation. Especially this morning, klieg-strength yellow light seems to be searching our minds. Lance silently studying his hands as if they are auditioning for some role. So I look around. The posters of Shakespeare productions we thumbtacked up are from other times and places. Our own new Shakespeare repertoire troupe, wholly sponsored by that impulsive recent patron of the arts Mr. Lester Laeme, has not staged even one performance yet.

The suddenly financially embarrassed sole backer Mr. Laeme completely forgot his love of Shakespearean production. Just two days ago he departed to live pants-down in Rome with a rumored Eurasian sorceress definitely named Veronica, definitely not named Valerie.

There is a big empty space on the wall beside the door. A TSF poster would have looked perfect there if it existed. Trenton, with its new public relations slogan, "One Hurricane from Greatness." Lester bought this concept of the area's future then skipped out on the bill. But now I see another absence. Years of strong daylight have left bright paint under a removed form. The missing large sculptured crucifix outline is sharp-silhouetted there, glowing like an emulsion photo negative. Mean armies killed each other quarreling over the exact shape of its incorporeal holy spirit. But now the old convent here is just very tangible real estate. That TSF rented on its own incorporeal assumption.

I sit silent, thinking my flitting way about the nailed transcendent figure gone missing in a ruined convent leased at ruinous rent from a disappearing religion. Of which I not so young now was an altar boy. Thus am slow to hear Lance. "What?"

"I said the play's the thing. Wherein we catch the conscience of the Queen."

"Conscience of the King. Claudius, right?"

Lance is talking to his hands, being quicker than me. "Harry, our Queen is Valerie Farnsworth, who was also Lester's Queen until she cut his head off. But she doesn't want us as her subjects." That is sure so, at the beginning meeting I saw Valerie cared nothing about Lester's Shakespeare vanity project. She was just in sex thrall to her gorgeous bad boy toy. Valerie's only about science. Later she was always away in a business meeting, unless off somewhere harassing wild creatures.

Lance says to himself, "Valerie could be cast as one of the egos in a history play. If all the world, to coin . . . ." Self respect checks him.

Lance hasn't looked at me again these minutes. I say toward his turned wavy, slightly grizzled mane, "So we have to get her to like Shakespeare because now she hates Lester. Snatch his pet project away from him?"

Lance's thumb touches his pinky tip. "Not her thing. Instead we need to catch our Queen Valerie's particular conscience."

This good light is encouraging me. "Sure, Lance. So you appeal to her conscience about dumping thirty actors out of work. Kiss her ring. Sure, she'll never miss TSF's overhead."

"Wrong. Wrong thinking, Harry. You wouldn't know her type from all your school life. A type not dreamed of in that philosophy.

"Some people who make a lot of money on their own work grow new strong principle. It's unmistakable in them. Some particular eccentric principle appears over time jutting out visible as an unbuttoned new sexual feature. Being nice is not enough to get Valerie's type to spend money she will never miss. Her kind of rich only extend themselves beyond self-interest on their own private principle." Lance pauses listening to his silent self. "Their ego consciousness is like the normal conscience little people feel."

For someone who I heard has been fired in anger quite a few times, Lance does have his flashes of insight. "So . . . . so? What in Queen Valerie do we have to catch?"

"The mousetrap was your idea, Hamlet. You put a play within your own play's real time. The mousetrap, the Murder of Gonzago story, that messed with the King's mind. Right? A few special lines inserted blew Claudius's perception wide open. So. Conscience in the sense of consciousness is what we need to catch Valerie's interest in TSF."

"So we rewrite the Gonzago lines to speak to her in the opening night audience? Saying, as actually Hamlet already does in a line, take good care of these worthy players?"

Lance cast himself as Hamlet's ghost father. Old murdered Hamlet's black-hooded cloak hangs on a hook at the window. Lance was an actor before a director. He stands and pulls it on, turns toward the door as if waiting for his son to appear to get haunted again. "No, Harry. I told you already. Valerie's character does not yearn to be nice to ordinary people." He's big now in the padded cloak, sunlight bounces off his outline as I look up in a squint. The room grows three beats silent, the way Lance stylizes lines onstage.

"Harry, this woman is a narrow scientist. She drives a big business with a hard edge. Her craves are mental fascination and winning in competition.

"So there is the itch that is our . . . rub. We need to reach Valerie's money by dangling a breakthrough big prize for her ego. Lester was just an aberration that's probably scarred over already."

From the other side of the door I am hearing dozens of murmuring happy greetings. Before Doom arrives too, weeping.

I just wait. Lance has got himself lost in his worry, then "How that can be done . . ." He can't help himself, really who could, "There is the question." A knock on the door. "What?"

"It's Ophelia, boysies. All the actors are getting fat on pastry waiting for you."

"Get thee to a nunnery."

"Already in one. Come *on*."

"Five minutes."

Not listening, I am still staring at the crucifix's lit shadow intaglio. Doubly hung over from this overnight crisis of our troupe's bankruptcy. At 3 a.m. I foresaw another losing hand in my personal life's poker game.

Looking at the crucifix space first dimensional, then shadow. Yet in surprise now lit as personality.

"Lance, do you know much about the Earl of Oxford's basis to be the real Shakespeare? That Oxford was the ghost writer of it all but the game got way out hand. Sort of like which dude was Jesus's real dad?"

I'm looking at my director with a Hamlet countenance, one

brow raised, which I do not consider corny if the smile is bitter.

"Of course, Harry. Most Shakespeare players have heard something about Oxford. Why?"

"Well, I know a bookshelf worth. One of the reasons I dropped my graduate work at Princeton was a professor who mocked my curiosity."

"Sheppard Germaine, right? A rough don in the Stratfordian man mafia. They whack young scholars for disrespecting their plaster saint Shakespeare."

"Oh yeah. I learned about that. I had started to realize that Queen Elizabeth actually was part of all the spectacular messes Oxford made of his life. I sensed that connects to why his identity as a writer would have been suppressed by her government. But then Germaine rejected my dissertation thesis proposal final as a bullet in the ear. He said it would put me on a track to unemployability by any decent university."

"Too bad. You could have dared to be great. The Queen did selfishly cause a lot of grief for Oxford. But. But her forty years of volatile maneuvers as to Oxford ironically enabled him to produce Shakespeare's writing. I'm an Oxfordian, Harry. But keep silent because I like to be employed. Directors too get blacklisted for nut stuff."

Lance has never revealed anything personal to me. It must be the bullets whistling over our foxhole as bankruptcy's line advances. So I am frank back. "I know that feeling. I chickened out. But my research was intriguing. What Americans let you learn as a kid, the good Queen Bess image, that's a child's cartoon. As I read deeper I saw everybody was afraid of Elizabeth's changeability. Especially with her being surrounded by violent thugs at court who amounted to real Italian mafia."

Lance nods knowingly so I go on. "Everybody in England was afraid big time. Her psychotic dad's head chopping off was continuous with Elizabeth."

Then my director turns back to the window, gone quiet to think our way forward.

So I think on too, going backward in my way.

Much of my scholarly reading is still in me due to a painfully good memory, though I stopped cold after bailing from my Ph.D. work years ago. For me the big takeaway is that Elizabeth's new type of made men capos were ambitious nobodies who got rich ripping off the rich. The wolfish Earls, Walt Whitman called her favorites. This Tudor-era turn against a thousand-year-old feudal order began with dad Henry's greedy predations. By Elizabeth's time anybody who crossed the borderline illegitimate Queen some way, or failed to pay due vigorish to her made guys, got their head whacked off fast. Martin Scorsese did not coin the term.

I recall more now, pulled out of the Harry Haines Memorial Trash Can Full of Melancholy Episodes. Part of my rejected thesis plan was to follow the consequences of Elizabethan literary controls. All writers got spied on by Crown agents. And heavy-handedly intimidated because they could stir up trouble. There could be no touching on the questionable legitimacy of Elizabeth as Queen. Or her covered-up sexual adventures and calamities.

So it came that very young Elizabeth had to step forward as Queen into an unsteadily ending feudal time. She had to assert her mysteriously God-given medieval right through her very shakily concocted lineage absolutely everybody knew all about. Including the part about her uncle beheaded for conviction on a charge of sleeping with her also beheaded mother. Everybody had already lived a half century under the Tudors as violent usurpers of old aristocracy. And then stunningly cynical predators on a beloved thousand-year-old religious culture.

This latest Tudor upstart ruler is a woman, to boot. Who as everybody knows lived most of her life declared a bastard under permanent house arrest.

Elizabeth, in such vulnerability, Tudored on. She oversaw her own 40-year maelstrom of fascist violence, publicly blatant as well as covert. The Tudor dynamic continued inflicting enormous miseries on most ordinary people in sudden swerves of Protestant and Catholic bloodshed. First under Henry VIII Tudors had backed Protestants going lethal on Catholics, then under Queen Mary Catholics going lethal on Protestants, then under Elizabeth Protestants back in power as a police state methodically tortured and killed recusant Catholics. Some Pope in Italy offered an immediate pass to Catholic heaven for anybody who offed Elizabeth *The Godfather*–style, and several unlucky attempts were made. Jesuit jihadis constantly on the move. Crown spies networking all of Britain and Ireland in thousands. The Crown employed a half-dozen spies and counter-spies embedded in each of France, Spain, Italy and the Netherlands.

It's quiet now inside our room of doom, I muse on. For England the latter 16th century was suffused in existential dread. Catholic Spain, rich on heartless plunder of both the New World and the Pacific World, was determined to invade and physically wipe out Protestants. In 1588 it finally tried and failed only due to a hurricane and one problem general. And too, decade after decade, huge rich Catholic France was another threat of invasion. The beleaguered native Irish actively invited Catholic invasion through their island.

All this in 60 years. Making an ordinary guy's head spin if he could keep it. A lot could not. Always through Elizabeth's long era a half-dozen or more grimacing severed heads rotted fly-blown on spikes over the South Bank entrance to London Bridge. They all said at once, "Remember this."

Now Lance is back mentally. And he's lightening up in foxhole camaraderie. "Harry, I knew I was right about you. Yes, all writers were scared of being tagged by the Crown. Chris Marlowe was killed at age 28 in a bar set-up because he habitually got drunk and talked too much about what he knew as a spy himself. And executed also because his chaotic violent spectacles were dangerously exciting big London crowds. He was deliberately stabbed through the eye. That was a brilliant theatrical touch for other spies and playwrights to remember. Marlowe's thug killer got rewarded with a government job."

I too feel camaraderie in this moment of garrulous unemployment. My hero Lance admires my scholarship. Thus encouraged, I show off to him a little. "You know this? Even silly comedy writer Ben Jonson was imprisoned multiple times for treason investigation, right? Some writers simply disappeared forever, and everyone in a small literary world knew the examples. For preemptive warning a few writers had their right hand chopped off, including Jonson's brother-in-law and his printer. Several authors had all their life works seized and ceremoniously burned, some on afterthought even after the Crown's censor had approved their printing."

When Lance looks up he's listening so I go on. "And . . . right, it's coming back . . . all that state menace and violence depended in any given moment on which direction Elizabeth's wind was blowing. But that direction was not always in her control, control freak that she was. She was prey herself.

"Beneath her bravado Elizabeth had to be terrified of populace disenchantment from some unpredictable source. There were always dark rumors. So Crown agents managed her image to be always positive. Fiercely eradicating any fact that might scandalize always volatile public sentiment. Such as, to pick one, that England's saintly 'Virgin Queen' had a baby at fourteen after a secret pregnancy."

"Yeah, man, a fellow conspiracy nut!"

"Well, Lance, not nutty if it's true. In plain historical fact Henry VIII's widow Katherine Parr immediately married Admiral Thomas Seymour, and Elizabeth was sent to live with them in Chelsea. In documented fact, spies for the Crown reported that Seymour was fondling the girl alone. Another extant spy document records Katherine Parr became so agitated that one day she herself took out a knife and cut off Elizabeth's dress in a walled garden, obviously to inspect her for pregnancy. And seeing it was so then in very big documented fact Seymour, despite being the aristocratic top Admiral of the Fleet, was immediately imprisoned. And quickly executed in the Tower on a boilerplate treason charge. Of course the proceeding strategically not mentioning his impregnating a very close heir to the Tudor throne."

The guy can smile big. "This is Internet stuff, right?"

"But no, Lance, that is real book history. Period records are also quite clear that Elizabeth was suddenly then sent to live in the remote residence of an elderly Crown spymaster. And it is plainly documented too that from that seclusion Elizabeth made no public appearance or communication whatsoever from June through December 1558. Then in January 1559 she reappeared in London back in Crown business as a virgin Princess."

I was saddened to learn this bit of horror. "You can imagine all the psychic damage piled onto the young girl. Her father Henry VIII had previously declared her a bastard expelled from joining the Court. That was after chopping off her mom's head on a charge of sleeping with her uncle whose head also got butchered.

"Subsequently to the dangerous secret childhood baby her

half-brother King Edward also kept Elizabeth essentially imprisoned.

"Then after Edward's sudden death Elizabeth's fanatic Catholic half-sister Mary as Queen for a few years also kept her locked away in a country estate. Actually, dying Bloody Mary got so far as preparing a death warrant for Elizabeth to prevent her taking England back to Protestant control. But by a tick did not get around to signing it before God called her to Heaven to help Him out killing Protestants."

Lance is looking into me with his director's ambiguous gaze, which is multiple gazes. Looking back in scholarly pride I add, "So there was always a lot of deadly stuff going on that the Crown kept secret." I am not going to overdo the raised eyebrow. "If the Tudor Crown needed to effect any cover-up conspiracy or to kill someone inconvenient, its agents had decades of expertise. You know about the Rainbow Portrait?"

Lance is just looking away. That means no in his vocabulary. I roll on. "Huge painting moved among the palaces with the Queen. Elizabeth is portrayed wearing a golden gown embroidered everywhere with large ears, large eyes, and moving mouths. The Rainbow portrait unmistakably says to every viewer, 'I am powerful, I hear everything and you be careful.'" It's on display at a London museum.

Now the smug sneer of Professor Sheppard Germaine blinks open before me. "To me, Lance, it seemed American-ivory-tower naïve to ask how ever the Crown, if it had vital dynastic reasons, could have managed to bury Oxford alive for his last two decades. While letting him write plays useful to the Crown in subsidized protection.

"Obviously Oxford was useful because he wrote stuff bolstering English nationalism through his many history plays. It was no accident they were performed during the twenty years of threatened catastrophic slaughtering foreign invasion of England. And also Oxford's work helped the Crown by supporting the Tudor reign itself. With all those popular romances, tragedies, and comedies starring feudal aristocrats. Of course this reflected glamor on the Tudor regime."

Lance asks the nunnery ceiling, "So then how did Oxford go so far wrong? If he was so useful to Crown power?"

I just bear straight in when I really care. "Because, Lance, his personality was unstable, his actions unpredictable. And because to some dangerous politicians his well-known scandals would have made him evidence of failed aristocracy. In Elizabeth's reign weakened feudal entitlement was increasingly challenged by rapid social evolution. Especially by the rising tide of strict religious Puritanism. Whose future direction wise Tudors could intuit. And sure enough Puritans eventually closed all theaters in England for twenty years. By 1650 a King was beheaded by new type politicians. If she lost control of matters, Elizabeth's head could have rolled first."

Lance nods across the Mother Superior's desk. "Elizabeth was so vulnerable."

"So, sure, Lance, some pseudonym beard was necessary to avoid controversy over Oxford as one of Elizabeth's lovers. Since he personally was a walking poster boy for loose morals. And was writing emotionally edgy plays, with about 2,000 people attending every performance. It would have been explosively dangerous if Oxford, that flamboyantly irregular senior aristocrat of England, became known as the populace's beloved author Shakespeare."

He replies, "So sure, some nobody had to be put in Oxford's place as the writer common people could love in the abstract. Or who commoners at least not care about."

Fellowship in the moment's foxhole. "Indeed, Lance. For the Crown agents that strategic suppression and diversion of identity from Oxford would have been child's play. The way I see it there can be conspiracy dolts. As well as conspiracy nuts."

This really is more fun than imminent dissolution in bankruptcy of Trenton Shakespeare Festival.

Lance's nod is in his tone, "So from what you read, Harr, who do you think Elizabeth's baby became? Or did they just smother it?"

My own checking account is overdrawn, I am real broke. "Actually right now we have to get big bucks or we stay beheaded ourselves." I have been observing Lance for the three months since he hired me. So I show him I know where he was actually headed as he half-listened. "Ms. Farnsworth is English isn't she?"

"Indeed. Indeed. It has to matter doesn't it, Harry? Even a maths nerd growing up in Britain must have Elizabethans in her bloodstream. It would be better if her name were Elizabeth. But still." And then he's turned away again.

I notice it has grown quiet outside in the auditorium. Then realize that of course somebody has just reported to the group that TSF is about to disband before it can open. That from triumph of joining a glamorous new troupe near New York City, each actor suddenly will be cast back drifting alone in the sad slack wide sea of unemployment. So I hear them out there, now at murmur low and tentative. Waiting for Lance to come out and tell them officially. That they are already dead in Elizabethan decisive swiftness.

The door swings open. It is Ophelia, it is Miriam. She is diaphanously gowned for dress rehearsal in the flirty early scenes. I look to the crucifix place. This is not a professional attitude I have toward my co-star. I have only been an actor for a little while. Miriam messes up my Hamlet's ambivalence. I just want her to jump on me as I jump on her. Lance seems to like the way Hamlet cannot bring himself to ever look into Ophelia's gaze. Harry does not like this feeling.

Miriam says, "Lance. It's time. If it be not now it be to come." My line of course. I believe I have mentioned that she is too much.

"Oh crackers, Miriam, this is serious."

"We're just actors. We need you to come out and tell us what is next. After that headcase Lester. I've actually met Veronica. A silicone job traded for Shakespeare. You couldn't make—"

"Sit down, sweetheart, take Harry's chair. Let's just be quiet a moment more. I need to look at you thinking." If Lance has ever hit on lovely young Miriam like Admiral Seymour on lovely young Elizabeth I have not seen it. And Lance has never come on to me or any of the other guys. Lance sexy-wise is in some other realm, maybe historical maybe not.

Miriam is only playful sometimes. "It's just so sad for everybody. Marjorie is crying and Gertrude doesn't cry."

Lance still has his dad Hamlet cape on. Turns his back again looking into the blazing clear liminal of the window. Just standing still silently silent the way he does. Thinking onward upward. Miriam watches hm. I may as well look safely at her.

And then Lance from behind is not the shape of defeated old Hamlet. For his arm pokes straight out of the cape holding his lit phone screen. He looks at the speed dial key, and presses.

"This is Lance, Gina. Is the great man in?" A pause, and then Miriam and I hear the beginning of the way both Queen Elizabeth and Queen Valerie just might save our pathetic Trenton Shakespeare Festival troupe from staying whacked.

*

*   *

Ethan Hawke's intriguingly odd *Hamlet* film is set in Manhattan. Denmark is a global corporation headquartered there, owned by a troubled family.

The Valerie Farnsworth show is set in Manhattan too. She has no family at all, especially thanks to Veronica. But Valerie does have a global corporation. Which, Lance told me in our cab to meet her now, is troubled. Where I come from troubled means drink or drugs, I don't know what a troubled corporation does to forget its problems for a while. But the way Lance spoke it sounded as if he does. He went to business school at Columbia before ruining his financial security in theater.

We are coming to this meeting two days after Valerie cancelled Lester's donations to TSF. I know the immediately prior conversation of Lance with her was a 20-second phone call asking for funding of TSF's bounced rent checks signed by Lester. In response to hearing Lester's and TSF's names in one sentence Valerie explosively told Lance not another penny ever will come from her. This only took seconds because it is time-efficient to then just say bugger the hell off and slam down the phone cracking hard.

Somehow golden-tongued Lance did speak to Valerie again, and finesse this meeting. Anyway, here Lance and I are again side by side in interrogation chairs, await for Valerie to finish torturing someone on the phone. She holds the receiver beside her ear like a butcher knife. I'm not much for dyed strawberry blonde on a woman maybe 50, but its chiffon does enhance the English face.

Long-nosed, strong-lipped, wide-set dark violet eyes. Which unreasonably are set in blazing anger at mute me as she commands into the phone.

"I never said that." Listening. "Don't play the flipping moron with me, Clive." Pause. "Well then he can try. Tell Sid to send him a threat letter. Copy his board." Pause, listening. "No. Absolutely *no*! I am done with the deal. Fuck 'em, Clive." Without pause the phone slams into its scarred cradle.

Valerie is wearing a warrior's cuirass. Tailored steel-color thick silk blouse instead of metal. But still. At the risk of offending those who disapprove of breasts I must observe for her age a high full chest line, in a sheer bra suitable for distraction of males and susceptible females. I think of old photos of Margaret Thatcher in her middle-age prime. As Valerie now turns her gaze to Lance I do too. He cleans up real good as they used to say in old cowboy movies. The navy suit is not hip, it belongs on a man of the world, not fantasies. His tie black, shirt white. He shaved, his hair is tamped down. Lance's just slightly aging good looks are British too, if you ever saw a Richard Burton movie. Valerie can see a peer not a beggar if she wants. He is directing her that way.

And Valerie is directing us to be intimidated. Her wide plate windows look out cloud-high among lower high towers. There is nothing to see or think but straight lines in the big room and on outside to serrated, shrunken blue yonder. I'm thinking how this is the worst stage set ever for a scene of mercy mild.

"Who's he?"

Lance, "Our Hamlet. Harry Haines."

"He's too old. What's your big deal? You have five." Valerie is too busy to say minutes and we're not worth the breath.

Lance has had 20 years of bitch leading ladies. I heard from Miriam of a Lady Macbeth he cast solely for type without any experience, as I suppose he did me for Hamlet. He stands and walks to the sill of a window looking up not down.

"Shakespeare can help Omniconal."

"He's too old too."

"But Valerie. That's exactly the start of your easy cheap sweet deal. Your software is under attack in Congress. Professional whiners are protesting that Omniconal's predictive artificial intelligence programming is . . . how to say? Finishing the sentence of electronic conversations like a nag spouse. Only now it's coming out that Omniconal has begun originating statements the sender actually did think but did not decide to send before it flew. Some say your company is an insidious threat to national security. Even a threat to what's left of society's politesse, but that's a fringe element."

It's not that you're supposed to think Valerie means it when she smiles. She means it when she shrugs indifferently. "People only have a dozen primary thought matrices. The idiomatic linkage interstices within them turned out to be highly programmable once we developed effectively reflexive algorithms using enough personal data scrape. From there we just need to comprehensively flash-scan prior communications within each subject's interfaces. Our step forward was from what cutting edge hedge funds apply algorithmically to business data—AI natural voice programming meshed. But our system instead uses personality algorithms. You're right, Omniconal is quite similar to a wife smarter than her husband. She who knows in advance what the poor slob is going to say and do."

"Congressmen with short haircuts from overweight States say you are playing God."

Shrug, smile. "Nobody believes in God including them. And

nobody believes in politicians or the whiny losers. For an entire generation now people have chosen to function through machines smarter than they are. Billions of people now consent and many pay to have their little tiny lives publicized to billions." She pauses, because of course we might quote her in press and she wants this next on the room's tape recording. "One of the few new social matrices since Shakespeare is that many people see themself as cast in a reality program that needs to excite ratings to continue life. We at Omniconal are just a public service to those who themselves healthfully choose to be revealed as they truly are in a given moment. We all must struggle bravely against society's controlling hypocrisies. Omniconal is here to help."

Lance, "And your—"

Omniconal CEO: "What's the *deal?* I'm going to send you a bill for wasting my time. But I didn't catch your name. I'll send it to Hamlet here." CEO Valerie is again glaring at me. I don't need cloud-based math to see why. Lance for whatever reason did not tell me to dress up like an adult in a business meeting. I sit there in my loser loner wrinkled T-shirt and grimed blue jeans, Jesus sandals and hair to match.

This is not Lance's third insufferable goddess. He looks seasoned as he wheels on his heels in a step forward that might get violent.

"The *deal,* Valerie, is that too many people with power dislike your smart-ass superiority. The *deal* is we can fix that big time for you. You will make yet another fortune from us doing so. Which you agree to share halvsies with Trenton Shakespeare Festival Inc." Lance smiling to her basilisk stare, "And all TSF records will disappear the name of Lester Laeme. Though we want nothing to do with his poisoning in Rome."

Valerie shrugs, "Now the fucker is in Verona."

Lance has a way of just dimpling like coolly admiring applause.

I seem to remind Valerie of another regretted offbeat lover. "Do we need Hamlet here?"

She sits down, crosses tanned arms I actually think are still cool. The wide-set eyes must be Norman blood. Very tough guys. And so gals. "You still have five."

A Lance signature move as director is characters refusing to look toward each other when they should if they were just ordinary people. He is back over at the window, looking up to what little to see of blue sky. "Seventeenth Earl of Oxford born 1550."

Pause. "Four."

Lance now places his metal tube chair alongside Valerie's chair at her black glass desk. In a low confiding voice after this stage business, "Your Omniconal software should be able to now somehow show that Oxford wrote the Shakespeare plays and poetry. A very bitter very important dispute about that has been going for a century. Involving suppression of the Oxfordians so harsh Queen Elizabeth's thugs would be proud. But now . . . Now, Valerie? Now Valerie Farnsworth with her gallant culturally woke Omniconal Friendship International Unlimited, Limited, in public service to the world at last breaks the case. To adoring applause of billions. And the clueless politicians back down due to your public popularity as a friend of the arts."

"You're Mark, right?

"It's Lance."

"Whatever. I have a computer science and statistics Ph.D. from Imperial. And I never saw one play all my time in London. I like facts. I like manipulating facts faster than people can think. And have zed interest in plays. All the lazy sods dressing up like children."

Damned if she isn't staring harshly at my T-shirt. I forget what's printed on the chest but am too suave to look down.

Lance in the counseling devil confidential tone, "Which is stone cold of you, Valerie. Which is why normal people don't like you, Valerie. So some want to disable your programming. Omniconal puts together so much so fast so tight that what it says for people is very hard to disavow. That's scaring too many people lately."

She has a CEO smile that would terrify small children. "'Just saying' is our corporate motto. A billion jerks at their screens love it."

"Valerie, everybody knows Omniconal is a cold bitch. You must realize resentment could round fast on you in politics. But—" This is *Godfather Part I* hammy, he even says it in low whispering reason's tone. "Look at me, Valerie . . .Valerie, with just a little money I can make you personally beloved by most of the world. And from your good deed make you richer off the copyrights and trademarks we will create. All inside three months.

"We have a great playwright. Our streamed production showcasing Omniconal will sell the genius-brilliant Earl of Oxford to the world as the true Shakespeare. Your people can come up with any bit of document fluff and we will shine it up bright, flashing as proof Oxford really was forcibly hidden behind a nobody beard guy not even actually named Shakespeare. I myself will be Oxford in the play. We booked Radio City already, streaming from there worldwide."

Her stone stare.

"And Valerie, there's you as Queen. At the explosive conclusion, we write in your cool cameo appearance for Shakespeare's great patron. So you come out to the footlights spotlighted in full Queen Elizabeth dress-up."

Lance should not do this. But he says enraptured to her chest not her eyes, "Sweetheart, you will dazzle everyone." Now he looks away, dazzled.

She says "Four." But that is a growing move upward at Valerie's glossed lip tips. "I deal one to one. Hop it, Hamlet." She picks up her quivering phone, pushes intercom. "Clarissa. Any caller gets a Number Two fuck off. Except Standfill, he's a Five and I want to hear your voice in here."

And then their real conversation began, after I shuffled away offstage. Lance told me of it later. But he is my director who does not explain well, in the opinion of some actors and readers.

*

*   *

"The Rockettes absolutely cannot wear skirts over their sparkly panties. In their contract since what the 1930s. Dangerous when they kick. And besides, you know."

Izadore Mocha is looking into Lance's eyes very earnestly. For 50 years at this desk off Times Square he has looked earnestly into the eyes of businessmen and women who were not business yet. Lance told me he is the agent who got him cast as an actor, and later hired as a director, over 25 of those years. Mocha is power speaking facetiously.

"Iz, this is not *Kiss Me, Kate*. It's *Hamlet*."

"Those girls can dance anything. Very competitive femininity. Fourth wave kids."

"Come on."

I can tell this is the way it is for Lance talking to the old fox.

Feigned Shakespearean misunderstandings then Iz was there all along. "We don't need dancing young ladies in panties. We're doing a new kind of *Hamlet*. This is our Hamlet, meet Harry Haines."

Mocha looks earnestly at me sitting beside Lance. I am wearing a rumply suit over a wrinkly T-shirt, Damon Runyan casting call style. "How old are you?"

"Thirty."

Mocha speaks to a wall in his confidence. "Too old."

Lance: "Come now. Hamlet was thirty in the play. And the Earl of Oxford was just maybe thirty-two when Queen Elizabeth began to dump him from her good graces after letting her gang rob him blind since he was a kid."

"Duh. Who what when? Look, my friend, you rent Radio City Music Hall for one night you are going to lose your ass this guy just moping for three hours. The girls could be a warmup act. Square dancing or whatever the fuck Queen Elizabeth liked."

"Okay. I appreciate your concern, Iz. But don't worry about me. I have my own Queen Elizabeth now. She's covering all costs. We're not even charging admission. It's a private party."

"Then invite some of the girls to liven it up. I'm seeing the crowd at a *Hamlet* party ... O ... my ... god. I went to a Götterdämmerung party at the Met once. Omi*god*."

Lance does his little stagey trick. He picks up his interviewee chair and carries it over to sit close at the side of Mocha. "Old friend, this is the most important gig of your life. You are going to be one of the brave band of adventurers who save the life of Shakespeare."

Mocha's life is like Yankee baseball. Sometime he pitches fast tricky, then it's his turn to get pitched to fast tricky. Lance's latest he just lets pass.

"Iz, you and I know our Shakespeare because we grew up with

it, were young men with it in our souls. We all have some Hamlet in our thinking and feeling."

Mocha is looking at me. I try to look three years younger. He looks away.

Lance is talking close to the old agent's ear like Claudius pouring stuff into old Hamlet's ear. "But with all the social change that new media brought, people are losing interest in Shakespeare. Now for most young people the plays are just odd old grandparents' stuff. The new generations want computerized impossibly buff superheroes. Everybody adores kickboxing red-hot women with goddess laser eyes. Cool is ninety minutes of monosyllables amid explosions.

"You're a twentieth-century guy, Iz. Me too. We know our Shakespeare. But dangerous language flowing out of complex people's emotions is just not in most people's awareness any more. Shakespeare's eloquent murderous royal courts a timeless time ago . . . just too weird. The young are drifting back into feudal mental serfdom. Chained for life to mass media that trivializes them by their own ignorant narcissism. Soon Shakespeare's subtle ironic insights could be lost as if never there to know about people's capacities."

Mocha does pay attention. "Yeah. That I got, Lance. Yeah." Mocha's shift of tone shows he sort of means to agree. Though considering his age and near departure from the scene, I intuit the future enlightenment of young ignoramuses is not really his thing. "Anyway, Lancey, I'm worried about your church gig in Trenton."

"We can be okay. There's still enough spirit left around New York for a few small Shakespeare theaters. But Iz, look at me, hey *look*, this is way more ambitious. Our commandos are going to juice Shakespeare back alive after 400 years. Like Frankenstein when the lightning bolt struck."

Mocha is not on the lightning beam. Real old to cast as one

of Lance's mental space commandos. "Yeah, I suppose, maybe. Kids now can't get enough monsters. And vampires. Probably reminds them of their computer dating scary hookups."

"Wrong thought, Iz. Shakespeare is not Frankenstein the freak. The freak is the man called Shakespeare who actually was absent from all that intense writing. Dangerous writing. Leaving a sense his ghost is hiding below story and words. But now instead the plays are mostly just presented as odd artefacts drifted to Earth from Mars. Some productions a little bit more cleverly colored in between the lines than others. But you know real theater, Iz. You know good plays are written from the author's real blood flowing out of his pen. Written in blood still welling out from under scars.

"That's our mission, Iz. We will put that shocking blood back into the plays. And credit that to a computer's commanding intelligence. Since computers have replaced both civil authority and religious authority. By the magic of our new vision, the young will be transfixed by newly supercool Shakespeare. Who we reveal was ignored as a kerflooey wastrel. But is *now* suddenly revealed to be the super-brilliant jousting champion and Queen Elizbeth's dancing stud, the longhair redhead rebel Seventeenth Earl of Oxford. A Marvel plot, isn't it?"

Iz turns back from his confidante wall. "Lancey? This is all from a one-night gig at Radio City? Come the hump on."

"Twenty-first century calling Izadore Mocha. We will film our night and adroitly flood the Internet for years. Replay will jolt billions of jaded people into seeing Shakespeare again anew. Meaning far cooler than the old plaster saint, far cooler than yet another new boy band or showoff girl. Cool as a reality show. Fascinating news for the jaded young and also the older crowd who did not know what they were missing. By our gig at Radio City everybody gets special new glasses of perception below his 400-year-old brittle surfaces."

Iz must have terrorized women when young. Sort of pensively: "As Mick said, 'the real love, the kind that you feel.' Kids are zeroes today about emotion. I have a granddaughter . . ."

"Good. So you *can* get it, Iz. Shakespeare really was not like some twentieth-century Broadway hack with a knack for cute stories. We can make Shakespeare real in real time to kids today. And also all the older people who tried Shakespeare's plays but couldn't get into the intense language. Because they didn't know the really deep emotion involved in it. You on the team, bubba?"

"I got this, Lancey. I got that you got an artsy problem. I have told you and I have told you."

"Wrong thought, Iz. Yes, just artsy is empty. But this Shakespeare revelation is for *real life now*. Because knowing that great mind newly deeper is a mental sunrise. It can bring more energy into an ordinary person's own life dimension."

Mocha has been staring steadily at me instead of Lance. "Hamlet, you had a mental sunrise?"

One should not be judged by one's T-shirt. This annoys me. I say evenly, "Lance is right. When I speak the lines I visualize what in Shakespeare's real world caused him to write them so. I feel the writer's anger from the writer's own experience."

"He write you a letter?"

"The Earl of Oxford lived among particular people detailed in history books. They made a dangerous society that entrapped him. Knowing those people's history plus Oxford's life events within their world, we can feel his emotion that is in play in his plays. And how he morphed that reality into codes."

"Eh."

Smug old lizard. I say, "T.S. Eliot."

Iz back, "They were buddies?"

"Before Oxford was discovered in 1922 as the hidden Shake-speare, Eliot wrote a famous essay. Saying the *Hamlet* play clearly seems to be thinking about mysterious things other than its own storyline. Eliot named this the missing 'logical correlative' but looked no further."

"The story's enough."

Lance: "Harry, give Iz more. He's just pretending to be asleep."

I know pregnant pausing. "Oxford's deceased father the Sixteenth Earl was probably poisoned. By an agent of Robert Dudley, a rumored serial poisoner and sly murderer of his wife. Dudley then was Queen Elizabeth's hot lover. Who she unjustifiably appointed as guardian to control a lot of the wealth of the orphan little boy who just inherited to become the Seventeenth Earl. Which Dudley then stole from him majorly over years.

"Elizabeth was so sexually bonded to Dudley she went along. Actually in the same way Queen Gertrude does with bad-boy Claudius in *Hamlet*. Dudley in actual history gets himself made an Earl and lives in a king-size castle with his new stolen wealth. And, like *Hamlet's* Polonius, Burghley as the Crown's top fixer constantly spies on young Oxford. Lays fake new impossible taxes and penalties on him. And then Burghley manipulates twenty-year-old Oxford to marry his teenage daughter with threat and a huge big dowry. Plus clemency from execution of Oxford's first cousin and boyhood best friend. Both promises were defaulted. Instead of paying the dowry Burghley made Oxford take a big loan which he later foreclosed on, keeping a lot of mortgaged land."

Lance: "Good, Harry. Ring-a-ding, both stories. So Iz, for you *Hamlet's* now no longer just made-up stuff. It's coded anger of the playwright about his own real-time entrapment by powerful people who kill and steal."

Iz is back. "That would be dangerous."

He's on the line. Lance: "Very dangerous for Oxford but the guy had bollocks. There was a production in the mid-1580s at Hampton Court palace, for big courtiers only. Oxford probably managed and paid for the whole event as a surprise gift for the Queen, since Elizabeth never paid for her entertainment. At this early version Hamlet's end all the coded bad guys plus Hamlet's coded confused mom wound up sprawled dead on stage. The lights went up and all copies of the script were immediately confiscated and burned. Only after 1600 when both Burghley and Dudley were dead, and Elizabeth grown fragile, did Oxford's mature re-creation of Hamlet appear in print."

Lance: "So Iz, now you know why there is a rumor of a lost "ur-Hamlet." It was Oxford's completely suppressed first production from 1585. When by the way that Stratford guy was only 21 and still living there poor."

Mocha sits silent. Then smiling yellow teeth: "So with Oxford as author you see Shakespeare characters deeper through to real people there under them."

Lance: "Smart guy, Iz. The Shakespeare writing comes in high def dimensional if you connect Oxford's biography to it. Big fun."

Mocha is of course a professional bullshitter too. And does he know actors and directors. "Lancey, get your money up front from the new girlfriend. Radio City plays with real knives about rent."

Part Two

If this were a movie scene it would look like Lance and I are runaway lovers, on a squanderous toot in a honeymoon suite at the Waldorf Astoria Hotel, Park Avenue at 50th.

But Queen Valerie has turned out to be as mercurially generous within life-long parsimony as Queen Elizabeth. Project expenditures became unlimited once she bought into Lance's plan to give Omni-conal the global glory spotlight of computer science, proof that the fascinating 17th Earl of Oxford, Edward de Vere, was secretly and tragically for him author of Shakespeare. Pocket lint to a technology billionaire, now TSF actors' salaries are doubled, our convent gym theater rent is paid a half year in advance, the global media pr team is contracted, the elaborate performance streaming production team is contracted. Lance's own financial reward as incorporator of TSF, Inc. is not my business. Considering his two meetings with Valerie over dinner it may not be business. Again like Queen Elizabeth and her favorites. Until they were not favorites.

And a writer for the play has been hired. Me. Lance must have had his undiscussed reason. Nothing to do with credentials for sure. He knows about the careening among disappointing personal nullities despite my IQ. The actual level of that IQ depending upon the interviewee, and whether I slept with them or borrowed money or both.

My job is to personally voice Edward de Vere, the basically infamous 17th Earl of Oxford. Onstage in performance speaking as himself, from his experiences transmigrated into his art known as Shakespeare today. Enigmatic Edward the man there onstage amid his characters who reveal their own ghosts speaking below their literal lines. The author of Shakespeare freed from all poses of fiction. This naturally will be searingly emotional for Oxford. He will speak as a confessing Prince of his own immense long-suffered realm of disasters. Will be heard as the artist in open reverie.

That's all. Simple. My new gig, as even Elizabethans said. Lance as usual is not much for guidance. I was just hired for a small-fortune fee paid in advance by Queen Valerie. Once enthused she has seemed to regard cash as trash. Which may be tidal, and once I almost drowned in a rip tide.

Lance cast himself to play Oxford onstage. How he will tonally pitch the tenor of that real-life chameleon I have no idea yet. And too Lance, whose last role as an actor was Prospero, convinced Valerie to perform briefly in the crucial epilogue. I am to write Valerie's lines. Simple gig. I am terrified.

Money being no object now Lance rented the Waldorf suite because of its view of the street scene in Ethan Hawke's striking modern staging of *Hamlet*. This is our writing retreat. Somehow overlooking Park at 50th should imbue my imagination. In Lance's opaque opinion. Anyway, now on my first day as writer employee of Valerie Farnsworth, very new patron of the arts, I sit alone waiting for Lance to come talk story.

One can be very alone in the Waldorf's repellently beige anti-septic suite. I try to bring back some of what I know already about the Earl of Oxford. And Queen Elizabeth. And their concurrences in history. My memory from university reading now is reemerging spotty, like my own bio. Meaning there are some sunny warm lit spots among sharp-edged dark cold shadows.

That dark cold memory part sums up how my Princeton doctoral program experience ended. To me as a scholar Oxford seemed biographically obviously like a complex Shakespeare character. And that led me to propose a doctoral thesis addressing Oxford as possible hidden author of the works of Shakespeare.

But my mentor, Professor Sheppard Germaine, being the Mr. and Mrs. Financial Fiddlesticks Chair of Early Modern English Literature, told me dead flat in tone and gaze: no. Full stop.

I already disliked my fat smug master on a fat salary in a smug university. I was ready to go anyway. So suddenly I fully stopped studying literature. To become a fat lawyer and so got into NYU Law. After a year not for me. Then on to become a skinny actor. And so. Pleased to meet you.

Just arrived at my and Lance's Waldorf script composition retreat, I'm feeling like my character Hamlet I was ready to perform before things went off course. I just sit here getting ready to get ready, mind moving in various directions. One forward.

Beside me in this beige oasis sits a big black wheely suitcase full of Lance's Shakespeare studies books he sent ahead. Yet to be opened it looks just like what a terrorist would leave in an airport lounge. My own library of dozens of Shakespeare books, with their thousands of markings in my studenty code, disappeared a couple years ago. Lost flotsam of another sunken romance.

I have to open that suitcase and intensely study its books to write our play properly infused with scholarly history. That I must get correct for an instant army of critics. But am still stunned by receipt of a $250,000 playwrighting fee from Valerie. Maybe the always glib Lance did not tell me of some barbed wire string on my fee obligation to scary Valerie and her mind-gooning company.

*

*　　*

I remember enough to already know that when I unzip Lance's Shakespeare library rancorous arguments as to who the writer really was will tumble out.

The Oxfordian scholars since a revelatory 1920 biography have accumulated hundreds of contemporaneously documented facts about Oxford. These they tie to intellectually corresponding content of Shakespeare's literary art. From their now dozens of published books and thousands of journal issues and web blogs thus stacked up, Oxfordians say, to those who will listen: Here behold circumstantial proof to the roof.

All this Oxfordian work has not been welcomed by Stratfordians, proponents of William Shaxper of Stratford as really Shakespeare. Stratfordian leadership is primarily university English Department professors, and their curricula tend to entirely avoid comparative biographical analysis of Oxford and the Shakespeare canon. Leading Stratfordian academics insist that no Elizabethan period writer of plays expressed his personal life or emotions. Biography connection, they thus say, is irrelevant at best.

Stratfordians further insist Oxfordians threaten grave damage to the magically gifted imaginative texts of Shakespeare. Believing that modern 20th- and 21st-century biographic-centric literary sensibility actually distorts the nature of Shakespeare's superb 16th-century literary sensibility.

Stratfordians look to the 30-play compendium published in 1623 known as the First Folio. Its cover says their author is "William Shakespeare." Editor Ben Jonson's preface materials refer to both Shakespeare and Stratford, though ambiguously. There is even a portrait of William Shakspeare. For the Stratfordians full, full stop with sneer.

But now some Oxfordians step up to the noisy crowded bar at the Mermaid Tavern. One waves a reproduction of the 1623 First Folio, the initial collection of all plays of Shakespeare. Noting that it was produced at extraordinary cost paid solely by the brother Earls of Pembroke and Montgomery. The Earl of Pembroke was then Crown Chancellor, who controlled publication authorization through the Censor.

Thumping the sticky bar of the Mermaid, the Oxfordian shouts the major fact that the Earl of Montgomery was the doting husband of Oxford's youngest daughter, Susan de Vere. Susan, recognized as a well educated intellectual, was at the center of a close family circle of in-laws, both very rich and powerful. She was thus friendly with her brother-in-law Chancellor Pembroke and with the brothers' mother. This mother of the sole publishers of the First Folio was Dowager Countess of Pembroke, a famous Elizabethan intellectual salon hostess and an old friend of Susan's father the 17th Earl of Oxford. Her sons Pembroke and Montgomery were both also friends of their peer the Earl of Oxford.

The de Vere girls, poor as church mice due to their father's perpetual bankruptcy, must have had special qualities. Susan's sister Elizabeth was happily married to the Earl of Stanley. Stanley, a brilliantly educated and Italy-traveled personal friend of Oxford, as well as his son-in-law, is rumored in a surviving letter to have been secretly writing plays for the commercial theater.

Thus Oxford's daughters' married families had their wealthy and powerful ways and means to a sophisticated manipulation of the First Folio misidentification to the Stratford man. By 1623 the recent rise of militant Puritans, hostile to aristocracy and theater, risked political trouble by Folio public connection to controversial feudalist aristocrat Oxford as revealed author, even though long dead. This diversion proved discreetly wise. Since soon theatrical performance would be banned for 20 years, much theatrical and other writing offensive to Puritans would be destroyed, and class warfare beginning 1639 would culminate in the beheading of England's King in 1649.

The track of the Folio project is documented. Chamberlain Pembroke's Crown multiplied aging Ben Jonson's modest stipend 10-fold for no stated reason. Jonson as Lord Pembroke and Montgomery's editor and ghost writer then prefaced the Folio ambiguously. For the first time in print ever linking just by inference of terminology the shadowy author William Shakespeare to the man William Shaxper of Stratford-upon-Avon. Jonson's preface received necessary prior clearance from the Crown Censor under Pembroke's authority. So of course the family acquiesced in Jonson's misleadingly pointing to Shaxper and not to his long-time tavern friend and competitor playwright Oxford as the man really Shakespeare.

No record has been found showing how the Folio came to contain a dozen Shakespeare plays not previously ever mentioned anywhere. Oxfordians say, well, obviously Oxford's daughters and son-in-law the erudite Lord Stanley directly brought them to Jonson as executive compiler of the Folio. Those plays were Oxford's drafts preserved by the family after his sudden death in early 1604, likely from a plague surge that killed over 35,000 Londoners in one year.

This past century, from the 1922 first proposal of the Earl as being really Shakespeare, has hardened the back and forth assertions of the Stratfordians and Oxfordians into mutual rancor. A dynamic rather similar to the Elizabethan late 16th-century era of bitter Catholic versus Protestant conflict. In that religious war one contesting dogma would put a crucifix on a nunnery wall. The other alternatively would smash it gone. Both sides at blooded sword point insisting their theory far beyond palpable fact. That bloodshed was literally so in the 16th century.

It is figuratively, literarily you could say, so between Stratfordians and Oxfordians. Mark Twain around 1900 wrote of the Stratfordian credo that they take one bone plus a thousand pounds of plaster, then model a huge dinosaur. A paper war continues from the times of Twain, Henry James, Sigmund Freud, Walt Whitman and other early sceptics.

Some propositions of the opposing proponents are plainly substantive.

For instance the Oxfordian analysis of improbable dating. They scorn Shaxper's presumed profuse immediately mature output as soon as he first arrived in London about 1592 at age 28. With at best a rote Latin junior high school education in a market town of about 1,200. Oxfordians point to vestigial evidence of plays produced at Elizabeth's Court in the 1570s that by topic or title seem to have been early versions of what later appeared revised to become the final canon work. In the 1570s Shaxper was barely a teenager. Full stop say Oxfordians. So it is they see that huge practical improbability of time as being much like medieval Catholic saints' wildly made up magical deeds, now universally disbelieved.

For an opposite instance, Stratfordians thump the biblical First Folio. Its editor the playwright Ben Jonson surely would have known who Shakespeare was. And right there up front he calls Shakespeare the gentle swan of the river Avon, which runs through Stratford. Plus there is his portrait right there on the frontispiece. Full stop say the Stratfordians.

So it is each side of the Stratfordian and Oxfordian dispute in one degree of scholarly politeness or another calls the other side to be like those medieval Catholic deluded fabulists. Naturally each side hopes for some contemporaneous document in their favor, for one thing that simply settles the open wrangle. But for now mere circumstance and inference reign the binary question.

*

* *

I sit on the bland beige Waldorf sofa waiting for Lance to arrive and direct my writing. Without opening the jihadi-size suitcase. I already know much of what is in there. To find a surprise in there is my fear of conscience.

The William Shakespeare name first appeared in print in 1592 and again in 1593. In two long sexually unusual poems dedicated to the then teenage 3d Earl of Southampton, Henry Wriothesley. These dedications are very fishy even to many Stratfordian scholars. Because, in Elizabethan society's basic reality, commoners like the young nobody Shaxper in 1592 legally and socially were not allowed to address senior aristocrats in published writing. The Elizabethan Crown kept class lines very restrictive the better to barrier aristocratic privilege. Royal sumptuary command even regulated how both lower- and middle-class individuals could or could not dress as to garment and materials, with punishment made for violating upper-class barriers. Unapproved publication incurred severe penalty, possibly including jail and disfigurement. But if the Crown knew "William Shakespeare" actually was an aristocrat's new pen name, mandated by the Queen's councilors, there would be no repercussion.

Thus debut of the Shakespeare name when about 28-year-old Shaxper first arrived in London greatly affects authorship credibility. No record indicates Shaxper ever even met the then teenage Southampton, who as still an orphan ward of the Court lived chaperoned, under control of Queen Elizabeth's top official Lord Burghley.

On the other, Oxfordian, hand the 17th Earl of Oxford demonstrably from historical records very well knew this Earl of Southampton. Documents show Oxford long urged Southampton to marry his daughter Elizabeth (who also was granddaughter of the Queen's top minister Lord Burghley). A French foreign agent's report says, otherwise unsubstantiated, that subsequently Burghley imposed and collected a huge punitive fine when young Southampton after a year of entreaties declined to marry the girl. The numbered first 17 of the *Sonnets* urging marriage are considered even by most Stratfordian scholars to be very probably addressed to young Southampton the formal dedicatee.

But there's more Elizabethan dish. Because some sonnets among the 145 or so veer off into an apparent homosexual crush of the poet on the same "fair youth." Southampton was a notedly effeminate late teenager. A recently confirmed portrait of still teenage Henry Wriothesly for centuries was mistaken as one of an anonymous glamorous young woman, fondling loose long hair at the chest and adorned by a garish large earring.

After word of the content of the sonnets was reported by spies, Oxfordians can guess the Queen and Burghley's exasperated response to this sexually scandalous behavior by Oxford. It was clearly existentially dangerous for the Crown. Radically doctrinaire Puritans would drive the English Civil War within five decades.

Already the 1590s were a time when scandals of dysfunctional feudalism had become a destabilizing issue in English society as it began to modernize. So of course mercurial Oxford, the wastrel seemingly gay definitely bankrupt embodiment of purely hereditary aristocracy, must not be allowed to pull the Elizabethan Crown into more controversy.

Severe warning followed. The recently widowed Oxford, who had been a notoriously troubled and troubling husband, received a miniature painted by a royal artist named Thomas Hilliard. It portrayed him touched warningly on his shoulder by a delicate woman's hand reaching down from Heaven, that would be Burghley's by then deceased daughter Anne. A Latin inscription warns that pederasty leads to Hell.

This Oxford episode is a very Shakespearean ironic twist. Sardonically comic, here is a dad gone gay for his daughter's fiancé. But in real life that scandal would be deadly serious in the unstable reign of the Queen.

Elizabeth, her right-hand enforcer Lord Burghley, and her left-hand spymaster Sir Francis Walsingham all must have seen the conundrum Earl of Oxford problem coming to a head. Previously Oxford's popular history plays had provided morale boosts for the unpredictable illiterate populace throughout the decade-long '80s period when European Catholic invasion ominously threatened. And his comedies and romances of exotic ancient aristocrats had bolstered imagery of the Tudor usurpers as prestigious royalty.

Here is what some Oxfordians deduce as the root of the Crown's imposition of a mask on Oxford's identity as an author. They surmise that by around 1590, additionally to the leaked homoerotic private sonnets, spies also showed Crown insiders that Oxford was capable of taking Queen Elizabeth's personal image into danger.

They reported that the still-unpublished text of Oxford's *Venus and Adonis* portrays a handsome young god considering and casually rejecting sexual pleading from a lonely aging love goddess. That was too close to Elizabeth the professional Virgin Queen, since everybody knew of Elizabeth's fascination with much younger Oxford in the 1570s.

Lord Burghley was Elizabeth's most trusted advisor and personal friend. Burghley's beloved only daughter Anne's life had been ruined by Oxford in stubborn anger. And the immediately suppressed circa 1585 "ur-*Hamlet*" play that Oxford previously produced to privately entertain the Queen at Hampton Court had transparently ridiculed Burghley as Polonius. Oxford as author even ignominiously killed Polonius at the hand of his obvious doppelganger Hamlet. With pen in hand this bipolar man Oxford was plainly a loose cannon politically.

The Queen had only to nod. Oxford could die efficiently as his good friend of same age Christopher Marlowe, stabbed in a bar room by an exonerated future Crown employee. He could be disappeared simply as a shrug.

But the Queen would not have that, whatever her hard men urged. Though harried by fate as Elizabeth always was, Edward meant things from her youth that caused her to protect him long and finally well. Young Oxford actually had been Elizabeth's doted-on favorite. Gallantly colorful above the other gallantly colorful handsome stylish courtiers the Queen preferred in her Court. Brilliantly eloquent and erudite Oxford. Mesmerizing performance dancer and musician Oxford. Oxford the Court's two-time jousting champion. Oxford the legitimate, elegant plume of ancient noble social order, so unlike the rawly arriviste destructive grasping Tudors.

Considering this overview of persons and events up to 1592,

an enforced government plan to hide Oxford's authorship from the public does seem to originate logically in Elizabethan circumstantial political practicality. The Queen's advisors were obviously correct to warn her that there was no telling what the dramatically bipolar Oxford might write next. And possibly thereby risk upset of already unstable rulership order itself.

So to Oxford simple choice rationally could have been put by the Crown's hard men. To either continue writing quietly but die as a publicly un-acknowledged author, or to just die. The Queen, likely touched by the pain Oxford previously expressed in the "ur-*Hamlet*" to "catch her conscience," had granted him from 1588 a unique personal pension. Generous but revocable, it allowed the then indigent Oxford to write in peace disengaged from Court struggles. But by around 1592 both the pension and Oxford's physical endangerment had come to a precipice edge due to all the spy reports about his writing.

Oxford was a hopeless bankrupt due to huge fee, tax and fine debt arbitrarily imposed upon his inherited wealth in Tudor predation. But even ardent Oxfordians acknowledge that the man's deep insolvency was compounded by his own extravagant expenditures from youth into middle age. He spent fortunes on generous housing and monetary subsidy of writers and actors, and subsidized two acting troupes as long as he could. In gratitude about 30 books were dedicated to this Earl of Oxford. Beyond reckless borrowing he made disastrously foolish sales of ancient illiquid agricultural properties of the Earldom to raise ready cash to embody his romantic vision of how an artistic Prince should behave.

Not the first or last advanced intellectual to have advanced poor financial sense.

So there Oxford was, past age 40 around 1592. Caught in a cat's cradle of impossible seriously threatening debt and likely deadly political threat. Thus he had to agree with the Crown to only write anonymously, using a false name as a diverting public shield. And anyway as a deeply traditional feudalist at the beginning Oxford may not have even wanted his real name known. In the Elizabethan period no true aristocrats were writing for the public stage in their own name. Such a breaking of the major class barrier, by serving the public at its pleasure, was culturally and governmentally proscribed anyway.

But brilliant Edward would be so brilliant at choosing his required pen name. He chose an in-joke commoners would not see. Oxford's second major title was Viscount Bolbec, whose armorial shield emblazons a rampant lion shaking a large spear.

And too this writer's pseudonym also gracefully salutes Athena, the classical Greek goddess of arts who was usually portrayed brandishing a spear.

Also Oxford could privately recall already being obscurely complimented as himself a writer who shakes a spear. For back in 1578 the well known University of Oxford intellectual Gabriel Harvey had dedicated a Latin translation to him in thanks for career support. Harvey wrote in Latin that his friend the Earl's own literary talent "shakes a spear." Harvey was alluding to Athena, as literati then understood.

So clever a veil over the author's name. Yet even all that was still not enough wit for Shakespearean complexity. Oxford had been a two-time jousting champion at Court pageants, where lances were also called spears.

There it is to easily understand even today. In witty flourish Edward de Vere, Earl and Viscount, submitted to Crown command and chose the jokey pseudonym of William Shake-speare. This multiply coded new pen name would have been amusing to Oxford's inner circle.

A pen name choice fit the culture. The Elizabethan Age was a golden time of witty pseudonyms of writers generally. Oxford's choice of Shake-speare satisfied practical Crown overseers because it sounded close enough to a shadowy minor actor and theater hanger-on newly arrived in London named William Shaxper.

Further amusingly for the notoriously often punning Oxford, the name "William" also was old slang for a country hick. A name which Oxford later played on. In *As You Like It* Shakespeare poisonously ridicules "William," a posing rural nitwit who aspires to steal a writer character's artistic muse.

So the acceptance of the name William Shake-speare was a complex matter for Oxford. But it served purpose for the Crown. William Shakespeare the commoner cover name had nothing to do with the Queen and her all too vivid courtiers including the reprobate Earl of Oxford.

*

*   *

Young Shaxper logically could have received from the Crown a substantial hush money payoff, paid with strong threat terms from Walsingham's hard men. Because in documentary fact, in all his lifetime, Shaxper never claimed of record to be the author of any work of Shakespeare. Or ever even used the name spelled Shakespeare instead of his lifelong legal name Shaxper. No evidence otherwise is known after centuries of search efforts.

When texts appeared in 1592 and 1593 and then 1597 and 1598 bearing the William Shakespeare name, Shaxper was silent. Being then safely back in Warwickshire for recorded periods.

For changing reasons, as English history rapidly evolved after Oxford's death in 1604, retention of this fictional "Shakespeare" shield remained crucially useful to the Crown. And also to the elite inter-connected families linked to his collected work in the Folio, who designed its diverting camouflage by the Shaxper ruse.

Very many Elizabethan and Jacobean manuscripts perished in the coming decades of English social turmoil leading to war destroying theater for a generation. And consequently much unwritten private knowledge of the 1570s through 1590s disappeared from English culture. But Oxford's life works had been thus preserved. This is an intelligent story of a caring and wise family, intuitively understandable today.

And a story of friendship among writers. Ben Jonson and Oxford are recorded as boozing together in a tavern with mutual friend Christopher Marlowe, in a letter written by another respected writer whom Oxford supported financially in his early career. There is no record Jonson ever met Shaxper and he obviously carefully never wrote so. Yet Jonson's Folio preface and accompanying ghost-written recollections do intimate that Shaxper was Shakespeare, swan of the river Avon. Stratfordians insist that of course Jonson would have known the author. His wording of the Folio preface is perhaps the single core document proof for centuries of Stratfordian conviction. Though even within the period its language is odd and the connection allusively put.

But then, quite to the contrary, one can argue that of course Jonson actually did know better. There was good reason, beyond his personally needed fee money, for Jonson at the direction of Oxford's politically powerful extended family to help shield Oxford as author of the Folio works. After an Elizabethan imprisonment Jonson bore a tattoo on his right thumb authorizing the death penalty for any further offense to the Crown. And anyway his old friend Oxford was long dead. Aye, Jonson could say into an empty echoing tankard at The Mermaid, aye, saving the plays from the Puritans is the thing.

And too lots of people still alive in 1623 knew about Oxford. Jonson consolingly could have thought the author's credit would come true in time. But Jonson could not have foreseen that all contemporaries would be dead long before theater escaped the Puritan complete prohibition in the mid 17th century. And so it was political expediency after political expediency came to harden into artistic gospel of centuries to come.

*

*   *

As to William Shaxper, a cash payoff for playing the role of silent stooge seems likely. It would have been paid by a Crown agent or the very wealthy marriage families of Oxford's daughters Susan and Elizabeth. Payments for no service but silence would have been made between 1592 and 1604, those years being between the first use of the pen name "William Shakespeare" and when Oxford died. Some 90 printed works bore the name William Shake-speare, or the easier to set in type. In the same year 1604 that Oxford suddenly died Shaxper left London forever.

Some Oxfordians think hush money likely because soon after arriving in London surely poor about 1592, always without any record whatsoever of any payment for writing or acting, Shaxper somehow became owner of a share in a Crown-controlled acting company that premiered most of Shakespeare's plays. That troupe traced back to Oxford's own sponsorship of it before he became destitute.

And, as mysteriously as this sudden ownership in an elite troupe premiering Shakespeare's plays, Shaxper was able, within about just six years from arrival in London poor and totally uncredentialed, to buy himself for cash a landed 24-room manor house back in Stratford—although he was the son of illiterate bankrupts and although Elizabethan playwrights did not become quickly wealthy on fees for a few plays.

Anyway, surviving records of Shaxper activities once back permanently in distant Stratford from early 1604 are clear as to his activities. Shaxper evidenced no literary or even literate activity whatsoever. But he was a busy man. Multiple third-party documents show Shaxper speculated in grain hoarding during plague and famine times, for which he was fined. And wool trading in violation of guild rules, for which he was fined. And loan sharked, for which he was once made subject to a London court restraining order protecting a terrified debtor. In Stratford Shaxper entrepreneurially contracted to collect taxes from distressed neighbors in a recession for a share of collections. And was documented to have corrupted local government by buying preferential protection from its seizure of Stratford community acreage, which seizure he then supported against his neighbors. He sued many times even over tiny sums, but never sued over any play despite abusive theft of scripts.

Such a hard, often shady, businessman. So here indeed for Stratfordians is replete contemporaneous documentation substantiating the personal identity of their man Shaxper. It abundantly shows their man Shaxper personally was a real asshole.

Of record Shaxper never wrote or received a single letter. Not a note to or from him about his multifarious business dealings and certainly not about any theater matter at all. Although thus seeming just an Elizabethan-style rough small businessman, Shaxper somehow also had extra cash to buy himself a gentleman's coat of arms, from an official later censured by the Crown for taking bribes.

This coat of arms was a scene Oxford would have loved to parody in a play. And that his good friend Ben Jonson hilariously actually did. What a story. This next is plain fact. Shaxper's cooked up family motto on the new shield is "Not Without Right." In Jonson's play *Every Man Out of His Humor* a pretentious parasite country hick is grossly mocked as the disreputable charlatan character Sogliardo. Sogliardo also buys a gentleman's coat of arms for himself. The fake family motto reads "Not Without Mustard." Sogliardo's shield display's a pig's head. Note that the DeVere coat of arms features a fierce tusked wild boar; ironically the ancient family motto is "Nothing Truer Than Truth."

*
*   *

From thinking so long I need to stand. It seems I need to walk to the Park Avenue window view. That streetscape presents hard facades relentlessly aligned. Its buildings likely full of Stratfordians. My job now is to ignore them, just to voice Oxford. So that the long occlusion of his wounded name by Shaxper will become a disappearing very odd dream for Oxford and for the world. As Bottom awoke amazed from long sleep in *Midsummer Night's Dream*.

New York appears so non-Elizabethan out there to behold. Humanity has gone on and on curlicuing since the 16th century. Oxford standing here in the Waldorf window with my job as a writer would not set out now to write TSF's new play exactly as he put tales 400 years ago. No, being so talented he would immediately use some new evolved idioms to express himself to us moderns.

The taxis below dart adroitly. Their drivers live by flow and so become themselves the flowing parti-color pulsing river of traffic. I stand as audience to Park Avenue's constant processions across the macadam and concrete stage. The moment's enormous cast all amove, from drivers on roadway to walkers on sidewalk.

Those walkers varied as in a pageant performance. Walking a woven stream of beauties and beasts, of youth and age. Some congenitally kind people, some bad to the bone. From distance or up close, so difficult to sort them apart. Many the mask artfully promenades the hardened heart of Manhattan. *Commedia dell'arte*, that's what New York is.

But *commedia dell'arte* wasn't the only big new influence for rapidly developing English theater. While living in Italy for nine months Oxford sought out foremost writers and artists of its Renaissance. Some he himself had previously translated from Italian or Latin to English, or would later sponsor their translation. Oxford learned of Renaissance intellectuals' high value on seeming to be casual about serious work, seeming at play. Easily parking off excellence in quick flashes. In their new word . . . *sprezzatura*.

Oxford was summoned home by the Crown in 1576. Soon thereafter comic works without an attributed author bedazzled English play audiences because of their daring freshness. Some of those new plays amounted to anglicized *commedia dell'arte*. The likely dynamic was performance first for the Queen and Court. And subsequently in a public production by a licensed troupe, usually somehow connected to Oxford's past sponsorship.

Suddenly, from 1576 when Oxford returned home, in these new *Commedia*-style London comedies men dress as women and women as men. Twins abound. Disguises abound. Rightful noble identities are lost and found. Lovers overcome foolish obstacles. Clowns are wiser than normal folk, who happen to be all nobles. Genders are good-naturedly fluid as hearts beat.

All is *sprezzatura* in spirit, in fast-paced and sharp-edged dialogue that shocked the English as a new kind of brilliantly casual wit. A workaday English audience felt the thrill of being drawn into a new realm of verbally reverberating wit. Who has not wished she-heorit could speak as casually brilliantly as a Shakespearean character? Then or now.

So on I mull. How would Oxford express himself in one of his plays now? Surely would be alert to the potential of technology. So maybe use it in lighting effects to allow characters to express like chameleons. Surely he would break the fourth wall creatively beyond prologues and epilogues. And for our modern-time audiences there certainly would be no necessary tether to unity of time and place.

And yet Oxford writing today would still structure a Shakespeare-type play. It would be woven of his trademark psychological and theatrical elements. His Shakespeare play written now would sparkle sardonically witty caricatures. Would trace lines of hidden or mistaken identity. Would impalpably vibrate anger under the edges of its comedy. And would shock laughter out of a viewer's tired self.

This all is too much for Mrs. Haines's disappointing son Harry. I am not spending any of the $250,000 fee. In case an Omnicronal goon reasonably demands its refund since I am not really a playwright.

The regimented hard facades of buildings across Park Avenue look like Stratfordians lined up. Glaze glaring at my preposterous role on stage here as playwright, they have upset me. I turn away. For all I know there are books in Lance's library in this room that make me a *commedia dell'arte* stock figure, that being The Loser.

I have to find out. Lance's black suitcase is too big to lift and open. In there the Mafia could stuff a garroted stool pigeon, a prison rat, an Oxfordian heretic. The suitcase soft cover unzips quick as a serpent hiss. Some books tumble out. Then I upend the case, noisily shaking all out. The confetti-colored pile of scholarship is a foot high and a serious leap across.

But still I do not want to start to read or write. I want my director Lance to come and just tell me my lines to write. And yet he does not. That's Lance. I think he has perhaps alternatively staged *Waiting for Godot* and cast me.

*

* *

Oxfordians say Shakespeare's work obviously contains advanced linguistic erudition. And evidences an author with actual extensive personal experience in royal Italian and French courts. For perspective, history dramas aside, over half the Shakespeare plays are set in Europe, not Britain.

How odd really. Why would Shakespeare so very repeatedly intensely portray European feudal nobility? Ordinary Elizabethan theater goers were wholly ignorant of European people and places. For there was no legally permitted casual travel due to Catholic country issues and war there was constant. English was not spoken on the Continent in the 16th century.

Minimally educated impoverished Shaxper, however intelligent, is known to have lived only in Stratford and London, a three-day ride apart. No evidence shows he ever traveled anywhere in Britain, much less to Italy. Medieval Catholic saint impossible miracles have been quietly abandoned by the modern church. But the miracle of the Saint Shaxper cult lives on solvently.

The Oxfordians say please look at the actual contemporaneous documents as to the Earl. Fluently speaking French, Italian, Spanish, Greek, and Latin, in his European sojourn Oxford sought out famous intellectuals. It is obvious common sense that Oxford's well recorded year-long sojourn in European capitals became his writer's capital. Writing as Shakespeare in his reflective later life maturity, he repeatedly mentally revisited his muse of perceptions gleaned in Europe. Just as he repeatedly reconsidered his muse wife Anne.

The authorship answer can't be so simple. I am going to have to look through Lance's library for what I may have missed years ago in school. Or what may have vitally changed the Shakespeare world since. That Pandora's rollie suitcase actually could hold even some fact that kills the Oxford theorem decisively as a dagger through my brain. Poor Chris Marlowe who misjudged his audience.

Now is my responsible time to write fiction true enough to advance "things standing thus unknown." As poor Hamlet put it in his last-gasp plea for a rewrite of his life.

And I also somehow must use what Valerie's Omniconal machine mega-mind turns up in research. Maybe it will be some thrilling plot turn. But I do not want to collide with a thrilling plot turn at this high speed calendar to the Radio City debut of TSF's explosive play.

*

*   *

The door swoosh is Lance breezing in at last. His it's-a-fine-day smile deployed, he declaims for the back row, "I love *beige*."

"Don't they have an Elizabethan suite here? That would help."

"Beige walls do not a prison make, Harry." He's looking at me a little long. "Cheer up, some good news. I came up with an ace title for our play. Ready set smile: *The Which of Shakespeare's Why*. We are producing what Hamlet asked good old Horatio to write explaining him 'absent from felicity awhile.' And here, Horatio Harry, you sit looking glum. So it's all good."

I do remember stuff unpredictably. "As to Horatio, actually, Lance, get this. Oxford's uncle was famous as Fighting Horace de Vere. He wrote poetry while not commanding on a battle field. I saw somewhere that after his time in Italy Oxford nicknamed Uncle Horace as Horatio. And Oxford had another de Vere soldier cousin named Francis. Dot-dot to the guard Francisco . . ."

"You go, Hamlet. And in keeping with our hidden figures in the text theme our title *The Which of Shakespeare's Why* is a sensitive literary reference. From a line in the Coen brothers' re-make of *True Grit*. With Jeff Bridges? Cool, right?"

"Well. Okay." Esoteric movie cool is not the issue now.

Lance is indeed my director, another name for puppeteer. "Put on a T-shirt, Harry." Waiting for Lance I have buttoned up the Hamlet costume's velvet doublet, my gray cat's hair subtly patterning its blackness. I like the puckered shoulder roll. And the thing is great for a waistline problem. I'd wear it everywhere from now on if I could.

"This is for inspiration."

"No. No, Harry. We're not playing cute any more. Everybody in TSF will just perform in their own contemporary clothes. Same as Elizabethan men did not think they looked quaint in bright colored tights and a lace ruff while carrying a rapier they really used. Hawke's movie got that 'real time is no time apart' sense dead right. When you're the wonder boy on stage you'll wear your usual East Village grunge. Claudius will be Brooks Brothers dark suit, white shirt, and show-off tie. I'm going to have to think about Ophelia."

Taking direction, as the phrase goes in theater, I'm rooting in the backpack for my Cannabis Forever shirt. That's the one I wore to meet Valerie. I'm as superstitious about good luck as a certain historic Yankee catcher with a sock problem. But I need to work amid good vibrations. "Please turn off the overheads, Lance. I couldn't fill out the room service card in this light."

T-shirt in hand at last, I say, suddenly as a mugger, "Lance do you even like this guy Oxford?"

It takes Lance a while, but he replies, "No, I don't like Eddie de Vere. Not in any simple way. How could anybody easily? De Vere's an impossible personality. A 'passing strange' guy to some people in his own real time. Probably when young he acted out manic-depressive. Though I do, Harry, I really do believe from his special mix of qualities somehow came the Shakespeare plays and poetry."

Fine, Lance. But now how to write a play starring mysterious Eddie himself as well as Shakespeare's dazzlingly complex characters?

I say, "Well, there is our big danger. Right, Lance? To construct a path to the genius writing from a guy who seems pretty jerky in his own actions. Isn't that going to make us . . . kind of like Stratfordians actually? I mean similar to their fantasizing in huge mental leaps.

Stratfordian professors have turned out hundreds of books competitively over-articulating the assumed utter magic of Will Shaxper."

Lance is smiling out into 50th Street. "Harry, you've got maybe too much professor still in you. And I myself also know too much to be simple. But we have to clean forget the library full of Stratfordian constructs now. *The Which* must come alive solely in the Oxfordian world.

"Our play cannot argue with Stratfordians. That would just muddle our clarity. Anyway, for decades now the university professors' competing Shakespeare text theories have been moving confusingly fast. For even fellow Stratfordians.

"There's New Criticism for the old hands. There's New Historicism for the hip. Deconstruction for the incoherent. Whatever Postmodern Theory is supposed to mean shape-shifts rapidly. And now Neo Factor which seems to be for short-term rent cheap. The professors make kids buy these piles of their knitting. But general readers do not buy these wordy theory books. Normal people want just a simple story of a hero genius whom everybody loves start to end."

Usually glib, but now there's an edge in Lance's baritone. "Bubba. The Stratfordian academic complex is an overbuilt house of cards we can tumble."

I have a case of hero worship for Lance. I want to impress him. So I say "It does get rough just among the Stratfordians. Have you read a book about their constant critical conflicts, *The Shakespeare Wars?* In the whole long study all the intensely arguing professors do not even mention Oxford."

"Hilarious! I do know *Shakespeare Wars.* One Stratfordian professor using ancient Greek called another quarreling Stratfordian professor a giver of fellatio to goats!"

That's a fine way Lance starts to smile then stops, taken aback by absurdity. But the dimple shows the smile is still there just turned ironic. Like Mark Rylance performing when I saw him from a first row. So very far beyond my acting ability.

But still we must get straight on this if I am supposed to write Oxford's lines in *The Which of Shakespeare's Why*. I persist, "Lance, really. Don't we risk being laughed off like the guys who get paid salaries to tell indebted students paying them it's really not even interesting who put pen to paper? That the zeitgeist of a period in time actually produces the author function? And also, all my personal friend teenagers, please give me an A on your faculty review report card so I keep my job."

"Chill, Harry, chill. Your are out of school now. And anyway we don't have to convince that type. Like Shakespeare you are writing for a common-sense crowd. Ordinary Londoners came numbering a couple thousand to each performance of an Elizabethan play, especially his. And not one single English professor among them. Since there were none yet.

"Relax, man. Your hurdle bar to astound a 21st-century crowd is very low. Actually present global perception of Shakespeare is mostly just from Harvey Weinstein's chick flick *Shakespeare in Love*."

Naming that stunningly silly movie and stunningly ugly man took Lance's breath away. After long pause: "We're ... we're really *not* going to theorize, Harry. We're going to script historical *fact*. And merely by connecting it to the play texts galvanizes them to new life. The characters will register even more intensely because they are more deeply accessible in their feelings."

This pops. "Lance. I'll try. But I pretty much don't like Edward de Vere either."

"You don't have to. You will do best to present him in aspects of his various inglories. Actually that is the same way Shakespeare himself wrote most plays' characters. Within Oxford's, being Shakespeare's, creatures the lines of what a normal person would call likable or call contemptible swirl around each other linking endlessly. Like DNA. That's a good emblem for our project, Harry. We will wrap the facts of Oxford's life around the facts of his Shakespeare characters in continuous lines that are recognizably linked. To anybody rational."

"Okay." It's just a sound I make sometimes.

Lance is flapping in fast flight, "Oh *yes*, Harry. Suddenly understandable as a specific highly articulate human's highly evolved life experience. Oxford wrote expressively in bursts of extraordinarily educated uniquely energized eloquence."

Maybe the room is bugged he thinks? "And we in truth are not threatening Stratfordians. All those salaried English teachers still will be in business at their old stands after Oxford is broadly accepted. They can go on publishing their explanations to the world of mankind and art. But as to works of Shakespeare academics can educate to a more richly and deeply compelling perception of the work."

This guy Lance Gulliver is a piece of work, I think Hamlet would agree. He turns around away on heels his bravura way. That is my cue to shut up for a while. And I do, turning away myself into thought.

Reader, I am 30 years old. Thirty can be a breakthrough age. All these guys were age 30 when they stepped upward into another mental dimension: Confucius, Siddhartha, Jesus, Zarathustra.

So . . . so what. I'm Harry Haines. So so-so. The likely what of *The Which*.

But still. "Lance, are you sure we can count on Valerie?"

"Sure as sparrows fall in the fields. But only after their time ends."

Whatever that may mean. "Well, we know hellfire is going to rain down from the sky from Stratfordians. Do you trust Valerie not to have another explosion and drop us again? But with reputations shot. Branded as unreliable outcast cranks? Like de Vere was in his lifetime actually."

From behind I see Lance's shoulders shrug. Shrug again. "Iz's near-in cancellation slot at Radio City is a blessing. We're a closed set until then. You and I both already know enough to write and play lines without much more research. Valerie's engineers will be lightning fast finding or making up Omniconal's digital McGuffin to insert into our script to make for her bragging rights about discovering who really wrote Shakespeare. So. It. Is. All cool, my friend Harry."

"I suppose." I'm not much of an actor in my own life.

"All good, guy. Queen Valerie I will be famous as a major benefactor to world culture like Queen Elizabeth I. She's not going to dump us so fast. Even if some Stratford goon somehow gets to her before the show. And remember too Valerie doesn't give a hoot about Shakespeare, much less any right or wrong theory. Contemptuous of all theater as you heard yourself."

"So we do have a real Virgin Queen."

"As to theater, yes. She's actually kind of girlish about getting to say her lines dressed as Elizabeth on the stage of Radio City. With all the golden balloons suspended overhead waiting to applaud her brilliance. Monster ego."

"But she wants to be not a bellowing bitch now?"

"That's our bet. I've been really frank with her. That being likable just a little while is key to getting her deal done. But you need to keep her lines short and close to what we know as fact about Elizabeth."

We're at the rub for me. I say, "You know, I'm kind of concerned whether Valerie is going to work well with me. As her script writer."

"Because she immediately read you as a loser twerp."

"Well. So."

Lance: "There is no personality problem at all for you with Queen Valerie. You will not talk to her again. She doesn't know I hired you as playwright and anyway she only wants to deal with me while flirting. My budget lists the playwright fee as payable to a guy named Arch Bottom. Who I told her is a top playwright using a pen name to avoid alimony. She smiled."

"But Lance, no. Arch *Bottom?* Bottom is the fool turned into an ass in *Midsummer*."

"Harry, *Harry*. Don't overthink like a Stratfordian professor."

And now Lance sits to write notes into his director's notebook. Which I am going to sneak a read of sometime.

Sure Lance. *Arch* Bottom is a Shakespearean pun touch, the arching of a body ready to be screwed. Shakespeare only came up with Nick Bottom, Arch is funnier. Lance and Oxford would have gotten on fine with a pitcher of Nut Brown and bowl of nachos between them at the roaring Mermaid Tavern. An Elizabethan playwright wrote a letter about his and Ben Jonson's mutual tavern pal, the flamboyant Oxford. That playwright friend wrote admiringly that Oxford was in contempt of both weak beer and plain grammar.

But stop, old world of memory.

Spin now, new world, spin true fantasy very fast.

Part Three

We players are waiting in TSF's convent gym for Iz Mocha to show up. And read through his Puck-like address to the audience before the Radio City Hall curtain rises.

I got the idea for it from Puck's sweet apology for any offense to an Elizabethan audience delivered as the last lines of a *Tempest* performance. This prologue will be a good way to break it to the expectant audience that a normal performance of *Hamlet* is not what they are about to receive. Lance's offbeat casting of Iz at age 82 for his maiden Broadway performance is inspired. Shrunken short, combed over white bald in a 1990s suit he thinks still looks okay, Iz packs a professionally polished fake sincerity my lines require.

I'm still tinkering with this prologue. It must be short as it is shocking. It must come so charmingly delivered in radical content that it does not cause audience members to head for the aisle. They need to receive sufficient understanding to be receptive. And thereby, when the concluding curtain falls, we must hope and dream, the audience will arise to crown Badboy Eddie deVere as a new global superstar. Producer Ms. Valerie Farnsworth, Omniconal owner and CEO, will give her thanks to all the unnamed little people who helped this breakthrough of computational largesse to society. Omniconal that just gave a grateful world the real Shakespeare.

I went with Lance to pitch the Puck-like role to Iz at his office. It was touching to see the old reptile unable to hide young thrill. At being the sole voice opening a historic theater event that will assuredly go to billions of screens. But that brain clicks very well still. He must have some deep deal or deep remembrance with the Rockettes. His yes was immediately conditioned on hiring those athletic young ladies to bear Elizabethan halberds and serve as usherettes, and also to militantly block exit aisles if necessary. Iz recalled a Radio City Merrie Olde England production back in the 20th century whose Beefeater jacket costumes in storage will be perfect. Of course there were no Beefeater trousers, so no safety impediment to the sparkly panties.

As we wait in our convent gym for Iz, Lance fiddles the lights down to a warm dimness. We summoned for this readout just Lance playing Oxford, Iz playing Puck, Miriam playing Ophelia, me playing Hamlet. And Marj Morningstar playing Queen Elizabeth. James Jace as Polonius comes in an hour. An actress cast as Gertrude (who Oxford wrote to half-mirror Queen Elizabeth) is missing, it is a shoot day on her soap opera.

Over the past weeks Lance did decide about Miriam's Ophelia wardrobe. She arrived in a cream cashmere sweater set. Golden girlish pigtails coiled in womanly sophistication atop her head Princess tiara style. Stunning, stunning both Hamlet and Harry. Bosom could be just a little fuller but I would not argue the point. Ophelia is dressed as Daddy's girl, pearl necklace from him included. This is wise of Lance since Ophelia is fatally her daddy's girl throughout our production. Sylvia Plath, another suicidal father obsessive, wore a sweater set all along her troubled way too.

Lance seems to like how Oxford's speaking interpolations initially focus on the writer's obsession with his 15-year-old bartered bride Anne Cecil, portrayed with confused ambivalence as Ophelia. Anne is beloved daughter of Queen Elizabeth's chief strategist and fixer William Cecil, knighted Lord Burghley, a near-photocopy from real life as the Polonius figure. Many documents track Anne Cecil's relationship over two decades to her troubled and troublesome reluctant husband Oxford.

Poor Anne will surface again and again recognizably sourced as a character in the Shakespeare plays. That troubling muse Anne was artistically permutated into major Shakespeare females of varying but intensely imputed characters. Each is a different vision of womanhood. Yet each recognizably acutely derived from aspects of Anne's historically known personality traits and sad fate.

That, perplexingly, was a mild woman's fate. Because here comes an opaque quality of our complex protagonist Edward de Vere, Earl of Oxford. Oxford evolving through his plays kept sequentially reconsidering Anne in uneasy conscience as he matured in age. In the heat of youth he had seen her only through the eyes of his own torment by her father Burghley and other Court predators. As their tool. But, after Oxford's emotional rejection of the forced marriage, then reconciliation producing three daughters and her early death, different conceptions of Anne opened. And opened again. And opened again since he was after all, above and below all, a brooding literary genius.

Across 20 years Oxford wrote and rewrote these surrogate characters embodying varying perceptions of their poignantly failed relationship. The principal woman as sweetly tender teenage lover. As treacherous wily manipulator. As catastrophically pregnant. As tool of a domineering father; and yet in no less than eight plays, Oxford dreamed up women dramatically disobeying their father's authority over their life. Then a play portrayed a woman as incoherently refusing proffered love. Another woman as tragically slandered. Then another as triumphantly superior in spirit and mind to men; Anne was the well-educated daughter of a noted mathematician mother and master lawyer. Then the woman is raped. Then murdered. Then she is mother of three daughters who cruelly reject their needy widowed father.

Twenty plays in whole kaleidoscopically revolve these shifting emotional shards of insight and inspiration from Anne and Edward's disastrous long marriage.

The audience of *The Which of Shakespeare's Why* will see them carrousel in brief cameo. As imagined by a man whose emotions touching Anne's own pale, gentle self somehow long engendered roiling impetuous tempests. And reveries. And obsessions. And regrets. And, finally, poignant resignation that led the late version Hamlet to leap into poor Ophelia's grave so boundlessly remorseful.

From all that double toil and trouble, all that fire burning and cauldron bubbling, came stage plays made of questions. Because even I can see this plain: in the works of Shakespeare questions of mistake in circumstance and questions of forgiveness indeed are warped into weft of main characters.

And beside Anne there was Oxford's confounding 30-year relationship of vicissitudes with his mother of sorts, Queen Elizabeth.

Lance, dressed in uncompromised black, his own real beard now close-trimmed young man style, says to each of us, with long glances sweeping like a search light, "This play is about dangerous tone. All of us know there is no one method in method acting. Just one effect. That is the written line bespeaking a whole life lived come to an utterance.

"So whose life is welled up for each of you players? You each know the submerged biography of your character that Harry wrote up. So your method is to play your lines continuing the real-life person who Shakespeare obviously lightly disguised as a Hamlet principal. You speak your lines in a mental continuum of the ongoing real life of that real person whose life story you know well enough.

"Good scholarly job with the bio squibs, Harry. Maybe after *The Which* Princeton will invite you back."

"They'll send out a Jersey hitman, Lance."

Lance looks off four seconds envisioning how to stage my hit-man scene. "Miriam, sweetheart, when Harry speaks to you he is Hamlet who upsets you at every turn. So do *not* ever look right at him. Hamlet is way too painful for you. You are a shy bookish 15-year-old girl. As your first boyfriend this guy is turning out an incoherently abusive monster. Your dad Polonius thinks he's plain crazy. But Dad is making you spy on Hamlet for his boss King Claudius. It's all so, so confusing for too young you."

Miriam says, "Sorry you're such an asshole, Eddie."

"I get what's coming, Annie."

Lance, "Marj, ring your bell." Fiftyish Marj, dressed in a matronly Eileen Fisher knee-length sweater over young at heart red velvet jeans, desultorily waves her long-handled silver bell.

Lance, "**No!** When Elizabeth breaks into the text she must snap the audience out of spellbound within the literal play. All the historical real-life speakers breaking into play text . . . you will first all ring real loud to freeze the show in mid-speech."

I recall Queen Valerie with a telephone receiver. Lance is a good director. He has prudently decided now that Valerie will not have any lines for me to write in *The Which*. At performance end she will simply glide onstage during Horatio's epilogue gratefully addressing smiling effusive gratitude to her and good old Omniconal. But for fun, hers, she still will appear in a replica of the gown portrayed in a famous scary surviving painting of Queen Elizabeth, that Rainbow Portrait.

A photo of this concoction, one of 1,326 outfits inventoried at Elizabeth's death, was love at first sight for Valerie. The aging entrepreneurial founder of globally snoopy Omniconal Friendship Unlimited, Limited saw her own dream. Because the golden velvet torso's fabric is decorated with oversize lifelike woven images of eyes, ears, and speaking mouths. Queen Elizabeth's image wordlessly says, "BEWARE ME, I WILL KNOW ABOUT YOU." Valerie immediately visualized that flat-chested Queen Elizabeth's decolletage line will play great on her own plenitude. Stella McCartney is sewing away. Like ordering a special pizza Valerie asked her for extra pearls and rubies.

Lance: "Okay guys. Before curtain up Iz apologizes that we are going to skip *Hamlet's* early bits. He announces we'll then play some *Lear* bits. And that in further mind-spin *The Which* will carrousel on in bits from several plays in the Shakespeare canon. Each scene in a play tying to the actual life of their actual author. Iz Puck-style casually announces to the audience that Oxford will be speaking as a character among his own characters. Talking to them about what lives within them.

"So Oxford talks straight through the characters to the ghosts of the real people they are based on. From Harry's memo you have overviews. Oxford originally wrote plays for performance at Court. Queen Elizabeth really loved to watch arena bear baiting. That carried over into her taste in plays. Oxford, her lover in his 20s and as you saw some scholars say her hidden son from a child rape, was allowed to write characters that almost rhymed with principals in the theatrical life of the Elizabethan Court. She liked to make a little fun of her courtiers. Elizabeth didn't even get angry when she was almost caricatured, or when in a Shakespeare show a ruler was overthrown. Remarkable because if it had been any author but her boy Oxford the Crown people would have sliced of his ears and branded him, maybe cut off the writing hand as a message to wise guys.

"Oxford was in his early years brilliant but manic-depressive. He made lots of colorful big mistakes and big enemies. That is what happened with the 1580s performance at Hampton Court, some say it was then called Avon, of the 'ur-*Hamlet*.' He offended almost all the top courtiers. Polonius was transparently the awful slippery manipulator Lord Burghley—who imposed false taxes and debts that bankrupted Oxford for life. Robert Dudley knighted the Earl of Leicester was transparently King Claudius—rumored to have poisoned Oxford's father to steal some of the Earldom's great wealth. Queen Elizabeth—she who would not acknowledge Oxford as either her heir or her lover—was the confused mother Gertrude. Burghley's son and successor in power Robert was Laertes. Christopher Hatton, Oxford's cloying rival for Elizabeth's affection was the lackey Rosenkranz. And of course Burghley's puppeted browbeaten young daughter Anne was wretched girl Ophelia.

"You can imagine sardonic Elizabeth laughing as 'ur-*Hamlet*' played for a small private audience of only elite courtiers. And you can imagine that as soon as the torches were lit again Burghley's Crown agents moved in to seize and burn all copies of the script.

"*Hamlet* did not appear again until long after the deaths of both Burghley and Leicester, when Elizabeth was near death. This most autobiographical of Oxford's plays must have benefited profoundly by rewriting during the long period of Oxford's internal exile and artistic maturation.

"So there is your method, guys. Speak your lines knowing the real person behind them. Like Omniconal flashed you a message about what your character is thinking under what they say out loud."

Miriam has been listening plus, as is her way. "Lance I don't think I should wear lipstick for my role."

"No, Miriam, do not. Hamlet is supposed to be furious with you. With lipstick how could he be?"

I think this would be like the real Oxford and real Elizabeth, they are playing within a play exchange.

Lance: "Okay, so that is how the show will move. But before the curtain rises Iz like Puck says casually that the actual author of *Hamlet* is appearing here tonight. And by the way that author most surely is the badass pretty boy the 17th Earl of Oxford, Edward de Vere. And do we have more surprises for you ahead!"

Lance has a way of looking one second too long from actor to actor to actor. It focuses our attention.

"Then, Harry, look sharp. The curtains explode open on you standing here frozen by centuries. And you go, you deliver Hamlet's lines your own way, Harry. Straight up. But **stop** at the exact syllable every time you hear Oxford's or Elizabeth's bell ring. Go, man, go."

And so. Voice passing a bit tight over heart in throat,

To be or not to be, that is the question:
Whether 'tis nobler in the mind to suffer
The slings and arrows of outrageous fortune
Or to take arms against a sea of troubles—

Lance calls loud from offstage, "**Harry, stop.** You're doing it way too fast again. Struggle for the next thought like for next breath suffocating. You need to stutter existentially in this introspection. You are a terrified prey hid this dangerous moment from pursuing hounds. Okay?"

I say, "Sorry, Lance. Got it."

My hero: "Good. You're close, guy."

And so:

And by opposing end them. To die: to sleep,
No more. And by a sleep to say we end
The heart-ache and the thousand natural shocks
That flesh is heir to: 'tis a consummation
Devoutly to be wished. To die: to sleep.
To sleep? Perchance to dream. Ay, there's the rub;
For in that sleep of death what dreams may come,
When we have shuffled off this mortal coil,
Must give us pause. There's the respit
That makes calamity of so long life;
For who would bear the whips and scorns of time,
Th' oppessor's wrong, the proud man's contumely,
The pangs of disprized love, the law's delay,
The insolence of office, and the spurns
That patient merit of th' unworthy takes,
When he himself might his quietus make
With a bare bodkin? Who would fardels bear;
To grunt and sweat under a weary life,
 But that the dread of something after death,
The undiscover'd country from whose bourne
No traveler returns, puzzles the will,
And makes us rather bear those ills we have
Than fly to others that we know not of?
Thus conscience does make cowards of us all,
And thus the native hue of resolution
Is sicklied o'er with the pale cast of thought,
And enterprises of great pitch and moment
With this regard their currents turn awry,
And lose the name of action.

Oxford/Lance rings his bell loud and same instant Elizabeth/ Marj too. So I freeze arms folded on my chest looking nowhere, I suppose toward the bourne.

Mask lit Oxford/Lance, "Well, I first wrote these lines around 1583 when I was about 33. After suffering so much grief from my enigmatic Queen and her shifting greedy boyfriends and Crown capos. All stealing my wealth after I became a helpless orphan at age 12."

Mask-lit Oxford/Lance is looking to mask-lit Elizabeth/Marj: "Your viper people had long ago bled me into indebted poverty. No wonder I had the Prince Hamlet speak of suicide. That was for you to hear, Majesty. A plea to catch your conscience surprised by the play I produced at my cost."

Oxford/Lance is coolly regarding his dangerous aging Queen across the darkened stage. "So your Highness could understand why I wrote Hamlet as my same self."

Elizabeth/Marj holds quite a long stare, a Queen can look at a cat. His tone warms, Oxford is a very emotional man. "Thankfully you did eventually realize all I meant. I bow gratitude to you again, because in conscience you did by 1588 give me financial recompense as well as protection from your hard men. You understood what I wrote in my pain ruined from boyhood by your wolf pack.

"But Burghley's men understood me too and burned all copies of that script and concocted a belittling fake review. You smiled with your mocking sense of humor at the fun I made of my tormentor Burghley as Polonius. But anyway my profound rewrite of *Hamlet* after he finally died was far better."

Elizabeth/Marj, "Oh *stuff*, Eddie. All your inherited 40 farms and the Arden forest bit were always subject to taxes to the Crown.

And fines for late payment. Plus all the wardship costs billed by my right hand man Burghley.

"Billy Burghley from his own advances provided money paid to all your famous tutors. He bought for your use an extraordinary classics library good as at Cambridge. Which as also the university chancellor he enrolled you into early recognizing your precocity. As well as later Gray's law school. He paid for your most broad and sophisticated education in your generation in all Europe. You owed much for your excellent care through a decade of wardship by the Crown.

"Don't, do *not* pose with me, Eddie. We know one another too long and well. In fact by age 21 you had run up ten years of high-life bills on your own egotistic judgment. And when you then were graduated to assume control of your Earldom you did legally owe the Crown a big due fee from wardship. Which when you could not pay incurred a further big penalty debt to the Crown by simple law. Yes, this was all brand new under my reign, but still it was law also applying to others."

Marj is playing big as intimidating Queen Elizabeth. She walks over and looks imperiously close up to Oxford's face. "Completely unearned inherited great wealth. And high cost of orphanage. Those, Milord, those are just two sides of the same coin. Deal with it."

Oxford looks back long and steady. "That coin was fake, Liz. That deal was fake. And you well knew it. Half my wardship properties' revenues were assigned to your wife-killing enemy-poisoning boyfriend Bobby Dudley. Who was a middle-class stud you named Earl of Leicester on the spur of your hormonal moment.

"And your sticky-fingered lawyer Bill Cecil helping himself to the other half of my wardship property long before rendering his padded bill on top. What a heave, scribe Cecil, his grandfather a mere footman to your father, but who you obediently appointed Lord Burghley so that his daughter Anne would be eligible to marry me since I was senior Prince of the realm.

"That hypocritical rat promised a huge dowry I needed to pay my Crown taxes which he himself had imposed. But then he glibly defaulted and turned my due dowry payment into just a big loan to me instead. Which he later foreclosed and took my collateral farms. The truth is Cecil and the viper Dudley competitively puppeted both you and me. Deal with that, your Majesty."

Elizabeth is looking off to some other time. Oxford has become more intense after her cool foil. "And of course Liz, your Highness, you well knew the brand new Crown fee for being an heir younger than 21was just your courtiers' invention to prey on feudal wealth. More money for Crown expenses and graft was needed. Because your father had dissipated all the Catholic Church's wealth he stole like a mugger with a knife."

Oxford steps to speak in his Queen's ear just the way Lance does when he's bearing down on a character. "Of course you knew that new law of your Crown was soon followed by several suspiciously early deaths of nobility with heirs under age 21. For red letter instance, Regina, I know you are already thinking what's next, my own robust father John de Vere suddenly dead at 41 when I was 12 years old. That very conveniently creating my nine-years-long wardship that both Cecil and Dudley looted mercilessly since I was just an orphan child."

"I heard no complaint from you."

"I was an orphan teenager. The Tudor hypocrisy was breathtaking. Let's get more straight in this new light. Remember, the Third Earl of Southampton's father was an enemy of Dudley. Everybody knew that the father Southampton also was poisoned after your hard men finally let him out of the Tower on a paranoid charge. Just as the courtiers all knew Dudley had his wife's neck broken in a fake accident so he could hope to marry you. Which of course probably would have been eventually fatal for you too, Liz. Then during Southampton's son Henry's consequent wardship under Burghley that Earldom's wealth was also predated by Dudley."

Elizabeth, "I . . . we . . ."

Oxford is at her close. "People ask what is wrong with Hamlet! For four hundred years people think he is a crybaby. But Hamlet knows what monstrous things were done to his youth. Dudley's sexing you up got him a gift of the finest castle in England not already yours. That he over-decorated with de Vere stolen wealth."

Elizabeth, looking down then up: "Bobby confused me. He was very dangerous to fall in love with."

Oxford looking out to the ghost of audience: "What is wrong with Hamlet? Is he crazy? Why can't he stay in the old revenge play?"

Elizabeth has recovered her verve, "Poor Willy. Your grievances always circle wealth. But since death has made you so flat-footed frank to speak with, the main fact is you never had any head for money. You were a genius of language. And a genius of imagination, always several fantasies in mind. But you had no practical sense of life's mechanics.

"In reality royal life is expensive as well as complicated. My Crown always had trouble covering its costs. Every year three fourths or more of Crown total revenue was spent straight back out preparing to fight the Spanish or the French or both. And always the Irish inviting Catholic invasion of us their ancient tormentor. Italian thug after thug called Pope was egging on every Catholic to kill me the Protestant witch, promising immediate passage to Heaven as the reward. I had to worry through four decades of all this. Forsooth!

"The Crown had to avoid triggering a tax revolt from the common horde, always grumbling hoeing away on their soggy land. So we needed all the cash we could get away with from the fat cats. Many of whom anyway had just recently got rich looting Catholic property after my lethal Dad's hat trick to head the new Church of England."

Oxford/Lance: "Which still was the Catholic Church just in depressing dressed-down drag under Crown puppetry. The nerve of the Tudors was always stunning. You do know it was my ancestor de Vere's cavalry who smashed Richard III to death? Your Welsh cattle-stealing grandfather Henry VII owed his crown to us.

"I was supposed to be a military leader like the several great de Veres in history. Yet you forbade that. And also would not allow me to join the Privy Counsel or the Order of the Garter."

Elizabeth: "Eddie, you were too charismatic. We feared you would claim the throne with popular support. Anyway, you had fun."

Oxford's voice breaks: "When Hamlet is asked what's wrong with him he says 'I lack advancement.' Majesty, I loved you like a son, you did not need to fear me."

Elizabeth: "But I *did f*ear you prudently. Spies showed me some letters you signed decorated by royal crowns, not the proper ducal coronets. And spies said when you drank a lot it was politics, not art, your fantasies went to. Worse, you were too close to the Catholic aristocracy by blood and friendships."

Elizabeth goes on looking and sounding like steel, "And you must know I myself alone also saved your head and heart. Edward, I was your friend. In my own complicated way. Complicated even to myself,"

Oxford has been staring at the Queen, "Two complexities mixed can feel empty. My plays often were speaking of my outrage at how you allowed me to be denied my birthright fate. It's why I kept displacing the identity of Kings. At some—"

Elizabeth: "Enough of that. As your Hamlet says of twaddle."

Oxford: "My birthright . . ."

Elizabeth: "Still at it dead or alive!! The dead must face account. You yourself actually did not ever earn any ownership of anything. You simply got born like magic to be a high aristocrat. Five hundred years before you were born William the Conqueror had simply given away huge stolen Saxon lands to create the Oxford Earldom. In gratitude for de Vere-led military success at Hastings. You were not there.

"But. But Eddie, the Crown always kept a valid legal string on revenues from all that land. You are a lawyer, my Lord, thanks to the elite education we provided for you. So do not pretend ignorance of what is not convenient for you to know. Like some prattling university professor.

"My Lord Oxford, all things considered your heavy fines for late payment of Crown taxes and fees were fair enough. Come see my own view of you as a fickle friend. Walsingham and Burghley had foot-thick volumes of reports on you. Two dozen spies wrote them.

"At any time I could have just taken back all your Earldom's land for treason due to your unwise flirting with Catholic insurrectionaries set on killing me. 'Come to it,' as you wrote your Hamlet's chilling phrase. You drank and gossiped and wildly fantasized too much among my own Crown spies all around you.

"So of course the Crown did not trust you. Though you were fun. Until you got angry. Like me I suppose."

Oxford: "Well of course I became angry. You above all knew what I meant by Hamlet's gratuitous lines. Of 'oppressor's wrong' and 'proud man's contumely' and 'disprized love' and 'law's delay' and 'insolence of office.'

"Say what you will, Majesty, I deeply realized I was just prey in your Court world. I wrote the 1580s private *Hamlet* for your own awareness. To win your help at last."

Elizabeth is scanning the audience her usual way, looking to see who dares not pay attention. Then with a high shrug: "Eddie, you always went for flamboyant turns of phrase. Because you were flamboyant in your nature. Actually you could still have had plenty of wealth after paying all your obligations for Crown taxes and fees and penalties. Bobby Dudley's, I should say the Earl of Leicester's, it's hard to keep track of all my made-up titles, greedy extent of graft was hidden from me.

"And nobody told me about his poisonings. Now I do see of course I would have been in line if I married him as he begged. But the rumor everywhere about his poor broken-necked wife Amy had Burghley pull me away from him. Bobby was a very different kind of bad boy than you. But I did give you recompense, Eddie. In kind by my personal protection of your vulnerability among blood enemies at Court.

"And I generously gave you a small fortune every year, out of reach of your creditors. Fourteen years straight until I died. You never would have finished your canon without my physical protection and financial security. You and the world owe the works of Shakespeare to my tough love for you."

Oxford: "Emphasis on tough."

Elizabeth: "But come now, Willy, Eddie. You have looked back and back by now. So you realize it was by your own demons that you chose to live so very extravagantly on borrowed money. And recklessly sold property in your family for centuries. Squandering so much on so many clothes you could have been your own acting troupe."

"I was."

"And you supported real acting troupes until you were indigent. And all the while also covering the expensive living and printing costs of your drinking pals the hangers-on writers and actors. Dozens of scholarly books dedicated to you in appreciation of your generosity!"

Oxford: "But I learned playwriting craft from all those actors. And I learned poetic expression from all those writers. After extraordinary education from all those tutors. That in sum is how I became able to write Shakespeare. To quote my Lear, 'Nothing comes from nothing.'"

Elizabeth, "But in '75 you went on sheer over the top. Walsingham's spies couldn't believe it. Burghley was shouting furious. You blew what was left of your fortune all the way off in that two-year toot showing off in royal courts of Italy and France."

Oxford, "I was gathering writing material. Anyway, there wasn't going to be much wealth left to me after all your vultures fed further on my father's estate. And I sanely anticipated getting killed before 35."

Elizabeth, "Well. One also must be fair in death's perspective. It turned out that European sensibility you transformed to English theater was magic. I really did love the elite scenes played at private performances. You put good old feudalism in such pretty lighting. Everyone talking so cleverly unlike the reality. Even my Privy Counselors thought it was good politically that the boozy common horde still liked stories about Princesses and Kings.

"And certainly the Crown men saw it was especially good that your history plays stirred England's patriotic spirit. Play after play through the entire decade Spain was approaching its invasion war in 1588, and then threatened to return in 1591.

"So all this is why I sternly protected you from the hard men.

You were an important Crown asset, however inadvertently. And besides I was Queen. And just liked you from in the '70s when you were such a gallant stud in my young Court."

Oxford, "Our '70s times seem like a dream now. I could have written more about then. But I would not have lived so long."

Elizabeth has slowly circled where Oxford sits in black on his invisible chair. It comes out. "Yes, Eddie, your Lordship, I am your heroine really. I kept the killers off you. And when you went completely destitute I did move to take care of you with my special pension though I had too many bills to pay myself.

"Actually, dear Eddie, since really you have no head for figures, I must tell you I certainly was never rich as the Crown pretended to the world. I gather your clever blonde bombshell daughter Susan talked her admirer King James into continuing my annual payment until your own death. Even though Crown spies informed James you were loosely talking against his coronation before he arrived."

"I had no idea Susan was such a wonderful piece of work. I neglected her badly."

Elizabeth, "So there it is, Eddie. Indeed not all your luck was bad. Including your domestic exile at forty from exhausting and dangerous Court life. Because only that quiet time island allowed you many years to write and revise your great works."

Lance now rings his bell loud and is become the director again. Next will come Ophelia's mean scene with that unaccountable jerk to her Hamlet. Lance says, "Marj you tough bitch, you are very fine. Miriam sweetheart, is your mask comfortable?"

Miriam, "Sure. You can hear me okay through it?"

Lance, "Oh yes. Actually you are a little amplified. Show me again you can turn it on. Just wave your hand anywhere in front of your face."

Miriam waves her little Princess hand. Instantly her Ophelia mask softly but brightly glows LED-lit from within. The mask is a delicately lifelike princess face, barely pink cheeks on alabaster skin, with a lightly applied profound red lipstick Elizabethan women used if they could afford it. This is the identical mask a half-dozen Anne Cecil avatar characters also will illuminate in *The Which of Shakespeare's Why's* kaleidoscopic finale. Each masked character being an avatar of Oxford's child bride Anne Cecil. Each character's mask illuminates as she steps forward to speak or suffer.

In scripting the play's half dozen Anne avatar poignant spotlight cameos I surprised myself. For I found that lines which I knew as a Shakespeare student for years were . . . actually become now new. Just as *The Which* intends. Our actresses themselves have told me that knowing my gloss on the specific avatar they speak with a new penetrating internal feeling soon as the connective mask lights to speak. Reality has lit itself within the play as Lance and I intended.

That reality variously was made into artifice by a writing, remembering, fantasizing, remorseful, yet still resentful, author. An author who was himself indeed quite a character. A character. As one says of a person one neither likes nor dislikes and does not understand.

Lance: "Excellent. Now we do the mean scene." Lance rings the bell as if for a Madison Square Garden prize fight at Radio City, which actually did occur there in the scrambling 1930s. "Harry—go, guy."

Hamlet: *Soft you now!*
The fair Ophelia! Nymph, in thy orisons
Be all my sins remember'd.

Ophelia: *Good my lord,*
How does your honor for this many a day?

Hamlet: *I humbly thank you; well, well, well.*

Ophelia: *My lord, I have remembrances of yours*
That I have longed long to re-deliver;
I pray you now, receive them.

Hamlet: *No, not I.*
I never gave you aught.

Ophelia: *My honored lord, you know right well you did;*
And with them words of so sweet breath compos'd
As made the things more rich. Their perfume lost,
Take these again. For to the noble mind
Rich gifts wax poor when givers prove unkind.
There, my lord.

Hamlet: *Ha ha! Are you honest?*

Ophelia: *My lord?*

Hamlet: *Are you fair?*

Ophelia: *What means your lordship?"*

Hamlet: *That if you be honest and fair,*
Your honesty should admit to discourse to your beauty.

Ophelia: *Could beauty, my lord, have better commerce*
than with honesty?

Hamlet: *Ay, for the power of beauty will soon transform honesty*
from what it is to a bawd than the force of honesty can translate beauty
into his likeness. This was sometimes a paradox, but now the time gives
it proof. I did love you once.

Ophelia: *Indeed, my lord, you made me believe so.*

Hamlet: *You should not have believed me, for virtue*
cannot so inoculate our old stock but we shall relish of it.
I loved you not.

Ophelia: *I was the more deceived.*

Hamlet: *Get thee to a nunnery! Why wouldst thou be a breeder of sinners?*

Lance waves his arm toward Elizabeth/Marj. Who rings loud and stands, reading script since she is still memorizing. Young Jed the intern has turned a spotlight on Elizabeth.

Oxford/Lance to Elizabeth/Marj: "I don't want to talk about Anne."

Elizabeth: "Why not now, Eddie? For twenty years you couldn't stop drawing and then refining her many refracted images. I know them all. There's Miranda, Helena, Hero, Juliet, Bianca, Desdemona, Anne, Phoebe, Lucrece. And Ophelia, whom you bitterly named from the Greek word for debt and tax."

Now Elizabeth walks to the stage apron, speaking directly to the audience. "I should have been in this play from the start. But since Eddie put in his tongue-tied father's ghost, there's room for me too now. And at the outset I wish to make something perfectly clear. I was having my hair done when the 16th Earl of Oxford got suddenly unfortunate. As the Privy Council saying goes."

Oxford replies, looking long at Elizabeth over a bitter smile, "Majesty, you must have read books written in times after ours, as I have. So much was lost later. What the tongue-tied ghost in *Hamlet* referred to was very clear to us. Yet his meaning became inscrutable over even one more lifetime when the Puritans banned all theater for twenty years.

"However, in 1919 T.S. Eliot's 'Hamlet and His Problems' essay re-opened the way back in to understanding Shakespeare more closely to his specific moments of expression. That was so promising. But Eliot stopped at the edge of his brilliant perception. He had sensed that Hamlet's character was too big for his literal function in a re-treaded old foreign revenge play."

Elizabeth, "Yes, I read Eliot too. That good poet sensed the character Hamlet came from another world than the one of the play. To whose track of events his personality is illogical. Eliot intuited *Hamlet's* text was obliquely referencing present time, and dark, underlying stories. We in the Court certainly did realize that. The courtiers snickered and sometimes frowned through Eddie's private production at Hampton Court. I myself smiled at its cleverness like at a comedy.

"But his surprise play cut too close to us real people. So naturally immediately the Crown destroyed all copies of the script. There was almost no *Hamlet* for you, lucky audience."

Elizabeth turns her look back toward Oxford who again sits on an invisible chair contemplating his still ink-stained hands. "But Milord Oxford, for you reading books written later on in passed time must have been very bitter.

"Because Eliot's 1919 essay intuition of hidden figure in *Hamlet* was explained by Thomas Looney's 1920 book. Mister Looney's comprehensive biography of you, the 17th Oxford, factually tied to the features of the character Hamlet so closely it amounted to a copied door key. As did the detailed European royal court settings of so many other plays, which could have been described only from personal presence there.

"But Mr. Looney, a mere schoolteacher, was a nobody disdained by assertive university academics in 1920. So that new key then became misplaced amid annual floods of Stratfordian bardolatry books. But by now continued Oxfordian scholarship has also built up into an Oxfordian intellectual presence worth considering."

Elizabeth looking first to the audience and then to Oxford:

"But Eddie. Be careful what you may still wish for after 400 years. If and when your time of recognition as being the actual Shakespeare does come, then you will have a terrible image problem."

Lance as director rings his bell sharply. "Go, Harry."

And I as Hamlet resume beating up horrified Ophelia. Miriam sneaks what-is-this-creep looks at me as I flame on:

If thou dost marry, I'll give thee this plague
For thy dowry: be thou as chaste as ice, as pure as snow,
thou shalt not escape calumny. Get thee to a nunnery.
Go, farewell. Or if thou wilt needs marry,
marry a fool; for wise men know well enough
what monsters you make of them. To a nunnery
go, and quickly too. Farewell.
Ophelia: O heavenly powers, restore him!
Hamlet: I have heard of your paintings too,
Well enough. God hath given you one face, and you make
yourselves another. You jig, you amble, and you lisp.
You nickname God's creatures, and make your
wantonness your ignorance. Go to, I'll no more
on't, it hath made me mad. I say, we will have
no more marriage.

Elizabeth's bell rings three times, sounding annoyed. "Eddie, this is so awful. You at first had been sweet to this dignified girl, who naturally assumed you were romantically sincere. But here you suddenly turn on her in stunningly vicious anger. Is it really misogynistic anger as it sounds to be? This young girl surely had nothing to do with killing your father. Eliot is right, your coruscating vehemence does not make any literary sense within the play's context."

Oxford to Elizabeth, after three beats pause, "Correct, Majesty. It does not. It is pathetic.

"I had, until the fires in me died down, a terrible insecure jealousy and resentment. A tendency at the edge of paranoia. I also am the author who killed Desdemona. The one who created the poisonous slander of Hero.

"It just came out as my pen moved. I was bullied and tricked by Burghley into marrying his blank tablet girl Anne. But of course by now how could I blame her? That skinny fifteen-year-old religious bookworm daddy's girl. And I was angry too for a creepy reason. I did realize Anne would have been happy with mild Sir Phillip Sydney, the poetic war hero who had already proposed to her."

Elizabeth: "You were toxic to young women. Until you were no longer young yourself."

Oxford is not here for more pretense. "Yes Liz, you my fellow spirit in quirks about marriage. Anyone can see in these nasty lines just said that the author is a strange brew on the subject of marriage. Everybody notices that my only happily married couple are the sociopath Macbeths. I liked courtship but stayed away from marriage.

"My Hamlet saw marriage as a trap because I myself being also himself was trapped into one. And my parents were horribly estranged. My father's mistress's nose was cut off by my mother's cousin.

"Also what cannot be seen is that off the page Hamlet has impregnated Ophelia, with all that consequence ahead suspended in his incoherently angry denial. Because that was my own true story as Edward de Vere. I couldn't remember ever once entering my forced bride Anne, my plan was to get a nonconsummation annulment. And yet, infuriatingly, she presented me with a child while I was happily living in Italy. This destroyed my chance of annulment,

I had been doubly tricked into unwanted marriage. By being made a cuckold by Burghley's hypocritical tool of a daughter Anne, which was rumored to my humiliation high and low all over London.

"So I had indeed, as they say, I think they do in the twenty-first century, fucked down big time. I was played and played again over Anne. Yes, Mr. Eliot, that is all there to feel but not see in *Hamlet*. The author not being frank with himself twisted all marriage into being the woman's wanton manipulation of sex. Not the man's wanton sex drive. Not the result of animality among kind. Later, I deeper understood. Much deeper."

Oxford's voice is not supposed to be cool and it is not. He says to a stage wing, "Please don't do Ophelia's mad scene. Gentle religious Anne did allow me to try to reconcile when enough people had jogged my memory about the Hampton Court drunken dance party in October '74. But my damage done over Anne's pregnancy lasted until the poor woman died at thirty-one. Knowing how violently unkind I had been to that still hopeful girl Anne. That cost me tears of heartblood to realize and write."

At Lance's director's wave Queen Elizabeth walks over and faces me as Hamlet. Literal and psychological lines in our play *The Which of Shakespeare's Why* have just now blurred. As truth often lies blurred between Oxford and Hamlet. Elizabeth is speaking summarily to me Hamlet the Heel, as Eliot would suspect all the girlfriends of Ophelia called me off page.

Elizabeth: "Right. Part of my big problem with you, Prince, is that you were so needlessly cruel to the heart of tender young Anne. She was the nicest, most modest maid of honor I ever had. And she actually believed the religion stuff. Burghley tortured himself that he had pulled his only daughter out of engagement to the paragon Sir Phillip Sydney to marry oddball you."

Oxford from downstage, facing the wing like a confidante: "Sydney was a twerp next to me. Look who reads him now."

Elizabeth declines to even look at Oxford, speaking again out toward her audience. "Sydney was an excellent army officer. He would have killed Eddie if I allowed their silly hormonal duel over tennis court booking time. Everybody liked Sydney. But I had to take the 17th Earl's side. Because the Crown could not have the senior prince of England killed by a mere gentleman over a matter of personal grievance. That could put ideas into heads we would then have to remove."

Oxford also now has come to the stage apron, he too is soliciting the crowd's support. "Burghley tricked me into the marriage to Anne promising a huge dowry I really needed to pay all those false Crown debts. But that fat weasel never paid. Which made me worse insolvent, leading to my fire sale of ancestral lands. And he foreclosed a land mortgage on his loan made instead of paying me my dowry. So that manipulated marriage was a farce that exploded and exploded and exploded in my mind. I was exasperated to point of fury. That was the reason for my cruelty to Ophelia who was Anne."

Elizabeth to her public: "Poor innocent girl."

"Majesty, I couldn't get over the Court laughing at me as a cuckold. And furthermore even though that also was an important part of the dowry due me Burghley did not spare the life of my first cousin and best friend the Duke of Norfolk. Who was really executed to seize his wealth by forfeit to the Crown on a false claim of treason. All this spiraling betrayal made my anger violent."

Elizabeth turns, talking to him but airily not looking at him. "Milord Oxford, Viscount Bolbec, Lord Great Chamberlain, for all your other brilliance you never could do arithmetic. As to Anne's pregnancy period your outrage was pathetic, not able to count to nine months from my big Hampton Court party where you two had to share a suite. Fluent in Latin, Greek, and four live languages but an idiot at simplest math."

Oxford: "I just sanely wanted out of that travesty of a marriage on legal grounds of non-consummation."

"Oh, I know. Everybody at Court knew. Even Mary Queen of Scots, bless her silly heart, wrote to me from prison that she heard you were setting up for a divorce from Anne Cecil because you wanted to give me a go for marriage. Like half the men at Court, but it was flattering." Elizabeth is now staring blankly at Oxford and silently considering. Her stock in trade.

Oxford: "Also I was traveling in Europe with a companion named Rowley Yorke who insisted I must be a public cuckold since I said I had not touched Anne. He told me that back in England everybody was laughing at the both broke and cuckolded 17th Earl forever under the thumb of clever Burghley. Tricked then humiliated by his pawn daughter. And then I found this out. My own trusted spy accurately reported to me from London that Anne secretly had asked a doctor I knew for an abortion drug."

Elizabeth looks up to where heaven would be. "Yorke was a rogue Catholic secret agent. Who for cash later betrayed English troops at a disastrous battle with the Spanish in the Netherlands war. We immediately poisoned the creature."

Oxford is back to studying his hands. "And Yorke was gay for me, another problem of mine at the time. Just like my father the 16th Earl I had a taste for shady, disorderly friends. Falstaff certainly did not come from a scrap of paper. Nor did Prince Hal.

"Eventually with maturity before age forty, just like Prince Hal blooming to be King Henry V, I shed my parasites. And then I domesticated happily enough. I simply loved my second wife, Elizabeth Trentham, who you yourself orchestrated, thank you very much, Majesty. We and our boy Henry (named for our friend the Earl of Southampton) lived peacefully in a suburb near the theaters for ten years, until plague put me in an unmarked grave.

"But back in 1576 living abroad I was disoriented. I wanted out of all England had done and been to me. And Yorke devilishly poisoned my mind against poor Anne just like Iago. Just like Iachimo. That period was a curse of guilt, and yet inspired my best art.

"As you more than all know, Majesty, Liz, much of my life wound up inside literary paper. I could only write outward from life I had lived and felt.

"I became a wise older man. But was a great fool young. You were a wise old Queen. You, though, you never were young, were you, Liz?"

Elizabeth: "You already know why not, Eddie. My bad dad Henry declared me a bastard. I was raised under house arrest entirely without mother or father. But then on some unexplained whim shouty daddy put me in the line of Crown succession. Which was the sudden opposite of his whim to chop off my mom Anne Boleyn's head. But his putting me back up as a possible Queen excited Catholic plans to kill me. Me being of course a usurper heretic Protestant and a bossy redhead woman to boot. That's one of two reasons I did not have an adolescence."

Lance as Oxford is now at his stage business thing. He has crossed the stage to place his invisible clear plastic chair next to Elizabeth on her own clear chair, a ghost style thing. A cat can look at a Queen.

Oxford, "The other reason? We must speak truth about consequences."

Elizabeth, exhaling, avoids the audience's too many eyes. "Soon after my mean, mean dad died I was sent to live with his widow, Katherine Parr, and her very new husband Admiral Thomas Seymour. This is long before you came to London as an orphan yourself. I was 14. And so it came to pass Admiral Seymour put his man thing in me a few times. Which was upsetting but bearable until my flat belly started to swell up. Spies knew all. Furious Katherine pulled a knife and cut my dress off me in her walled garden to see for herself. She saw. My brother Edward's men took Seymour to the Tower and his horny head rolled immediately from a sham trial keeping my rape out of it. My strategic value was as a virgin. Crown agents removed me to a dying spymaster's distant house. I was held incommunicado for six months until past birth. The nurse told me my baby was stillborn. And I then resumed my 44-year career as a professional virgin with a cynical heart."

Oxford, his hand sympathetically on her shoulder: "Your cynical heart saw well. You were correct about my weakness, Liz. I was too volatile for politics, I had too much artistic temperament start to end. A loose cannon. But. But really we ghosts must be frank. You almost did more damage than I ever could have done as Shakespeare. Beginning to die without a named heir, that was dementia's grip on you. In final egotism seeing death come you forbade as treason any succession conversation by anyone. That selfishly invited even more Tudor chaos."

Elizabeth: "I suppose. I feel better now that I'm a ghost with hindsight instead of alive lacking foresight. But peaceful succession did work out well. As did your many years writing and re-writing internally exiled. And secretly subsidized. And protected from enemies. Mark you, all that came from me, my Lord."

Oxford: "I do. I do eternally now, Liz. The bargain was close to fair. But still I died believing that once I could write nothing more to trouble the Crown it would allow me to be recognized as Shakespeare. That the phony use of the nasty little Shaxper fellow would be abandoned as ridiculous."

Elizbeth, smiling proudly as she again turns to face the audience: "That set-up was a workmanlike job. Four hundred years is a long time for a successful sham. We Crown Elizabethans did a massive lot of competent deceiving. Including big dangerous matters. Like entirely erasing any record that half our own troops defending against the Spanish armada of '88 died of starvation and disease because of the stingy Crown's lack of care of them afterward. And like also disappearing any writing about the catastrophic loss of most of a huge English reprisal fleet attack against Spain in '90. And too, beyond cover ups, we did a lot of false propaganda. So fun to recall Burghley himself forging letters of a ringleader English Catholic pledging his loyalty first to the Crown over the Pope's Church, which we circulated all across France and Spain.

"And we regularly did so many deniable murders. Each at its time seeming necessary. Like the writer disappearances, the feudal heir deaths, and priest executions out of hand. The Tudor Crown was good at making all sorts of events erased to be non-events ..."

Oxford: "Anyhow Liz, I do apologize for using your sad second secret pregnancy in my Tudor-prince-as-heir theory. By it Henry Wriothesley, that gorgeous golden young Earl of Southampton, was really your child secretly fostered to the dying 2nd Earl of Southampton. And as you grew feeble I did urge my few remaining friends to popularize a movement that Henry should be crowned on your passing."

Elizabeth: "A very Shakespearean plot within plot that would be. Fascinating indeed, Eddie. That Tudor prince tipsy fantasizing of yours very nearly took off your graying head for treason. What a piece of work you were, silly man. Fantasy was your reality.

"Poor mixed up Henry Wriothesley was another doomed dreamer. Foolishly joining his hero Essex in rebellion plans. That treason's pathetic failure went to the heart of the Crown's power, so pretty Henry simply had to be properly sentenced to Tower Hill execution for treason with Essex and the others. Which I commuted later for Henry alone. Because you pled for him so movingly that even your brother-in-law Robert Cecil relented.

"You know after Robert succeeded his father William you were protected by him as well as me. Even though some thought you mocked his hunchback in Richard III."

"Well, I wasn't that suicidal. The Chronicles actually had the crooked back. Robert was not relentless like his father."

"Yes, I think as succeeding chief minister Robert Cecil had some sympathy for you because you both suffered under his father's devious hand. But there was a limit to what I could do to protect you, Eddie. There always was a lot of death swirling around me. You came close often to the flame.

"And you were expensive. Due to needing to competently shield your identity we had to twice send a Walsingham terrifying thug, probably their one who did for Marlowe, with a bag of gold to silence the greedy little nobody from Stratford."

Oxford: "I know what great good you did for me, Majesty. But you know too I lived up to our bargain."

Elizabeth: "That you did right up to your death soon after me. Poor frustrated Eddie. Always writing away in easy code. So obviously really about your obsession with rightful nobility that is confused, denied, and restored. So much exile in your work. Always so many disguises of identity. Your plays are quite the roadmap for those with open eyes."

"Speaking of roadmaps, I like the huge portrait of you in London today at the Dulwich Gallery. What bravado there was in you, Liz. You are poker faced mysteriously standing centered on a map of Oxfordshire. Your finger is pointing straight only to Southampton territory. And you look thick in the middle."

"Do not go there. Eddie I'm warning you. Do not go there ever again."

"Yes. Well."

"Well is not in it."

Lance's bell rings enthusiasm. "Done! Very *very* well done, people. Harry, we are keeping you in the Waldorf for the duration. You write great stuff there."

Part Four

Rain is sheeting, it is three moods at once.

This wet stone hill has been so abraded by deep time its protuberance is rounded breast smooth. Nothing wants to nipple atop it. A twisty evergreen tried but has not progressed in half a century. Here is Vladimir and Estragon's tree.

Up against this tree's trunk a body lies prone under a rain-glistening cape, legs spread wide. Raised a foot up on elbows, it grasps a rod held by metal braces like second elbows. The rod points toward the next hilltop over in a landscape undulating to far deeply misted horizon.

Valerie five hours on is at last in range of her stag. Who is otherwise enjoying a fine early afternoon snacking on always tasty white heather. This entitled male, a 10-pointer, looks to be posing for a whisky label.

Brrring!

"Alec!"

"Sorry Ms. Farnsworth. It's off now." Young bearded Alec whatever was chosen by Valerie as her guide on the basis that he looks as studly as a stag. But things have not been proceeding socially. Alec at 23 is sunk into deep phone screen addiction. Five hours in the rain is a long time to tag along behind some kind of Marvel character bossy lady. Alec will not be a hunting guide much longer. He doesn't see the point. He is Scottish but hates being rained upon. Today this new girl Nance in Edinburgh is sending him an Instagram like every half hour, each time with less clothing in the picture.

The stag raised its bearded head at the distant ringtone, but he is the diligent type as to heather pruning. Valerie is twisting a knob on her father's rifle. The Farnsworth family have been pruning stags in this range for quite a long time. Her legs straddle wider, her boot tips dig into muddy turf. Behind her Alec on mute is ogling increasingly shameless Nance.

KAPOWW—W-W-w-w-w-w echoes back across the glen.

Scientific shooting is Valerie's hallmark outdoors as well as indoors. The stag is perfectly heart-shot. Falls to ground limp as a hammy stage actor receiving very bad news.

Braaaa . . . Braaaa. Now it's Valerie's phone. She missed three breaths for the shot. A huntress's killing moment is intense going as well as coming. *Braaaa . . . Braaaa . . . Braaaa.*

Finally Valerie reaches inside her poncho chest pocket, looks at the screen. "Sod off, Clarice. I'm busy." But Clarice persists in speaking. She is just the age to be Valerie's daughter, and capable of a Force Five fuck off hang up herself. She is also comfortingly plain in looks compared to Valerie.

The boss is listening while through the rifle scope she checks the bullet entry point on her trophy. "No do not send anything in writing. Google will mine it in a minute. Jeff Bezos lost half his fortune counting on WhatsApp encryption." Valerie glances back to her reluctant guide who is not glancing at her. "I can't talk now, Clary. But this could be good. Tell Clive I do not want him to talk any further to anybody else. My jet will arrive in London tomorrow. Tell him to internal code both continental ops to collect the bugger where he says and bring him to our London warehouse. Two o'clock sharp. And decoy cover me leaving the plane."

She is listening. "Don't say any more, sweetheart. NSA could be listening from Colorado and looking up your skirt at this moment. I'll take all this over from here. The situation needs to be gamed out

Omniconal style. Just schedule the ops pick up, then everybody shut up tight."

Valerie listens to five words. "Yes, thank you for your concern. I did get my kill. Call Bernice and tell her a haunch is coming to London for the office dining room."

She listens longer. "Oh come on. What a wuss lot. They won't eat even chicken?"

Listening. "Who is he?"

"The office boy!"

Listening. "Fine. So whatshisname gets the whole haunch. Make a man of him. He'll be arm wrestling at desks and pinching bottoms."

Listening. "Yes. And tell Clive well done so far but go silent, the ops and I have it all now. Ask him if he'd like a lion bag of elk sent to New York."

Listening, listening. "How does Lester even know I am going to be in London? Tell him .... *aah! Aah!* Clarice how does Lester know to follow me there? *Clarice? Clarice, you reckless wuss!*"

And Valerie throws her phone through the rain at Alec since he is a man and there. Alec who is bent over his own phone screen now watching another one.

This scene in driving rain must have happened more or less so. Here I am only coloring around the unauthorized phone surveillance report that Call Me Bill gave me. How else would what I later learned make sense?

*

*   *

I cannot live at the Waldorf another six weeks without getting some of my stuff at home, including pharmaceuticals and music in that order. Once there I acted on a thought that had been growing within my hack writer's cocoon mind.

So I walked from my twelfth apartment in New York, that current rat hole being at Avenue B and St. Marks, to meet Dr. Arthur Arbuthnot at his home in Battery Park City. They—good old they—say everybody in New York soon completely forgets what fine old buildings were here once, but disappeared to wrecking balls of new greed. I much as anyone I suppose. But wending my way toward my appointment's particular gleam of tower it occurred to me this is a different spin of time inside Manhattan's globe. For Dr. Arbuthnot lives high over where when he was born the harbor still lapped ocean waves to shore. White magic for once.

That's how it began. And went.

"Do you think this is amusing?" Arbuthnot says that breaking in to my beginning explanation of *The Which of Shakespeare's Why's* premise.

I always have been too sensitive to strong light. I took off my sunglasses in the elevator so I would not look like some sinister interrogator in a movie. But now in the apartment's glass-walled corner living room I need to put them back on. Arbuthnot's eyes bore in. I suppose he just sees a love-handled hipster not a sinister agent of fate. Wearing another too cool T-shirt too young for me, I realize. Dr. Who Are You is wearing a cream linen sport jacket, turtleneck and not jeans.

This happens. I can't speak back to him now. I've read articles by professors of psychology and psychiatry that catalog the bipolar behavior incidents throughout Edward de Vere's well documented life story. Things like the manic playfulness of his jousting pageant performance as the resplendently all-gilt Knight of the Tree of the Sun. Where at age 27 he broke 12 cagily waving golden lances—some then called them spears, and so waving a lance is shaking a spear —on opponents. Fairly winning a second jousting tournament in dedicated honor of delighted still foxy Elizabeth. De Vere literally also shook his manly spear masterfully as he danced intricate steps with otherwise rarely smiling Elizabeth to intricate music, some of which he himself composed.

But then at this historically famous Court championship meet de Vere went too far. In his manic mode as gilt-armored Knight of the Tree of the Sun (Elizabeth his page had declaimed was de Vere's Sun) he went literally over the top. His planned lavish celebratory fireworks overshot and burned down several citizens' houses. Then for souvenirs a worked-up drunken mob tore apart the golden tree de Vere's page had stagily declaimed to them symbolized the Queen. At which point Elizabeth stopped smiling. Years later his depressive side of bipolar grew stronger. De Vere for all his youth's vivacity became increasingly, then wholly, reclusive.

Literally within Shakespeare's works bipolar is there plain to be seen. Energies swinging back and forth all through the plays' characters and indeed swinging across the array of the whole canon of plays. For Shakespeare wrote an intense comedy, then next an intense tragedy. Manic jollity surprises us within violent drama. Sudden complete transformations of identity occur obsessively often. The sonnets are eloquently low in spirit, sometimes followed by lively wit in the same poem

This is there to read within so many canon texts. And then reading the biographical record of Edward de Vere one also sees a similarly bipolar range of personality. That is an armchair psychology diagnosis easy to comprehend. But not why I am here. Dr.

Arbuthnot is a retired surgeon not a head doctor. And I stand here witheringly over-lit in his living room just on my whim, not calculated logic.

Now I stand staying silent. Frozen by a mental shutdown as has happened to me since childhood. When the future multi-volume biography of Mrs. Haines' disappointing son Harry issues it will report that, unlike his hero bipolar Shakespeare, Harry suffered from periodic severe autistic arrest episodes. Leading to lost opportunities and possible mates. And right this moment to a freeze in the steady penetrating gaze from Dr. Arthur Arbuthnot. Harvard, Harvard Medical School, New York Presbyterian Hospital, the Century Association, as real a deal as I am not. Of course I seize up in his scary critical dad eye, go inert as a pillar of salt.

So here is time to digress outside time. Lance has great notions the same way a ball in a pinball machine has good rolls. A good one until the next bounce to deal with. By his inspiration the unseen huge subsidizing hand of Queen Valerie is inviting all the American and English Oxfordian society members to the premiere of *The Which* at Radio City Music Hall. Plus all the living authors of a pro-Oxford book or article. And all the signatories to the online Declaration of Reasonable Doubt about Will Shaxper's actual authorship, signed by a cross section of American society in every state (except of course wholly illiterate Hawaii). Plus, and this was my own suggestion after experience under the hobbed heel of Professor Sheppard Germaine, several major university teachers under age 40 who cover Elizabethan literature classes. The invitations will be encrypted by Omniconal link for a voucher to cover airfare and an overnight room.

When I scanned the Omniconal-generated list of those 3000 invitees I had my own pinball bing-bing thought. As they wrote,

Edward de Vere and all the Elizabethan playwrights obviously knew the types who would respond to their work. So they wrote with intelligent anticipation of the social response to their impetus. And also considered the fascist Elizabethan authorities' response, which had to be correctly calculated or else. Only an idealistic fool of a writer moves his pages along without thinking who is out there to read or reject them.

Thus, being tasked to write *The Which*, I decided that prudently I should get to know a few of the invited Oxfordian audience. Dr. Arbuthnot, a member of the Shakespeare Oxford Fellowship, is my first contact. I just chose him because I could simply walk over to talk to him from my walk-up.

Perhaps I stood there in my seizure for a week, couldn't say. "What?"

In the luxury of retirement from operating rooms, the doctor has grown a spade beard, spoiled by being white so that a conditioned Santa Claus thought is tempting. But not for long. "I said are you people serious. I mean is this another perfumed fart like *Shakespeare in Love?*"

"No. We are presenting accurate Shakespeare performance excerpts. But accompanied by Oxford the author's actual biography cognates twining dialogue through. For this centennial celebration of Looney's groundbreaking book our play will bring Oxfordian conviction to life theatrically. First time."

Arbuthnot is looking at me arms crossed without crossing them. So I go on. "We thought we should interview some Oxfordians to help us express the tenor of their views. Just at random, Doctor."

"To see how nutty we are?"

"I have been wounded on the Stratford battlefield myself, Doctor."

He actually can smile. "They're good at ad hominem. Like Queen Elizabeth's enforcers I suppose."

"You Google as a surgeon and conservationist. Not an English scholar that I could see."

"That's correct. Like the majority of Oxfordians I have a solid education but not in English literature. Which is contemptuously laughable to the Stratfordians, who are mostly specialized Shakespeare university teachers. Their more crudely aggressive types like Sheppard Germaine at Princeton call us just cockroaches who keep coming back."

He's smiling so slightly. "But actually somehow Oxfordians do tend to be oddball personalities. Isn't that so, Doctor?"

Maybe people in glass-walled towers develop a special habit in speaking. After stepping over to his long view, Arbuthnot replies, "Some, indeed. But somebody is odd on any subject of dispute. And most subjects are disputed in this world of billions.

"But there are a lot of scientists, including some senior physicists. A number of physicians, including university-tenured psychiatrists and psychologists. Lawyers who have seen a lot of real life and sense probability, including six recent Justices of the Supreme Court. Women highly educated and achieved in some profession they have left behind. Some talented free-thinking theater professionals, a few are famous Shakespearean players. You say you know the Oxfordian writing—what do you think of its quality?"

I mean this. "Sober in tone. Factually punctilious. Intellectually coherent. That's why we are staging *The Which*, to spread that awareness in the general public." True. But. But also to get hold of an egomaniac billionaire's financial support. Failing which, Trenton Shakespeare Festival's 30 actors fall right back again into pitiful unemployment.

"You want to know what draws people to the authorship question." Arbuthnot is no actor. The pause is not art, he cannot quite find his words. "A common element is that they are not intellectual feudal serfs. They are modern minds not satisfied by improbability."

Now he's on. "In their own lives the professionals who gravitate to the Oxfordian movement have dealt with a wide variety of practical matters, successfully navigated a complexly open world. They have experienced a very different life from the sheltered—one perhaps could venture *priestly*—insulation of a lifelong English department professor. Or anyone else whose livelihood primarily depends upon continuing the myth of Will Shaxper as a saint of pure inspiration. Those others being the tourist trap and media mill trades."

The blunt old doctor is not even looking at me. "Magical thinking does not require absorbing factual life's complexity. That's the doom in it. Think of the huge now unreadable libraries of magical thinking in closely reasoned Christian theology." Some people burned for it and some become burners.

"Nailed it, dude. Excuse me."

"It's the thought that counts, Larry. I think next you should go talk to Aaron Aaronson up at Columbia. He's a physicist said to be in line for a Nobel. He gave a talk at a Century lunch of its Shakespeare fans. Ron offered the best opening to Oxfordian engagement I have heard.

"He said if you get Shakespeare's identity wrong you get his plays wrong. If you get Shakespeare's identity wrong you get the Elizabethan Age wrong—its culture, its politics, the balance of its literary context. And then he turned up faces in that grizzled crowd of intellectuals. Speaking from the top of applied research physics Ron told them that if you get Shakespeare wrong you get the fundamental nature of human creativity wrong. Because scientists have long ago proven from all history that acknowledged geniuses grow from their personal very long-sustained very focused effort. Not instants of inspiration. Pretty for lazy minds as that may be to dream."

"Can I tell Professor Aaronson you sent me?"

"Sure. On the other side you've read Diana Price's take down of Shaxper?"

"*Shakespeare's Unorthodox Biography, an Authorship Problem.* I looked at it. Impressive detective work but pretty dry. She aligns biographical information as to two dozen known Elizabethan writers. There is contemporaneous documentary proof they wrote for 23. Only Shaxper, who modern history supposes was well known as the famous Shakespeare, has zero documentary confirmation he was a writer at all."

That is a doctor's penetrating gaze. "But you fellows must not clown up your play. You could do great damage in public opinion. And to yourselves. They play with real knives in English departments. Ad hominem sharp as scalpels."

No. Indeed. There will be no chance of a clowned up amateurish mess from this T-shirt fellow here in red tennis shoes, no indeed. I hate this light because Dr. Whatever is brighter than me. And something is flashing I cannot see. I'm too dizzy in the instant. Not like a genius at all. "Can I sit down?"

"You may." He perceives something I am feeling. This is after all a medical doctor, not a doctor of early modern English literature. "I'll get you a glass of water."

Seated quiet alone I close sun-glassed eyes. And so see the idea that has been flashing under my horizon. Coming since I decided to break the fourth wall at the outset of *The Which.* Where, pending curtain rise, old Iz playing young Puck portends our subversive effect. Even as he feigns apology for it. Subversion of which Lance and I mean every word.

Now I realize Puck's apology for the coming play's transgressions will not be enough. More talent than I have is needed to finish writing *The Which*. This should be performance consequenced beyond anticipation. As came specially tragically to Oxford the tragedian, in his long fate of casual cruelties and calculated revenges.

When I've drunk the water glass deep wishing it were vodka I say to piercing eyes over that white squared beard, "I started scenes but it's only me. I'm not even very good playing Hamlet. I should not be writing Shakespeare. I don't want to crash this bike."

The doctor is looking at my childish T-shirt. I said bike but I did mean motorcycle. Of course this old man thinks oh sweet Jesus if only you could help. Two minutes on: "You like the comedies?"

"Everybody does."

"The comedies came from the same heart that wrote the tragedies, right?"

"Unless there were two Shaxpers or two Oxfords."

Pause, pause. "Who would play with that idea? Four within two that logically must be one?"

Yes. "Shakespeare."

"Shakespeare writing your play wouldn't preach or argue about identity. He'd come at it surprisingly. Yes?"

"Yes." This is like catechism when I believed. "Yes. Like the way he ran anger all through the comedies."

The doctor's eyes won't leave mine. He seems to be smiling under that wide white moustache. "So write playfully, Larry. Shakespeare would. And you are free to do so because you love him."

My name is Harry. But he's right, my own identity is not in *The Which*. "Okay." The sound that gets me into trouble.

"The binary form of the question who was Shakespeare freezes both sides. In modern science the freshest thinking tends non-binary as well as non-linear. New understanding follows new pathways. The Stratfordians do not actually consider how eccentric a man the writer of the plays must have been. Externally as well as internally. So let your audience feel that in the man Oxford.

"Audiences are smart. They can recognize more than normative straight line. Show a bit of the man next to a bit of the artful forms of the man and . . ." He went somewhere that spoke to him a moment. "And you will have performed your lines well enough for honor done. No actor can expect to force an audience to understand his character. It's up to them not to be fools of fate."

"Okay."

"They are called plays for good reason. Even the serious ones. So when you write your serious subject, play with it as Shakespeare would."

"Okay."

And then I am standing on a breezed stone plaza outside the doctor's building. It is a high tower now on water that was moving 400 years ago. This moment a glittering gleam of sunbeams.

I do not believe Arbuthnot was really a surgeon. Play doctor maybe.

*

*   *

Then they got me. It came sudden and harsh as passing through a Tower of London barbican gateway, pinioned by grip of hard hands. The Tower guards' Crown-issue bloodstained rapiers strapped to thick thighs. Though, as Hamlet said to Horatio, stopping one of his own overwrought embellished tirades, too much of that.

All morning of this day after consulting Dr. Arbuthnot the Waldorf has hulked silence around me like a pyramid tomb. I asked Lance to leave me alone in the suite so I can try to write.

But for hours now my pen has lain stilled. I am as if overwhelmed onstage, cued from the wing to declaim a momentous soliloquy not yet composed. My room service apple cube Waldorf lunch salad is browning to shriveled edges. Sleeping in my doublet did not help inspiration as hoped. Dawn's uneaten breakfast tray array expired long ago of old age.

It is because it was. It was and yet is to be maybe. I think and so it is. Or at least was. The 800-year-old de Vere family motto "Nothing truer than truth" is a twist in Latin on Vere and veracity. How heavy can irony get before it falls and breaks the writer's tap-dancing foot?

Ovid did not claim to know all the contents of Pandora's opened box of troubles. Lance's bland black wheeled suitcase looked just like any ordinary drug runner's travel accessory. Its dumped-out heap of books still centers the living room floor, yet to be consulted. About half seeming from cover copy to be Stratfordian, with the balance announcing themselves Oxfordian. I have noticed Lance's bonus selection of a few nut-job tracts.

I am nearly the same age as the character Hamlet. Who was conceived by an author about our same age, and I sometimes feel that in his texts. But this tiredness in us three at our far edge of youth is not final exhaustion. No, that is why our thoughts as words said circle so. I Harry must think as Hamlet. There remains readiness in him for what is to come. But we three, perhaps four of us, you withal, have suckled dread's trickle in our growth to mid-life time. Dread is part of our sustained readiness by now. More than hope. Yet less than wonder.

Go to church, go to theater. Clutch your wafer, clutch your ticket. Pray for wonder. Two, one. Call that religious feeling if you must.

But Dr. Arbuthnot has wisely prescribed me to write *The Which* theatrically woven from serious knowledge. So that elephantine mound of books in my Waldorf cell must be read through. What I write must structure from published fact. I owe that much to whoever Shakespeare was. And to who Sheppard Germaine is and will be to me.

*

*   *

I have no more made my book
Than my book has made me—
A book consubstantial with its author.

Michel de Montaigne

Montaigne's unpublished introspective essays were circulating in 1575 Paris when Oxford arrived troubled and thrilled. Fleeing Elizabeth's viperous Court in search of better destiny. Montaigne himself had just fled Paris because the plague was also new in town. Plague death would have to wait until 1604 to catch up with the 17th Earl in London. What a sad darkness for the world could have fallen in Paris in 1575.

I think I would have made a good professor myself, except for my basic personality and the punctuating autistic episodes. Like a proper academic I recall texts sharply. I certainly drink to standard.

This morning I put on my black doublet and shuffled and shifted through the book pile. Flipped through a Jeremy Japes Stratfordian tome touching beside my toe as if ready to bite an Oxfordian. I gathered it over-explains detail of classical text references in Shakespeare. Oxbridge showing off tedious as display of last winter's turnips.

Next I opened a book by somebody who from the dust jacket seemed to have slept with Shakespeare, who talked aloud in dreams which she is glad to now explain in English

Department jargon. That book dropped I picked up a thick fluff from a totemic guy of the Yale English Department about Falstaff being some wiggy way the complete sum of humanity. Both author and subject being way overly garrulous, way overweight.

But sitting down with my second cup of coffee I picked out from the scrum a book by one of my intellectual heroes, Professor Stephen Greenblatt of Harvard.

Will in the World. I had not read this, apparently a biography. If Professor Greenblatt, man of superb intellect, is writing a biography of Shakespeare I need to read it before I can responsibly write of the Earl. Park Avenue shafts sunlight between lit glass towers. I pull a chair to beside my street window.

Within minutes Greenblatt's *Will in the World* had paused my confidence in Oxford being really Shakespeare as efficiently as a dagger tip to throat. I opened first to the source notes and read them stunned by the number of books itemized as to their chapter by chapter context of use by Greenblatt. Each of those hundred plus books must have taken years of the writer's thought and effort, each had scores of believers in its particular worth to print.

I shuddered to anticipate what he has written from and above it as to proof Shaxper was Shakespeare. Be it to come as I read? Am I indeed out of a job?

Samuel Johnson called it "index learning," going straight to specific topics of interest for a new reader of a book. From the index I soon learned the Harvard professor had absolutely no interest in Edward, 17th Earl of Oxford. Not when he was writing his book in 2004 anyway. The sole reference in *Will in the World* to Edward de Vere regards his shouting quarrel with the forgotten poet Sir Phillip Sydney over use of a tennis court reservation. So a silly fellow. Nothing else in Greenblatt's book as to Oxford.

Greenblatt's bibliography has not one reference to any Oxfordian book of the several that by now comprise new scholarship inconvenient to the Stratfordian worldview.

Thus Oxfordians say that Stratfordians in effect prune Elizabethan history to fit around the empty profile of Will Shaxper.

But the charismatic 17th Earl was no blank space in Elizabethan society. He is extensively documented. Historical documents show him well respected by Elizabethan intellectuals. Dozens of books were dedicated to the serious arts patron Oxford. A 1612 book surveying English writers on its cover has a puzzle showing a hidden hand writing from between curtains and an anagram that decodes as "Oxford is the author." A 1622 book reprinted three times ranks Edward, 17th Earl of Oxford first among many historical English authors, and never mentions Shakespeare or Shaxper. During Oxford's lifetime cryptic or sly references in print were made to Oxford as a first-rate mature creative author. Of record as a scholar Oxford translated and prefaced various Latin and Italian texts. Including the then controversial new "Cardenas" Italian philosophy. Its distinctive Italian Renaissance intellectual elitism reverberates among various Shakespeare characters.

I pause reading the book of the professor whose sources do not seem to know of my man Oxford. Because new textual close analysis by Oxfordian scholars seems to show that the Earl while still a teenager actually was the first translator from Latin to English of Ovid. It is thought his tutoring uncle's name was used to get Crown censor approval. Ovid of course is Shakespeare's most prevalent classical source. There is a beard within a beard aspect here not likely to please Stratfordian professors.

Fascinating, it's coming back. Scholars have just recently adduced extensive textual matches between that first English Ovid translation and Edward Earl of Oxford's extant evidenced personally distinctive writing style and vocabulary. Furthermore, and overarchingly in common sense from simple historical fact, teenage Oxford's old Uncle Arthur Golding is highly improbable as the real translator of the very sensuously intense firs English translation of Ovid. Because in fact Golding in all his life never published anything else but Puritan religious pamphlets and classical period nonfiction translation

Oxford is known to have periodically housed and financially subsidized over a half-dozen noted professional writers of the Elizabethan period. And for years Oxford supported actors and his own two acting troupes that ultimately evolved into the one that predominantly first presented plays attributed to "William Shakespeare." Oxford's early youth companions included his father's acting troupe's beloved clown Will Somer. Some Oxfordians see this man as inspiring Yorick, who is a character not appearing in any precedent text to *Hamlet*.

So theater and writing surely were in Oxford's basic personality. Throughout his long years of reclusion from Court after happy marriage, he chose to reside just a quick walk to the South Bank playhouses.

Absolutely zero of all this factual substance is of any interest to Professor Greenblatt's tale in *Will in the World*.

I look out the window and across Park. See aligned hard-shelled towers. Then think of the hundreds of medieval stone-towered cathedral sodalities churning out immense ecclesiastic libraries. Those hundreds of densely intensely written treatises. All of them rendered now very peculiar indeed to consider after the Age of Enlightenment.

The 2004 Greenblatt bibliography does not include the scholarly 2005 *Shakespeare by Another Name*, a soberly comprehensive Edward de Vere biography by Margo Anderson. I do have to wish Professor Greenblatt had considered this very central new scholarship among so many peripheral old writings.

Anderson systematically ties the biographical facts of de Vere's life to features of Shakespeare's plays and poems. Moving through hundreds of text and life event overlaps and echoes. Not in general profile, instead always corresponding text to specifically Oxford's many specific life events. They do seem to fit as keys to literary artistry throughout the plays.

For some, anyway, this Oxfordian construct is as compelling as intellectual salty vinegared potato chips.

But for what I have of self-respect I must remain honestly scholarly. Or quit . . . before I crash this bike. I do not want to ruin by sloppiness this chance for all the TSF actors that Lance kindly entrusted to me. And I do not want to piss off Valerie Farnsworth anywhere near a throwable heavy object. Or a light pointed one. I've been out of work before but do still have the wealth of good conscience. And that I will protect.

*

*   *

For three hours I sat at the Waldorf window overlooking Ethan Hawke's *Hamlet* scene at Park and 49th. Absorbed but eventually realizing what gave *Will in the World* its persuasive charm besides Professor Greenblatt's masterful writing style. Greenblatt did not just make up events in any cheap way. The historical facts of Elizabethan life on into James's early reign are responsibly portrayed in detail. No Hollywood pandering nonsense like Harvey Weinstein's sexy coy simper *Shakespeare in Love.*

But Greenblatt's book really should have been titled *The World in Will*, rather than *Will in the World.* For while the profuse details of general events and circumstances paint a pedestrian historical tapestry, the professor's imagination inserts very many instances showing how Will Shaxper *would have* fit into it. Would have *if* he were a person of such extraordinary literary genius he could prestidigitate dozens of diversely worldly works despite factual lack of cognate life experiences, and despite factual lack of any cognate education.

Which of course is not at all the same accomplishment as showing what Shaxper *actually* did or *actually* was. I was reminded of the way bluescreening film overlay is assembled. Real background scenery can accommodate varieties of inserted presences and come out convincing as a whole. Tom Hanks in *Forrest Gump* is part of our modern culture.

Reading on I relaxed in that kind of pleasant persuasion. So I made the leap Greenblatt invites, jumping into his fundamental premise. I sat there for hours as if at a pleasant movie starring Tom Hanks as an uncanny genius named William Shakespeare (though in fact the Stratford man birth to death was recorded as William Shaksper, a common regional name, and never used that name Shakespeare for himself).

I became absorbed inside *Will in the World's* donnée, as Henry James put it of a novel's setting. That is the same Henry James who wrote that William Shaksper of Stratford as author of the works of Shakespeare is "the biggest and most successful fraud ever practiced on a patient world."

James published a wryly funny short story of a docent at the Shakespeare museum in Stratford, prudently not named, which is still today the second most-visited tourist spot in England. Shaksper's longstanding hometown tourism flows a Nile of revenue in billions of pounds annually to interests directly and indirectly vested in his worship. In James's tale a mild-mannered docent of the great genius's birthplace, after years spent rote repeating factually unsubstantiated myths, has begun to doubt their truth. His diffident asides to visitors upset their lazy simple image of a magically endowed saint of world literature. Finally the docent is reprimanded by his boss. And rather than lose his job, that hectored guide shuffles back into spouting simple credo lines to endless lines of happily ignorant tourists.

So *Will in the World's* graceful spell floated me along in a beautifully whole warmly colored portrayal of the greatest literary sensibility ever. But then at a page I froze. For I suddenly recalled a similar rapt feeling long ago. As a young Catholic boy in an old Catholic Midwestern community. A willing altar boy, I loved wholly accepted religious envisionment. I loved to believe that all which came to ignorant me explained truth completely.

But later as a man I lost that passive fascination and became wary of comprehensive fables. For I became appalled to know that, over two millennia, millions of everyday people died bloody in wars and persecutions. All asserting arbitrary but comprehensive abstract religious dogma in some now preposterous claim of being exclusively true Christianity. In just Britain's tight little island of the 16th century, so very many thousands of souls were mercilessly slaughtered quarreling over true belief in an imbued religious sect improbability. As opposed to actually a close alternative imbued improbability.

So then I ceased enjoying charming, self-assured academic insistence as to Shakespeare's identity delivered to impressionable general readers.

Seven years at Princeton. Now the phrase "specious paralogism" has just popped into my mind. Because I sense tricky mirrors of sophisticated rhetoric propelled this *Will in the World* to bestseller popularity. But that opinion of mine sitting on a couch, like showoff academic vocabulary, is coin I cannot spend.

*
*   *

The phone rang, my screen showed a head shot of Lance 10 years ago, show biz style.

"How's it going today, Harry?"

"It's not. I'm all wrapped up trying to deal with *Will in the World*. That Greenblatt guy is so suave he makes me feel like a nut."

"Just ignore him the way they all ignore us."

"But what if they attack with big media on autopilot support? With all their fan awards and university prestige nobody will believe us. Written off as nut stuff."

"Harry. Consider how the Stratfordian writing magically

vanishes a tower of documented hard fact that we Oxfordians can show. Those professors actually are very vulnerable now to a shift in public view of Shakespeare. Because their plaster saint worldview is both stale and pale.

"So forget the old Stratfordist prayer book. It's really not our problem. We will simply let the fascinatingly transgressive Badboy Eddie de Vere story rip. And the world audience will have a great new time discovering it. A Marvel hero who can write like lightning strikes."

"You're puppeting me. Aren't you, Lance? You have a career as a controversial director, you'll go on however The Which lands. But there is no Harry Haines career. If I get branded an irresponsible clown in international press, there never will be a career for me in theater. From this I could get banished to behind the counter at a deli. And Stratfordian death threats for sure."

"Perspective. Perspective, bubba. Valerie is paying you what you might not have made as an actor in a decade. And anyway without The Which TSF is dead right exactly now. And so you would be again an unemployed absolute nobody. But if The Which makes any kind of splash, then Iz can re-make your image for whatever works in the moment. Downside it might be Australian musical theater, dinner-in-tents-on-the-road kind of thing. Iz's done that for box office poison here. But also consider your Harry the Riverboat Gambler upside. You might become resident star of Trenton Festival until you have worn out two wigs."

So I laugh. And he laughs. That makes two hands seen of four in play. "Did you like the Lear segment?"

"You bet. Way above sandwich order quality. I sent it straight on to the three very mean girls. We do a run-through on Friday. 10:30, be there or be square."

"Larry as Lear?"

"Sure. But not just on the basis of being a geezer. Larry actually understudied Lear at a Young Vic run. But alas, as we say a lot in theater."

"Okay. Okay. But stay out of the hotel until Friday. I really don't know what more to do yet for conclusion. Greenblatt has me spooked."

"The best writers are scared of something. Embrace it, Harry."

"Are you buying a sailboat with your fee from Valerie?"

"Cigarette job, baby. Oh look. We need a hot sequence put in somewhere near our end at *The Tempest*. Leave space for something about Elizabeth's mercy big pension at last to our man."

"Why? There's nothing in the plays about it."

"Being a dangerous Crown secret, natch not."

"Lance, we need theater with felt motion and felt impact. *The Which* won't work if we turn it into a thick cold stew of Oxfordian theories. Or an amateur fruitcake of confused delusions. Which of course is what the Stratford hit men will call it if it's any way weak scholarship. We have to be accurate on the hard facts."

"Go, Harry, go. But you will need to be able to stick in a few lines somewhere showing off what Valerie's boys, machines, whatever, turn up. Like Hamlet did in the Gonzago murder scene within the main play. Just write fast when Omniconal's bell rings."

"I should know what Valerie is trying to do."

Lance has weaponized dimples even over a phone. "No, Harry. You should not. Not yet."

*

* *

*Good Lord, will you see the players well bestowed? Do you hear,
let them be well used, for they are the abstract and brief chronicles of the
time. After your death you were better have a bad epitaph than their ill
report while you live.*

Hamlet to Lord Burghley, I mean to Polonius

Oh good Horatio, I'll take the ghost's word for a thousand pound.

Hamlet to his Uncle Horace, I mean to Horatio

I should not know what Valerie is doing. I should just somehow
insert a dozen or 16 lines into *The Which* about the small fortune
value of £1,000 annual payments from Elizabeth to Oxford.

Actually I need to doze off a bit and get out of the box of writing *The Which*. The beige sofa under me is humming beige lullaby.
Bucked up as usual by Lance's cavalier attitude, I throw Professor
Greenblatt's Pulitzer-winning cavalier fantasy as far away as archi-
tecture allows.

My name downstairs at Waldorf reception is Mr. Bottom. This
Mr. Bottom has dreams as did his ancestor four centuries ago. For
both of us characters sometimes the past, the present, and the future
become churned together in disorder. "A dream past the wit of man
to say what dream it was," said my ancestor Bottom in *Midsummer
Night's Dream*. Sometimes dreaming works that way for me too. In
this moment I doze into imagining that might be foretelling of a
"dream what was" written in the future. Bottom stuff happens.

So.

Valerie's strong cheeks today are English rosy. Her hair has not
begun to recover from Scottish weather, she is fresh arrived into
London on the Omniconal jet. A hundred pounds of still bleeding stag haunches and slabs aboard were chauffeured from the

London Airport tarmac by stretch black Audi to the office boy in her Gherkin office. But the CEO herself was driven in an unmarked old beige Toyota sedan straight to a Cheapside bankrupt start-up's rusting corrugated warehouse far off any corporate books. She wears a kerchief à la Queen Elizabeth II to hide the strawberry blonde wavy eruption.

Valerie sits now alone in an empty chamber, unless you count the thick-shouldered man with a Guy Fawkes mask pulled down on his neck. Or the little fellow in the little room next door. Or the seven-foot tall Omniconal special ops agent in there leaning over him.

It is quiet. Valerie on a tablet is scanning through Stella McCartney's design sketches of her Queen Elizabeth outfit, which copies the famous Rainbow Portrait dress. With a cursor edit the Omniconal CEO lowers décolletage a little and adds even more pearls and rubies to the wig. Suddenly a hand loudly pounds a table in the other room.

The man with the mask stands up. "I'd better see."

"Yes. Put your mask on, Cameron. Why did you pick an asshole?"

"The asshole picked himself more it. There is no regular basis to examine Crown bursary records from Elizabeth's time. The archive clerks are determined not to be bothered to work. And they self-select as shy anal-retentives. So we picked one of only two of them guarding the 16th century. Otherwise, Ma'am, Omniconal could have spun permission wheels for a year."

"That would have upset me."

"Yes, Ma'am." Cameron is a retired Commando. Seeing no more reason to smile idly than Valerie. His job is secure.

"No, wait. Tell Nial to step in. We're at the point of breaking the little willie's goddam fingers."

"Yes, Ma'am." The former colonel does simply agree. Facts are facts.

Now Cameron and Nial stand attention in front of Valerie.

"The bastard is still locked in?"

"Yes Ma'am. He peed himself. But took it like a man. There's some steel not you'd know to see him."

"What's his predictive analytic?"

Nial: "He'd fuck you. Not really I suppose. But really. Pardon my French, Ma'am."

"Fuck is not French."

"Il voudrait vous en foutre forciblement, Ma'am." Valerie does not like employees who smile. She sees to it.

The Omniconal CEO does look queenly right now, headscarf knotted under her chin. Just the wrong Elizabeth. "Where's the number now?"

"Down to five mil cash just right now, Ma'am. Two hours to get from ten. I had to slap him twice."

"That's his bedrock?"

"That's the analytic probability, full databased. He's got the only photo on his phone, which our scan confirms has not been forwarded or saved to a file. He seems to be lazy and stupid as well as a little crook at heart. And he's got the torn corner to prove it's real zippered in his anorak pocket, which our scans show he did not bother to photo. Technologically this here is a real old times pecker, like from all the way back in Mr. Big's time. But the little berk's got a good hand of cards, better than he knows. Media would make him a world star in a blink. Hard for us to kill him if he reaches celebrity."

"You picked the wrong asshole."

"Clive approved, Ma'am. Up to the ten he asked. You were at

sea spear-swordfishing. And just then the Panama cellular sky got scrambled by the CIA for some assassination thing they had in op."

"I'll speak to Clive."

Neither of these former combat soldiers is brave enough to joke with Valerie. Probability full database odds are less than zero that one will say, "Actually the problem was you were off shaking your own spear. Ma'am."

Instead, "But Ma'am. We only had two bogies. His was a blank nobody, previous jobs all chain sandwich shops, no education, a Beatles Nowhere Man. Our only other inside job choice in the Treasury archives cellar was some woman who the Ministry pays enough to feed a cat. And she still donates a tenth of her salary to save the whales. Her predictive was terrible. She has a projected principle streak a mile wide. Just mentioning an offer to her was odds on five-one she'd go to her bosses. Who would then down from command five-one lose the file for good to protect Britain's Mr. Big. And then three-one MI6 sics CIA on us. CIA has been very nasty lately under their latest weirdo President. Tudor-scale nasty. You might say."

Valerie is staring unhappily as usual. "Five will do. We get his phone with the only photo. We get the torn page corner. He signs legal's release and NDA, on video reading them out with today's *Times* front page in the frame for a date. Then he does get five million pounds in unmarked small denominations. Down from wasting ten we're making money. How's he going to carry all that weight?"

"He brought one of those black wheely suitcases like the money launderers go for. The guy does have some moves."

"One peep from this clown and it's goon time."

Nial, "Yes Ma'am. For a lazy weasel he's coming out amazing. He even looks like a smug weasel."

"Whatever a lazy smug . . . Nial. Show me his face on your

phone. Which you will remember to shred after you print his mug shot if we ever need goons."

Nial opens his phone. Valerie frowns at the portrait of one lucky weasel. The phone looks back scared.

"Corblimey, he *is* from central casting. Did he lose the other earring when you roughed him up?

"No Ma'am. It's a special kind of bar thing you can suppose looking at his shoes or whatever they are. Bar code you could say, code for bars you could say. But his little goldwire earring does look like what teenage girls put through a nostril to upset their parents. I know. But at least girls don't have his male pattern baldness too, which would be really . . ."

"What's wrong with your camera? It looks like he has two right eyes."

"Camera's fine. He looks like that at the world. You see it in famous writer photos, Ma'am. My teen daughter has a photo of Jean Paul Sartre over her bed, exact same dodgy pervert squint. Makes sense for writers but this guy has never written a postcard. Out of a crap council school at twelve. Somebody must have ghosted him in the Civil Service exam. Or he's one of those *idiots savants*."

"Your French pronunciation hurts my ears, Nial." Then quiet. Valerie is fascinated to regard this man who at the moment has her world-shaking spear in his dark pocket. "Then what's wrong with his little shoulders under his big head? It looks like he has two left shoulders."

"That's the anorak, Ma'am. Too small and rides odd. Even without cloud backup we figured out it was a gift. You can see when it's zipped up the chest reads Save the Whales. That would—"

"Yes. The office lady's going to miss him. He'll wind up living in Cyprus instead of this bronchial hellhole. A sunny place for . . .'

"Yes Ma'am." These veteran soldiers are both action-oriented. "Even SpyEye couldn't get a bio squib together on this drink of water. A nobody from nowhere doing nothing but the sandwich shop jobs. Not even fingerprints. Ma'am, by now he might be fiddling the lock. No telling what else he did after his bit of schooling ended. But if you want a wheeze his council school was in Stratford. Like—"

"I do not want a wheeze. All right. Now we plug and play. Nial stays in here. It's good he hasn't seen you yet, Cameron. Shock him. Wear the Fawkes devil mask and shout like cannons."

"Ma'am."

"His other payment is fear of sudden death. Give him that now."

"Ma'am."

"I want this joker to pee himself again for the money."

Seconds later Cameron bursts into the little room roaring at that odd rogue secret agent of Omniconal Friendship Unlimited, Limited. Roaring because Omniconal's sheer wizardry of computational detective deductions across 400 years commanded him as independent contractor stooge to do a simple job simply as a robot. For a fee equal to three months' salary as a basement records clerk. Just to take a photograph of any page with any of certain words on it in a span of a certain few years of Queen Elizabeth's personal household accounting. And just walk away with a torn corner of it and call your contact.

Well, what kind of shifty weasel would try to parlay that little job into his own world fame? He will be paid his cash price. But only after threat of death following mutilation, made in coarse language so loud it shakes the cardboard wall behind which Valerie waits. Impatiently but smiling at the only theater she enjoys.

Her phone is on buzzer. She opens it. Clarice has sent a defensively minimal text about dinner at Claridge's with Lester tonight.

Valerie sighs and looks to the past and future at once.

*

*   *

From *The Tragedy of King Lear*, registered with the Crown authority 1604:

Lear: *What can you say to draw a third more opulent than your sisters?*
Cordelia: *Nothing.*
Lear: *Nothing?*
Cordelia: *Nothing.*
Lear: *Nothing will come of nothing. Speak again.*
Cordelia: *Unhappy that I am, I cannot heave*
My heart into my mouth. I love your Majesty
According to my bond, no more nor less . . .
Lear: *But goes thy heart with this?*
Cordelia: *Ay, my good lord.*
Lear: *So young and so untender?*
Cordelia: *So young, my lord, and true.*
Lear: *Let it be so. Thy truth then be thy dow'r!*

The de Vere family ancient motto from time of its origin in Normandy being "Nothing is truer than the truth." A play on "ver" in veracity's, truth's, Latin root.

Susan de Vere, youngest daughter of the perennially bankrupt 17th Earl of Oxford, as a teenage lady in waiting to Queen Elizabeth performed in simple skits, masques, at Court gatherings. As part of a 1602 show each player was given some gift from the Queen accompanied by a personal couplet. But wittily the Court poet John Davies who wrote the masque presented nothing to Susan. Everybody at Court knew Susan age 16 could offer no dowry from her famously improvident father in the financially competitive aristocratic marriage market. This thus is the Court poet's couplet read to her before assembled nobles:

Nothing's your lot. That's more than can be told.
For Nothing is more precious than gold.

Many hearing this would have known why "nothing" could be spoken of about her lot as a daughter of an insolvent recluse. All hearing likely knew the witty official court poet was calling her Cordelia as in her father's play *The Tragedy of King Leir*, previously privately performed in 1594 before Queen Elizabeth. (That play titled *Leir* was not same as the yet-to-appear 1604 *King Lear*, which was a dark late revision). Wit aside, it must have been apparent to the Court sophisticates that this scholarly girl had special qualities not dependent on a monetary dowry. And so indeed it turned out.

Within two years the 1602 witticism as to Susan needing no dowry had become a big laugh at Court due to her wedding. Which occurred just months after her father Oxford's sudden death. Susan de Vere married Sir Phillip Herbert, imminent next Earl of Montgomery. And with his brother the Earl of Pembroke leader of a truly wealthy truly aristocratic family.

The Herbert family's lavish wedding festivities included the performance of four plays in sequence. All four were ultimately ascribed to "William Shakespeare." Most everybody at Court knew the necessarily discreet which of that obvious why. All those Shakespeare plays at Susan's marriage saluted the de Vere heritage. But as the Court poet had put it precisely, "that's more than can be told."

But then. But from then onward through socially tumultuous 17th-century history the rest remained silence as to the Earl of Oxford's authorship of the Shakespeare works.

From the time of King James I's accession after Queen Elizabeth's 1603 death the favored Herbert family would officially control Crown authority over publications. By far later in 1623 the wittily sly old 1602 couplet had come to be a hilarious howler of irony. For in fact Susan and her husband the Earl of Montgomery, with his brother the Earl of Pembroke, were the sole funders of publication in that year of the First Folio that comprehensively included all the plays of "William Shakespeare."

That printed volume is more than half a foot thick. Previously Shakespeare canon plays had only been printed individually in bootlegged cheap pamphlet format. It was a labor of love at a cost then very far beyond financial means of any ordinary commercial publisher.

Remarkably a dozen of the Folio's works had never appeared in print before. And the Folio contained a multitude of authorial revisions from more crude versions that had appeared in anonymous apparently pirated printings back in the 1580s and 90s. How that plenitude of both new and superior revised material was gathered for printing has never been adequately explained.

Oxfordians say, "Calling Susan de Vere." Of record she lived in her father Oxford's house in 1602. And in 1604 married his friend the Earl of Montgomery. Who subsequently published the Folio under his brother Pembroke's control of the Crown Censor.

The enormous cost of printing the massive Folio clearly was not remotely achievable by the couple of retired actors who fronted it for the Censor's record. They realistically would have had no acquaintance at all with the Earls of Pembroke and Montgomery. As apex aristocrats they lived barriered from low-caste commoners, of which actors in the time were lowest.

The Earls as sole funders of the Shakespeare First Folio compilation also hired the then financially hard-pressed old Ben Jonson to ghost-write those actors' dedicatory page, and also to write a preface compliant with his command new job from Pembroke's Crown to keep Oxford's identity away from Shakespeare's name. Jonson's meager Crown stipend as an artist was increased 10-fold at the time he undertook this Folio task. Jonson and Oxford had been drinking companions. But Jonson's misattribution to the Stratford man was a Crown command job for high pay. And the Jacobean Crown was as dangerous for a writer to cross as Elizabeth's had been. Her Crown jailed Jonson three times to intimidate his irreverent writing.

Stratfordians have long proffered the Jonson Folio preface material as their most substantial evidence, calling it proof of Shaxper's authorship of Shakespeare. But in also documented historical scholarship it is apparent that Jonson's writing job was wrapped in pressing historical circumstances "more than [could] be told." Those circumstances are clarified by unfolded history.

Susan de Vere was raised in the London palace custody of her grandfather William Cecil, Lord Burghley. As had been her father Edward, from the time of his becoming an orphan at 12. Like her two elder sisters Susan was largely ignored in childhood by her preoccupied unto beset father. But as a precocious teenager she was on good terms with her aging, long-reclused father. Writing letters around 1602 from Oxford's house near the South Bank playhouses, Susan was known to have strong literary tastes.

And elder sister Elizabeth de Vere also must have been literarily inclined. For she was chosen for marriage by the Earl of Stanley, a close friend of Oxford. Stanley was, similarly to Oxford, both erudite and sophisticated from Italian and French travel experience. Heading this extended family was the Earl of Pembroke, Susan's brother-in-law and long the very powerful chancellor chosen by James I.

This compatible family group included the Dowager Countess of Pembroke, mother of the brother Earls Pembroke and Montgomery. The Dowager was famous as an aristocratic salon hostess and was a loyal sponsor in society of both Susan and Elizabeth de Vere. That intellectual old lady had long been a personal friend of their famous father the 17th Earl of Oxford.

Thus historical records show a tightly knit English social circle bearing both wealth and power. And all within that circle were long affectionate toward Oxford. By Oxfordian predicate they would have been very well aware the Earl wrote the pseudonymous canonical plays. A letter from the Dowager Countess survives inviting someone to visit her because "the man Shakespeare is here." One may guess. Would the Countess have meant Lord Oxford father of the Countess's two protégés, the de Vere girls. Or the very rough-cut socially barriered Shaxper?

As to daughters, what goes through the mind of a loving father when his tells him she is going to become an actor. At 10:00 Friday morning we actors of *The Which* are gathered on the convent gym's trim stage. Each of King Lear's three daughters here is a lovely young woman. Nikki, Chloe, and the unspeakably fine Miriam. I would gratefully make love to any one of these three beauties. Not happening has long now been wordlessly obvious to Harry Hopkins.

At some point their parents perceived these striking daughters here on stage were not destined for security. Not law school, not medicine, no salaried cubicle, no rich enough husband to grace her life. No, for each of these girls it had to be the open road of acting. In a special world populated mostly with theater people. So go such daughters. Voyaging in their fluently memorized widely diverse roles so far, far, far from fireside Scrabble and cookie baking. Becoming in their chosen future others' imagined pasts.

And then too, so much of life being obverses, you could wonder at a daughter's perturbed view of a parent's choice of a life defined by theater. A daughter assessing a theatrically obsessed personally unstable father in the cool straight perception of wounded youth. Like Cordelia.

No. Truly like Susan de Vere. For *The Which* I decided to summon the ghost of Susan, being the logical inspiration for best-loved daughter Cordelia, to speak in due frankness to her father as creator of all those strange plays. Ghost Susan talking to ghost Oxford as a peer because both are now beyond relative age. And moreover Susan speaks as a key savior of her father's works for posterity.

So Lance's instinct to produce *The Which of Shakespeare's Why* to lure financial backing does base in commonsense fact. The Will Shaxper-as-William-Shakespeare fable requires multiple leaps of faith difficult for modern minds to accept upon forensic analysis. But the myth is very stirring. By it underdog Shaxper's uniquely purely intuitive literary gift created a one-off working class superhero. And this myth is so interesting too for university intellectuals. Because they can competitively embroider Shaxper's mostly blank biographical pages as if they were themselves creative playwrights. Though that the professors just are not.

*
*   *

But as Hamlet would say, enough of that. The leap across Shaxper's existential rap sheet s is not ours to make. *The Which of Shakespeare's Why* leaps instead deep into the case for Oxford.

This morning's rehearsal reading is my script twining Oxford's life facts around the literary content of the early *King Leir* and also the decade-later radically and darkly revising *King Lear*. I decided to let Susan's ghost directly address her bad dad's ghost off and around the script of *King Lear*. That is Miriam playing Cordelia, wearing her lit Anne mask which she flicks lit to speak as daughter-ghost Susan to her lit father ghost Oxford. Lance in continuity of our *Hamlet* passage staging will speak, mask lit, as the ghost of Oxford. Marj is still Elizabeth's lit ghost, monitoring the players. Lear is played by good old Larry Loessing who has just arrived looking like he needs two canes not one. His long askew hair freshly dyed white over dyed chestnut with undertones of mahogany, dyed over white.

Lance blew in distracted, as if still talking to someone else somewhere else about quite else. Everybody here has had two days to learn their emailed lines. So off we go with the early *Lear* scene of his renunciation of his crown and lands. Larry has just thundered, with an aggrieved old man's petulance, to that withholding type Cordelia whom he has just disinherited:

Thy truth then be thy dow'r!

Susan turns on her mask to speak directly to Oxford. "Father, this play is really about your Norman castle, isn't it? Hedingham, where you grew up in the Essex sticks. But why force it on your daughters? We certainly didn't ask you to give it to us. Not when you owned no other good home."

Oxford: "I was tricked, Susan. Again. I gave you three girls my

Hedingham last redoubt because the devil Burghley as your guardian insisted as a condition to a deal I thought I had. And which that unpredictable piece of work the Queen led me on to expect. Then she too dumped me. Again. In exchange I was supposed to get a big castle with revenues of farms in Wales. But after I signed they just changed their minds. I did also expect that after I gave you Hedingham and its income you girls would like me better for helping your dowers. So I thought that, thus in your good esteem as daughters at last, I could retire from London in my 40s. To go live and write quietly far away from my enemies at Court. Win win. But I lost. As usual among these vicious Tudor people."

And now Lance flicks off his de Vere mask, to say as director to us actors onstage, "Pretty good, guys. Harry I like it you are not trying to echo the play's elevated diction at all. This is emotional straight talk people today can really take in. A smart young woman talking to her father who for a long time has badly let everything down. Himself, his now dead wife, his three estranged daughters."

I say, "Thanks Lance. I went with seeing that Susan de Vere, considering her brilliant achievement preserving the works after her father's death, could not have been much like the theatrically inarticulate Cordelia. The real daughter plainly sees her father is the kind of erratic guy she herself would avoid. And did in marrying the gracious competent Earl of Montgomery."

Something is back on the director's mind. He has forgotten we all are here. So I add, "But Susan also appreciates and respects the magically better self her father Edward writes with as Shakespeare. So the daughter saw the two variant personas, the writer and the written. Like most great authors in history."

Some nod, some adjust their wigs. Miriam to Lance, "So how pissed off is Cordelia, really, with her dad?"

Lance replies after more pause, "It's a more in sadness than anger thing. But Cordelia's not taking any more nonsense. You as Cordelia are talking very plainly now with your odd father Lear who of course is really your odd old but genius father Oxford. You girls and he are all ghosts so there is no more need for family deference pretense in the moment."

Lear/Larry to his director: "I stay in Lear's bitch fit mood this whole passage?"

"Yes, Larry. Like the Gloucester figure. By the way that Gloucester bastard son story Oxford impudently stole from a work by his enemy Phillip Sydney. Lear like his counterpart senile Gloucester does not see truth until it is too late. And so both the naïve has-beens are . . . utterly . . . utterly mercilessly . . . ruined by viciously clever players. Once again we have a play ironically transmuting Oxford's take on his own relentless fate in real life."

I, just Mr. Writer for Hire, say, "But you know, Lance, *Lear* is one of those several plays where Oxford is probing around possibilities of forgiveness and so redemption. The man craved redemption, his letters and actions show it. Yet the final 1604 version of this story was a radical revision that denied anyone redemption.

"It reversed the ur-play *King Leir* that the Queen's men troupe presented at court in 1594. In that version Leir and Cordelia reconcile and he's put back on his throne. But by 1604 in an emotional 180-degree spin they both end miserably dead." Lance knows this but the actors probably do not, so I turn to them. "Maybe, then, when we jump to the last scene extract, Larry can strike a perceptible tone of asking forgiveness?"

Lance thinks it's now his script. "That's not in the text, Harry. Oxford was writing in very black ink by the time of *Lear*. In 1594's *Leir* he was still feeling optimistic about reconciliation and forgiveness from his daughters. But by a decade later, hobbling badly lamed from a streetfight stabbing, Edward had sunk into the depressive downside of his bipolar personality."

Chloe, "So he changed *Leir* to *Lear* in a turn to the bipolar downside you think?"

Lance: "Yes. Steep down. Oxford was beginning to fall apart physically from his bad wound. You may think Montague and Capulet revenge fights—if that rings a bell.

"But no, Harry. We can *not* tinker with his final text. Oxford meant it as his final vision and *The Which of Shakespeare's Why* stands for truth." Lance can't help himself sometimes. To all three mean girls, "Reality is our play' motto. Like the de Vere family's same motto for six centuries.

"Not that it helped Eddie, unfortunately. Anyway, Harry, we don't need to shade the performance. The way you wrote de Vere's ghost talk with his daughter here you opened to a far wider understanding outside the play text. Our audience from this encounter now can sense the author's basic hunger for forgiveness meta-text. And the audience already got the same perception from Ophelia's scene with Oxford's surrogate Hamlet in our preceding *Hamlet* passage.

"So they now can better understand from factual history how Oxford marionettes his actual disastrous life events to be his fiction."

This is my script, not his. I say evenly, "Then, Lance, I should make this dialogue more clear. The de Vere family facts under the *Lear* play facts fit like fingers in a glove. Three estranged daughters. The emotionally needy widowed dad who bankrupts himself trying to buy love.

"Come to think . . . that true story fit is like the true story fit of Hamlet's Gonzago play within his play. Because *Hamlet* in code was a replay of young Edward's ensnarement in wardship after his father died. Suspiciously to the benefit of a rumored serial poisoner, Robert Dudley. Who then with wealth stolen from young Oxford expanded his kingly castle given him by Queen Elizabeth. Some expected them to quickly marry."

Lance likes to impress the young women we stand among. "Yes, Harry's on to it. Shakespeare very frequently puts perspective tales within his basic drama. So they suddenly pop wide open in irony or illumination that overarches the main story. It's an essence of the Shakespeare magic for audiences. Ordinary people at a performance suddenly realize that they themselves actually are subtle enough to see in such doubling ways."

All six luminous actress eyes now focus on the sort-of-famous director Lance Gulliver flashing brilliance. He knows it. "Et voilà! *The Which* is our new Shakespeare-type play performed within— but now overarching—Shakespeare's own plays."

Et voilà. Et voilà oh crimminy. Usually I look away aside when I start to feel shaky. Like when I've drunk too much, or I have just heard too much jive talk. But Lance's glibness can be annoying. I say, "Lance, hold on. This all may be too cool for school. Are you sure our audience will be up to *The Which*? Shakespeare's audience would have been. But today nobody uses cadenced shaded meta-phor in everyday speech, the way ordinary people did in the 16th century. American English conversation sounds like grunts even next to Elizabethan chitchat."

"So far, Harry, your script works for me. Cheer up."

I suppose to them all I do look concerned. For I have obeyed encouragement to jump into a deep slow river running through Ivy League and Oxbridge English departments. Where fierce gargantu-an-ego toothy crocodiles patrol their Shakespeare territory jealously against intruders. I am bearing half-healed scars from my toothy mauling as a student by the 20-foot long Professor Sheppard Germaine. Now Lance has encouraged me into this river, waving from his safe shore as a celebrated gadfly director.

Miriam/Cordelia/Susan, mask unlit: "I get Harry's script okay. But as an actor, Lance, I have to feel your character Oxford's urgent unsteady neediness. Give me more to respond to. Don't be too suave." She is looking steadily at him. Flicks her mask lit on-off on-off. "As usual, sweetheart."

Lance isn't all that handsome but he has a silent film star charm smile, glow eyes and all. "Miriam is so right. And so. On we go. From the top, sweetheart."

Miriam's mask looks so different lit from within. A striking beauty in very sad mood. Miriam as actress has picked up Lance's signature pause. After two beats long so that words follow silent conflicted thought: "Dad, you spent forty years complaining you were tricked. I see the consequence upon you. It's wonderful how tricky your plays are. Disguises, twins loving twins, double crossdressing, deadly secret messages, shipwrecked enemies, smiling killers. Uncanny creatures. A volatile magician. But . . ."

Oxford lit, "Daughter, you are unkind. Unkind because you are not ignorant. You and your sisters grew up in Burghley House. So did I after your grandfather de Vere was murdered to seize our wealth. From both our upbringings you well know what a snake pit of deceptions Elizabeth's Court was.

"Those manipulating forces touched and bent every line of my life. My own facts are what I fled from in my writing. And in my too generous patronage of other intellectuals.

"But I did learn to write plays consulting my well-paid good professional writer friends. Those being Lyly, Munday, and poor Nashe. And learned from testing lines with wise actor friends in my own two troupes and others. So aside from my intensive education I had two very practical playwriting educations. Not none like that . . ." There Oxford blocks a false name.

"But Susan, *King Lear* was really closely about *me* as I revised it darker when I was approaching 50. *Lear* truly was *not* about you and your sisters."

Susan, "Come on, Dad. You usually wrote within your modus operandi. What about all those plays expressing some altered view you had over a long time of bedeviled Mom? All those obsessively revised versions of Anne Cecil your unwanted wife. You puppet-dress her into a dozen characters. From unknowable mystery to plain good to plain bad. We girls saw our mom ranging through *Hamlet, All's Well That Ends Well, Measure for Measure The Winter's Tale, Comedy of Errors, Merry Wives of Windsor, Cymbeline, Coriolanus.* And your horrible fantasy *Othello* . . .

"So Dad, of course we could not quite trust you with our affection. We were brought up by Grandad Burghley and Mom's family who all considered you an unreliable jerk. Actually you got no worse than coolness from your daughters. Yet being so artistic you projected us into being the cruel tormentors of innocent old you.

"Dad. Look at me, not your inky hands. You were so wrong when you despaired of your daughters and ended *Lear* in depressed bitterness. You had your dark moods, and we girls were wary of them. But we all quietly respected your genius even though you were so intermittent with us. The proof you know now.

"Lizabet and I charmed and pushed our husbands and dear Chancellor Pembroke to pull together all your plays for proper publication. Including the dozen that you and Lord Stanley were still editing when plague killed you in two days.

"So the Folio was published for love of you by your extended family. My husband Montgomery and dear brother-in-law Pembroke paid what no one else in England could afford to get its immensity printed. Talented Stanley made the dozen unknown draft plays complete in polished form.

"It was tricky sophisticated undercover business with the Puritan war on theater itself growing stronger by 1623. We in the family conspired hidden under Chamberlain Pembroke's Crown power like a secretive gang. Not of art thieves but of art preservers. We had to be stealthy because the awful Puritans were sure to pounce and burn everything if they found out super-scandalous you were the commoners' idol Shakespeare. But we did it, using the Shaxper ruse so cleverly. We beat those devils who never knew what happened. Unfortunately, our trick switch has lasted four centuries after the Puritans disappeared."

Oxford, back looking at those eternally stained hands: "It would seem I failed to appreciate the love of my daughters and their husbands. But you . . . . well. I never could portray normal family affection in my work. Because I grew up so strangely. An orphan in a hypocritical predatory entrapment."

Susan could have made a good actress. When she focuses a gaze it burns. "We girls knew about growing up in Burghley family clutches too. We forgave your mood swings.

"But my god Dad, those psycho sonnets! You should have known they would be leaked around the Court by two-faced friends. For all the artfulness, everybody knew the sonnets were about middle-aged you going some kind of gay for young Hennie Wriothesley even while urging him to marry your daughter Lizabet. Who you declared a bastard until you changed your mind years later. And Henry was not even gay though he sort of looked it. But we girls could tell. It was so embarrassing to us at Court after you dedicated that sexually confused *Venus and Adonis* to him, and right away *Lucrece* also."

Oxford: "Susan. Mercy now. I can get lost. But in my best drama I was asking for forgiveness from Anne and you girls. And personal understanding from unpredictable Elizabeth. I had to write. And it had to come out as it did. From my real life first before I possibly could alchemize it into art."

"Dad, your self-pity trapped you inside distorting myths. Your life was still very privileged. You did get a spectacular special education that Grandad Burghley carefully arranged. You surely could not have written as well otherwise. You had the very best education of anyone in the English Renaissance."

Oxford: "Finally I did realize that. Did you spot this, Susan? At the very end of all my writing, at the very end of *The Tempest*, I had me as the disappearing wizard Prospero thank his former enemy for the precious learning he made open to him. When writing that, I had thought back to Burghley's aspiring tutoring plan for me. Another strange brew man there."

Susan is smiling warmly. "We girls sneaked reads of what was on your desk and in that black lacquer chest from Venice. Lizabet had a special lens for you. She got us younger girls to see how many times in your works daughters rebel against bossy dads.

"You wanted Mom to renounce Grandad Burghley. And so your characters acted out as you fantasized. In *six* plays your daughter character starts submissive . . . but then you have her rebel against bossy dad. Miranda in *Tempest*, Hero in *Much Ado*, Bianca and Kate in *Taming*, Phoebe in *As You Like It*. Of course Ophelia the shaming suicide in *Hamlet*.

"Then—hello, Dad—then finally King Lear with his three gratuitously mean-girl daughters. Not at all like your own real three admiring and sympathetic daughters. Who in fact cleverly preserved all your writing for posterity when it so easily could have been lost.

"That right there is the problem with you, Dad. Your family just was not as real to you as your work. You couldn't see Mom or us because your imaginary characters took over your vision of reality."

Oxford looks shaken to be spoken to so bluntly. "I did realize that by the time of writing my final version of *Hamlet*. That a sensitive girl would want out both from the character Hamlet and from the author husband, being both ways me, Edward. So to tell true, I did write Ophelia's suicide thinking of poor Anne with tears in my dimming eyes.

"You know, Susan, several of the herbs and flowers she drowns herself cradling were then believed to induce a miscarriage? As was the willow tree she jumped from—it was for Church censors I had to say she fell. First I was furious as a cuckold knowing your mother in true fact had tried to abort. Then years on I understood like a lit candle that of course she wanted the nonconsummation divorce too, even though she knew the baby would be mine. Because I was such a disappointment as a husband.

"Poor Ophelia, poor Anne. You probably know in ancient Greek the word Ophelia signifies both a debt and a tax. I was so clever a writer. And so stupid a man. Both at once."

Susan: "We girls saw. Mom came to understand. We forgave you because of all your painful issues."

Oxford is glad his forceful daughter's tone has shifted. "Sure. I wrote many plays because I had seen the audiences also loved the idea of romantic young love. Marlowe's, Kidd's, and my revenge plays made decent people feel ill. A little of that was a limit."

"That's part of your greatness, Dad. You came to understand

people liked to envision warm attractive couples. Fun for men as much as women in an epoch when actually most marriages were based on factual practicality. Economic common sense having nothing whatsoever to do with lovely virgin princesses and lovable princes. Whatever real people's marriage evolved to be over time. Somebody clever recently said Elizabethan marriages formed around assets and often lasted into love. Whereas in the 21st century they form around love and often end in arguments around assets."

Oxford sounds like a dry smile. "Audiences like sexy. Sexy I knew."

Susan: "But you always stopped short of married love. There are no happy married couples in all your plays."

Oxford: "But hang off, as they say now. I did write female characters with perceptive warmth. Though somehow their marriage state—that I could not imagine"

Susan, "Dad, we women naturally always have liked your penetrative emotionality. And your focus on complex female character as much as male.

"At one of the Countess's literary luncheons she pointed out to us de Vere girls that there are many heroines throughout your many plays. But actually no heroes. No man in all your Shakespeare plays stands alone pure. There's no man in Shakespeare without entangled contradictions. None not blinded by lust or greed or vanity. Your key men all bear compromising baggage from their past."

Oxford shrugs. "Well." He has stepped to the stage edge to read the audience's faces. "That's life not even tissue-wrapped in art. What sane man sees a simple hero looking into a morning mirror to trim the beard? And so falling through the glaze of his image. Everybody contains multitudes. I just, I suppose, bore more than most."

"We did watch you closely, Dad. That's why Mom and us girls have our pet name for you. You are still our Mister Piece-of-Work-Man."

Just at these words Lance claps his hands loud, the actors freeze. "Good. *Excellent*, guys. Where the hell is James First?"

*

* *

There is a remarkably real world beyond those of fantasy stage plays like *The Which of Shakespeare's Why*. Indeed several plenitudes of reality all bite and chew one another at every moment. Omniconal Friendship International Unlimited, Limited, would eventually find in its trove of recorded phone conversations this following snippet of innocuous conversation picked up from a couple walking close to a mic at a basement doorway outside the Elizabethan archives of Her Majesty's Treasury. Its transcript dateline shows this passing snippet occurred the ironically same instant when James First, overplayed as usual by Butch Burgoigne, minced onto the convent gym's stage.

It was missed because the all too human Omniconal auditor operative had been diverted just then by *The Which*'s informative father-daughter-ghost conversations. I found this out over late vodkas with the Omniconal spy involved. Whom Valerie had terminated for incompetence though without bloodshed. He introduced himself to me out of the blue as Hubert. But after two refills asked me to call him Bill. That was his name as a boy, and a nice boy he was he insisted.

Anyway, Hubert/Bill appeared suddenly to give me the dossier of his Omniconal "TaskForceO" tapes. In some kind of penance. Hubert/Bill explained that he was leaving the espionage game, which is apparently full of unstable needy personalities. He will now enroll in acting school and wanted my advice. That was a difficult talk, not much of a quid pro for Bill since I am not myself sure yet if I am an actor.

I have paged back in time through that dossier printout preparing to write this memoir. Mixing its varying strands of others' past recorded instants with my own lived story. That record speaks always in a present moment. And so is mysterious to read in retrospect. Try this:

You're sure?

Very sure, Mommy. Or should I say Mamacita?

Ohhh!! You are my scrumptious muffin.

*

*   *

Onstage Lance's head turns to the opening gym door. "For heaven's sake. Where have you been?"

"Not for heaven's sake." Butch Burgoigne has gone over to fish out his chest-length curly-locked wig from the prop chest. He must have looked like young Peter O'Toole once upon a time past. Now he looks typecast for Casper the Friendly Ghost. Mortality being such as it can be and always is, Butch is understudying old Larry as Lear. And Larry is understudying old him as King James.

"Late is so lame, Butch. We have to . . . ."

Lance has paused himself because old Butch is grinning at him in a wiseass young Peter O'Toole toothy way. Because yes, obviously all of us are only on this stage this hour due to our *Which* story being . . . . 400 years late. Miriam in her sweetheart-of-a-girl-mode straightens Butch's wig and kisses his cheek. Apparently just because he may no longer be a merciless ravager of young women and men, or still may be, or she herself looks lovable in that mode. Make it the latter.

The reading proceeds. Butch and Larry exchanging glances meaningful between themselves.

> Lear/Larry: *A plague upon you murderers, traitors all,*
> *I might have sav'd her, now she's gone for ever;*
> *Cordelia, Cordelia, stay a little. Ha:*
> *What is't thou sayest? Her voice was ever soft,*
> *Gentle and low, an excellent thing in woman.*
> *I killed the flame that was a-hanging thee.*

Susan/Cordelia/Miriam switches her mask lit and says to Oxford/Lance: "Dad, you wrote this in 1603 just as King James's reign began. What kind of judgment was it to switch from the 1594 *Leir*'s happy ending with the King reinstated on his throne to instead put in a King, confusingly re-named Lear with an "a," dying in rags at the hands of traitors?"

"Dramatic judgment, Susan. It was correct dramatic judgment since *Lear* has been played for four centuries. But anyway I was thinking of myself as the poor rightful King betrayed by all he knew. I saw my death coming close. *Lear* had nothing to do with James in my mind."

Susan: "No, Dad, *everything* then was about James as unpredictable new King. The Crown's mean guys at that moment could have put you in the Tower for portraying the overthrow of an English monarch. Especially since apparently most of the country did not want the King of Scotland to become ours. It was a bigshot shady payoff deal. You yourself tried to oppose his choice, which of course the secret police reported to him."

Oxford: "I was in a mood. Midnight dark. But anyway I was functionally a hermit by 1595 and nobody at Court took me at all seriously. I heard later one of the Crown spies actually wrote that in his report to excuse me fantasizing about my candidate the Earl of Southampton instead. It blew over. *King Lear* was registered for publication."

"You really don't know what saved you and your work that time?"

"I just died peacefully that year. If you call two days of plague misery peaceful."

Susan: "No, Dad. My brother-in-law as incoming chancellor convinced James you were just a depressed harmless fellow. And then when you died a few months before our wedding, King James himself marched me down the aisle.

"James became more boy-gay as he aged, but was flirting away with both me and Phillip then in cute ways. On the morning after our wedding he came into our bedroom at the palace in just his nightshirt, sat on the bed and wanted to know how the sex went for us. But that was all."

Oxford looking wistfully to a stage wing: "Damn. I could have used that."

Susan: "The new King stood up to those fanatic Puritans and

allowed your sexy plays to stay in repertory. At his own risk. Everybody political knew the Puritans were capable of chopping a feudal monarch come to it, in Hamlet's chilling phrase. Of course they came to it within fifty years. And long before then terminated all theatre performances, for twenty years. That is another reason your identity disappeared, the populace of contemporary insiders were first terrified of raising the subject and then died of old age."

Oxford: "All too strange a coincidence for even a Shakespeare play . . ."

Susan: "Not really, Dad. You were like a Shakespeare character, so your life was your play.

"Anyway, publishing your complete works got permission by just another wave of King James's hand. Perfumed, yes. But that approval from the King was a brave and serious royal decision."

King James/Butch's mask lights and he says to Oxford/Lance: "Well, Susan might have also mentioned that when she told me how poor you were I immediately also helped. I told my watchacallits to convey back to you some of your Earldom's ancient properties. Stuff that Elizabeth's wide boys nicked away from you cheap for the Crown. The greedy old Tudor witch. My poor beheaded mom Mary Queen of Scots."

Oxford/Lance to Susan: "That was all you?"

Susan: "Indeed. That was my version of a dramatic necessity. Unlike your killing me as Cordelia and you as Lear. Instead of letting restored King Leir and his good daughter end happily. Leir had much smoother original dialogue by the way. In Lear you went off key with fake ancient diction."

Oxford: "Truly you were not Cordelia, Susan. Cordelia was a version of your mother Anne. Because in retrospect I so much wished Anne had rebelled against her manipulative father. By 1604

I was even angrier with the world, so I closed the same dark deadly way as my late rewrite of *Hamlet*. But obviously King James did not care about the new ending where the King dies."

Mask-lit James/Butch to Oxford/Lance: "No, Oxford, I just did not know that you had switched the plot to a lèse majesté conclusion. Even after yourself opposing my choice as King. I wasn't aware until after *Lear* was printed. By then you were dead. But after that bombshell my watchacallits read me the plot of *Macbeth* that they found in your papers.

"We made sure neither regicide play was performed as long as there was a Stuart King. Theater people long referred to tabooed Macbeth in code as just 'the Scottish play.' Which they could not perform or safely even name for fear of being prosecuted as traitors."

Susan/Cordelia/Miriam to Oxford/Lance: "Dad, King James did appreciate your very late edit of *Hamlet* as an apology for initially opposing him. When Hamlet lies almost dead he gratuitously pops up to tell Horatio, being of course your Uncle Horace the soldier, it is right that the leader 'from the north' is the rightful next King."

Susan, who has been called here, says: "Calling T. S. Eliot."

Oxford: "So you do see, daughter. I could come around to common sense. And I did write James a letter of gratitude for the surprise reconveyance of my two stolen forests."

James/Butch to Oxford/Lance: "Edward, I know something about unusual temperament myself. It wasn't just that the Herbert boys and your Susan were so cute. I allowed them to print the Folio over the whatchacallits' objections because I greatly respected your work. Just as I allowed my bible committee free rein to express themselves in artful language.

"And that worked out well too. General readers turned out not to be so lazy and dim-witted as publishers had assumed. Oxford, you never assumed audiences were dumb either, good on you."

Susan/Cordelia/Miriam, mask lit, to Oxford/Lance: "In better times the King would have allowed you credit as the real William Shakespeare. But we Herberts and he agreed to defer that in the current dangerously unsettled times, with the book-burning Puritans gaining ground every year, especially in attacking theater. Sanely we could not risk the consequences of revealing scandalous you to be Shakespeare. Ben Jonson was terrified of Puritan police coming after him. And you had already passed on anyway."

James/Butch to Oxford/Lance: "All of Elizabeth's old watcha-callits and mine agreed, Oxford. Plainly you were the wrong man to be Shakespeare. That always dangerous London throng needed a neutral figure as author."

Oxford/Lance to James/Butch: "But not forever. Surely not forever that asshole ruining my due renown. In Hamlet's last word, 'Oh oh oh.'"

James/Butch to Oxford/Lance: "But there it was, Edward. The Crown needed a blank author figure for your sexy and dangerous plays. Someone like the engraving of Shakespeare's pie-face by that ignorant teenage artist Drueshott. Who on counter-espionage instruction simply dreamed up the simpleton frontispiece portrait of the Folio like nobody real. If you look close at the chin, that's a mask edge at the chin line. The ear is a pull tab And the eye directions don't match. Nor do the shoulders. Every part a little askew like a manipulated doll.

"And the sketch is dressed in violation of a serious sumptuary law. He's wearing a nobleman's velvet. Shaxper most certainly was not an entitled noble and, Milord, you most certainly were.

"So clues were left in the Folio for history. Unless the world to come learned a wrong history. Or the world just forgot history."

Elizabeth/Marj, eye always on the rolling ball or head, to Oxford/Lance: "But by 1597 when pirated quartos started showing up with the name 'Shakespeare' on them, and the Puritans exactly the same year first threatening to wipe out theater entirely, my people told me we had to move on the situation quickly. So a big nasty Crown man with a bag of gold again went to visit Mr. Will Shaxper before he got more ambitious after his 1592 quiet money and Chamberlain's Men gift share windfall.

"The terms were simple. Shaxper would be quietly killed for one yap of his claiming or disclaiming authorship. And he could use the gold to buy a house back in the country, where the whatcha-callit people wanted him out of London attention. Shaxper was delighted, a commonsense fellow with no interest in writing since he could barely read. He immediately in 1597 bought himself a huge show-off house back in poky Stratford. Contentedly traded commodities while loan sharking and tax collecting in years of prolonged famine."

Ophelia/Susan/Miriam to Oxford/Lance: "Dad, it is such a shame you did not live another few years. You, the King, and the Herberts all taking care of silencing the basically illiterate Shaxper would have been perfect for a comedy setup. Think of it as what you loved to write. Another funny tour of mistaken identity. You could re-use disguised identity, a rural clown type, secrets under secrets. With of course the big happy reveal of a respected King just as you imagined so often. Very *Twelfth Nighty*, right?"

Oxford/Lance has turned gazing to the audience. "Yes, I could have had fun with that. I did ridicule that chancer hick Shaxper by characters in *Measure for Measure*, *Twelfth Night*, and *All's Well*. But four hundred years is a long time to wait for the right laugh from my audiences."

Now Lance breaks the ghost spell with a loud clap of hands over his head. "Well! I had fun with that. Very, very good, troupers. Harry you might try creative writing sometime."

"I have, Lance."

*

* *

Why, anyway, do people like theater plays?

All you have to do is listen closely anywhere and there is art of mind everywhere. But sometimes if you have heard and did not understand in moving time, it would be wiser to just erase a taped transcript. Especially if you work for Valerie. Like my sensitive new friend Call Me Bill, whom she fired shouting hurtful insults of his drooling monkey-low intelligence. That came after this Treasury basement surveillance printout he missed that eventually saw light within Omniconal:

> *But Squooger I like my fingerprints.*
> *Mommy you be a big girl.*
> *Ohhh. I don't . . .*
> *Mommy when you chew on my fingers, you know . . .*
> *Yess.*
> *That's his work. You'll love your new looks.*

*

* *

If I Harry Haines were trapped in a spy novel, this next moment shoved at me in the Waldorf would read something like this:

"My mobile rings its Omega tone, my Breguet shows 2 a.m. Dubai time. And so this is deadly trouble for the Countess waiting in my bed. Quickly I draw my Walther. With trouble since my pants are down and I am dribbling on the bathroom floor. The wet semicircle suddenly gleams up, like yet another Mandarin question mark."

But sadly that is not the Harry Haines existentiality. I am indeed peacefully on my bathroom throne in Suite 6A when the phone rings. And indeed answering with some aforementioned difficulty. But I am trapped in an unrequited love story, nothing more.

As Lear observed, softness of voice in a woman is lovely. I think Miriam must have gone to graduate school to get that voice just right. I think it was a school for scandal.

"Oh good, it's you." And then she stops. Now my turn to fire.

My Walther is made of wood. "Hi Miriam."

"Can you meet me now?"

The wood is jammed. "Now?"

"Yes, Harry, at the present time, sweetheart."

Often in international thriller movies the protagonist seen with illumination profiling him two-dimensional seems like maybe a loser dolt. I have been distracted by the spreading puddle of piss which I cannot control due to the phone being in the hand which is specialized for weenie maneuvers. "Here at the Waldorf?"

"Oh, no. You have no idea. Let's meet in Central Park."

"It's dark."

"Yes it is, Harry. Wear a black T-shirt."

"I have one."

"Oh, for heaven's sake, I know that. Do you know where the Shakespeare statue is?"

"Southeast end of the Mall." Nailed it. Now I'm feeling sharp. "What are you wearing?"

"Sweetheart, this is not that kind of call. You have a problem. I will be wearing a dark jacket. And a black lace thong. Just kidding."

"It will take me twenty minutes to get over there."

"Me too. If you find Shakespeare but don't see me just . . . whistle. You know how to whistle, don't you?" I've had quite a lot of school. This is a literary quote from Lauren Bacall to Humphrey Bogart in some potboiler. She purrs it like she is wearing just the thong.

"Yeah, Slim. It will be a tune from *Hamilton*."

"I refused to be indoctrinated. Just whistle 'When the Red, Red Robin Comes Bob-Bob-Bobbin' Along.'"

Then with thriller-quick scene change, here Miriam and I are standing in front of the greened bronze of somebody's idea in the 19th century of what William Shakespeare must have looked like. Which is exactly like King Arthur.

"Okay. Harry. Okay . . ." And time stops. Miriam has such a crush on Lance that in her real life she now pauses excruciatingly the same way he wants her to perform onstage. This is troubling for me as Hamlet. I am such a spotty new actor I just see luscious Miriam, not annoying Ophelia. And so pause too in what should be Hamlet's tormented fluencies. "Harry. To my eyes."

It was really the book she clutched at her chest. I've noticed a serious side to Miriam in the past but coming along the high hard Manhattan canyons to the Park have hoped this will be some sort of fun.

The dimness here is unique. Lamp posts ringing the terrace suffuse amber light up into the elm surround's arcing chartreuse canopy. So luminant verdance wells back down bathing both Shakespeare's and my male pattern baldness. A realistic touch in a fantasy is wise, so Shakespeare sculpted in 1880 was given a shiny bare crown like mine instead of a jeweled one.

On the other side of realism Miriam's honey-blonde tousle is so perfect a passerby could think it too perfect. Perhaps a wig wardrobe selection but not. I can read the cover of the book she has clutched at her chest. *A Year in the Life of William Shakespeare: 1599.*

"Do you know this?"

"No."

"It's by Professor James Shapiro at Columbia. I audited his Shakespeare course. When I was studying drama at Barnard."

"That's nice."

"Look at me please, Harry. Professor Shapiro is a top Shakespeare expert. When you open the cover you will see fifty squibs praising this book from press reviewers. It's an imagined season-by-season dramatization of what William Shakespeare would have seen and done and thought in the year he was thirty-five years old. And, as the Stratfordians like Shapiro think, peaking as a playwright."

"Okay." This is a noise I make to keep vultures off my inert mind.

"Well, it's not okay if you are an Earl of Oxford groupie."

"Okay. What's this professor say about Oxford?"

"Silence, complete contempt. There is nothing in the book's index or bibliography. Except in a simple listing of other candidates somebody thought maybe wrote the plays instead of Will of Stratford."

"How bad is this for *The Which?*"

"I just read parts. I'm always distracted somehow, Harry. You'll see the book fills out with a lot of Home Depot–scale historical wallpaper. About wars Will was not in and famous people Will did not know. But all that profuse but pretty irrelevant detail is actually dazzling. Like a movie soundtrack filling in for absent dialogue. Semiotic stuff. This Shapiro guy is a smooth operator writer. Reviewers love his professorial utter self-confidence."

"But Miriam. You must be aware any hip Elizabethan writer would have known and lived in that same canned setting. So is Professor Shapiro's *A Year in the Life* just like Professor Greenblatt's wallpaper book? *Will in the World?*"

I'm relaxing. She saw no proof. And Miriam is so goddessy there glowing emerald luminance. Miriam, the serious edition, "Well, as you said about *A Year in the Life*, there are yards of historical scene-setting and name dropping also in Greenblatt's *Will in the World*."

I say hopefully, "But it all lacks a killer document proof showing the book's elaborate doodles tie credibly to actual fact?"

"Well. Harry. You should be careful of *A Year in the Life*. Because it does more than doodle."

My throat clenches. "Shapiro's got some document I don't know about?"

"Not . . ."

I do like Lance. But he is a questionable directorial influence on the vocal stylization of impressionable young actresses. "What's that supposed to mean?"

Miriam laughs the half-way she does on stage. "Nothing shall come of not!"

"What?" Oh, come on. She's stealing King Lear's lines now.

"I'm your friend, Harry. And . . ."

"And *what?*"

"Well, you should build yourself an escape hatch in *The Which*."

"Why?"

A nervous, deflecting stage laugh. Miriam says low toward the big kingly statue apparently quipping only to her, "The why of *The Which* . . . ."

She's overplaying for a reason I cannot see into. I seem to invite people to toy with me. Like all my life. "Just what are you saying, Miriam? We are presenting *The Which* because it's true."

"Harry. You are writing *The Which* because you are dead broke and were led into it by Lance. Whose Trenton troupe is dead broke. And so he charmed Ms. Gotrocks to pay you both a big lot of moola to star her whole big lot of ego. There's truth."

Miriam is a born Shakespeare heroine because she has steel under appeal.

"No. I really believe in the world I am writing."

"Sweetheart. I've played a half-dozen Shakespeare figment women. I really believed every one of them every minute I was on stage. But I was on stage because I truly needed to be there and so away from my real life. And to get paid. I do understand your need. So, as a friend . . ."

"You're saying Shapiro does show some killer fact that makes nonsense of *The Which?*"

"Not . . ."

"*What??*"

"Harry, please do not shout at me in the dark in the park. Wearing a T-shirt. You'll get arrested. As to Shapiro's book, just take out a pen and note all the passages where he ties Will Shaxper to acting companies and theater ownership some way, and what plays were presented when, and how Will might have been paid without any record of it. And you'll see this guy Shapiro is brilliant in close psychological readings. Speculating how specific texts logically would have reflected real time context.

"You will read that Shapiro's basic conviction is Shakespeare was a flash brilliant genius at absorbing his time's information and reflecting it out as relevant art . . ."

"But . . ."

"But. Yes, of course. Oxford could have done the same instead. Anyway, Harry, remember. Oxford's biography also has no killer document proof despite a century of looking for it.

"So you need to take care sweetheart. Consider *A Year in the Life*. And I saw online Shapiro wrote another book, *Contested Will*, about the authorship dispute. I'll order it for you."

I'm looking over to the statue, that lump of deified metal. Which may as well speak up too, just saying more distress. "But Miriam I can't make Oxford both be and not be the author in *The Which*. He has to be or not be. To be, I mean. *Isn't it?*"

"Well, Hamlet, Harry. There may be more things than are dreamt of in your draft script. A draft which is, I'm just saying as Ophelia, Harry sweetheart right now just pretty room temperature. Mechanical, frankly, in your insistent underlaying of biographical facts. Facts which may be coincidental or used second hand or something more complicated. But actually not Oxford's writing.

"As Ophelia I'm supposed to pick up on a guy whose mind is so dangerous it drives everybody nuts. Read Shapiro's take on what shifting perspectives whoever the author was used for the character of Hamlet as he wrote and revised. Shapiro is intense."

"I see. So you didn't like my rehearsal performance as Hamlet even before *The Which* came along."

Miriam, being out forward along on the enigma spectrum as I am forward on the autistic curve, habitually does that actressy thing of speaking with only eyes. Some of those blue-robe soulfully gazing Renaissance madonnas on non-modeling work days must have been red frock *commedia dell'arte* actresses or whatever as well. Themselves artists of a kind.

But now Miriam does care enough to really speak to me. "No, not so much. Sorry, sweetheart. *Hamlet* is a revenge play that loses its way. It wanders into personally painful obsessions driven by death fear. I thought you as Hamlet were not suffering all that intensely enough. Sorry, Harry. And that was mostly Lance's fault. He likes to throw actors in the deepness and see what happens. A lot drown."

I say, not hot or cold, "And so far you do not like what I've written of *The Which*." Now I see back a gentle pitying madonna look. Regarding the squirmy infant already on his way to getting nailed up. "You think I am writing Oxford as too ordinary a personality and mind if he was capable of writing the complex Shakespeare plays and sonnets."

Here is her steel. "Just speaking as Ophelia, yes. So far, for me Oxford stays dead. I'm only an actor but I can dream of Hamlet writing his own author. Expressing as brilliantly as Hamlet his vision of his author's ghost."

This night air is now past all convection, breathless. "I'm not brilliant, Ophelia. Miriam."

"You are really a good guy, Harry. There is more around your . . . but I can't quite see it. Just . . ." Then the damn suspension. "So don't paint yourself into a dangerous corner. Because it seems *The Which* is itself within a play. That other people are writing too. And maybe nobody now knows exactly where that story is going. But you're not likely the star, sweetheart. That's just what I came to warn about. Sensitive actress stuff."

This is not damaged Ophelia speaking here. This is touchingly sane kind Miriam. Her lovely looks withal. Who bothered to come out here to speak seriously to me, Harry, pathetically adrift in spirit.

I say, "Miriam, let's go get a drink."

Of course she has an outstanding beauty's radar. "No, Harry. I'm only sleeping with Lance now."

"Oh."

"Lester and I are still friends but I did break it off with him over that flagrant Witch of the East Veronica. Who has become old news. Very deservedly.

"I'm not sure what those two guys are trying to do together now. But Lance says Lester is returning to New York soon."

"Oh."

"So."

And then Miriam walked away. I watched her turn into the broad highly lit Mall. Safe for her. But every one of those street footlights she passed went to black space for me.

I sat on a bench near the statue of Saint William. It took quite a while to breathe. A church bell on Central Park West rang 11, maybe midnight. I tried to factor this latest hour of my life into thinking as would a brilliant writer like Edward. Or Will. Or both. Think on as should Arch Bottom with *The Which* half-finished and deadline to performance creeping near.

Of course bronze graven images can see and hear in the dark. So we're not quite done. I call over to him, "Mark Twain had your number. Here's what he wrote in his book about your hustle, 'We are the reasoning race. And when we find a vague file of chipmunk tracks stringing through the dust of Stratford village, we know by our reasoning powers that Hercules has been along there. I feel certain that our fetish is safe for three centuries yet.'"

And then I fell apart fatigued every way. Too tired to open the ajar door to wondering why ever really Miriam had called me out here at 2 a.m. Dubai time.

*

* *

Time does not flow forward. Not always, for me anyway. Passing moments can turn down, turn to side, come back corkscrewy.

As a sort of playwright, in time to come I enjoyed paging through Call Me Bill's dossier entries, each in its misleadingly precise chronological bubble. Though it is shocking to read printed out how emptily Americans really speak. That is why writers of good snappy dialogue are so very valuable in America today. For instance here's a little chat I spotted in Omniconal phone surveillance:

Dateline 8/4; 12:20 p.m. EST; SW Mall Central Park, NYC, USA:

Me: *"It's Harry."*

Lance: *"Good. But it's too late."*

Me: *"My existence is good? Or my existence is too late?"*

Lance: *"Both reflexively unfortunately, buddy. Okay, what's up past midnight?"*

Me: *"I need another couple days to write now. We need to push the Daughters of God rehearsal back to Friday. Please. Best I can do, Lance."*

Lance: *"Sure. We need your best. You a little nervous, tiger?"*

Me: *"Why didn't you show me Shapiro's book?"*

Lance: *"Which one?"*

Me: *"Which one? A Year in the Life: 1599."*

Lance: *"Oh well. That guy's just tap dancing like all the Billy Boys. Harry, listen. You need to keep clarity of focus. It won't work to write The Which as you being Hamlet. This . . . what's that noise?"*

Me: *"Police chasing a mugger."*

Lance: *"Where are you?"*

Me: *"I'm looking at that creepy eight-foot tall Shakespeare statue in Central Park. Which looks like he is actually alive in the shadows here."*

Lance: *"That is the very wrong very dead guy. Be cool."*

Me: *"I am a cool guy, Lance. That's why you hired me, isn't it? A wised-up angry good scholar for your quick trick."*

Lance: *"I believe you have special talent, Harry."*

Me: *"Sure. As to your own jobs, did Iz find a Rockette who can act in the Daughters?"*

Lance: *"Yes, he did and more. We hired Rockette aristocracy, a second-generation stunner. And a Ph.D. You'll get along great with her."*

Me: *"And another three who can follow her lines in chorus?"*

Lance: *"Harry. Harry the Rockettes are chorus girls."*

Me: *"Okay. Sure. Okay."*

Lance after long pause: *"Have you been talking to Miriam?"*

Me: *"No."*

*

*   *

Call Me Bill's penance gift dossier transcript pages by now do read for me like eating salty potato chips. They go very well with vodka and solitude. I have found there is no true order of potato chips in a bag, a matter best left that way in perspective of ultimate potato chip destiny. In the end eaten sooner or too late the whole bag makes your head fat as your middle and the end is the end.

Know what I mean? Here's a nice crunchy page of savor. Overlooked in real time of speech by Call Me Bill. While distracted by personal musings about his possible new acting career.

Dateline 7/4; 221b Bermondsey Street, Southwark, London, United Kingdom (former)

Male 1: *"Mommy! . . . I told you not to just walk in."*

Female: *"Ohhh. I've been bad again."*

Male 1: *"Yes you are so bad. Shut the door tight. I can't have any shadow."*

[indistinct scratching noise]

[very distinct door knock]

Male 2 through door: *"The Turkey just called me. On his encrypted WhatsApp still using cute code words like he's in an old movie. Anyway, it's on tomorrow. Claridge's room 901 11:00. So he can be done by lunch. Actually said that. Our Turkey's oven-ready."*

Male 1: *"Well . . . Mommy, get away from that!"*

Female: *"Ohhh, I'm so sorry, Squooger."*

Male 2 through other side of the door. *"Fell like a hero for the ten. Who is Squooger in there?"*

Male 1: *"It's one of my aliases. Like Dickhead is for you. Sorry Mommy."*

Female voice: *"I understand. You are under so much pressure, Dear Duck."*

Male 2: *"Louise just called you Dear Fuck?"*

Male 1: *"You do your job and I do mine."*

Male 2: *"I do my job great, Squooger. I got him here. He wants the handover one to one, for his security."*

Male 1: *"For my security after the last time."*

Male 2: *"I did like your nose before."*

Male 1: *"It's okay. I have a Matt Damon model picked out. Did you have to go off script any way I should know?"*

Male 2: *"No. He thinks he's been talking to you. This guy made a billion quid so fast it's sticking a long pole out his leisure pants. Like a . . . sorry, Louise."*

Female voice calls through the closed door, *"I understand. You are under pressure too, Dickhead."*

*

*   *

"Hi. I'm Harry."

Silence is a quarter smile. She's as tall as me. All four of them are as tall as me. Each athletically hard-bodied, each in perfect proud posture. Each has wideset roundish eyes, from six feet away all these young women radiate confidence and mild curiosity. Iz Mocha has had his way with Lance and these Rockettes just came out onto the convent gym stage for the rehearsal reading kitted in their usual sequin panties. And Beefeater-style short jackets. Lance apparently won the point on halberds.

I am shocked finding these four allegorical women from a mid-16th-century morality play suddenly facing me as very taut flesh. A week ago I just made them up in a sleepy inspiration. I had been mulling Dr. Arbuthnot's saying modern scientific understanding is flourishing as it has moved beyond binary and linear modular patterns. And too I have been brooding over Miriam's too frank for me criticisms of both my acting and my writing. Obviously she expected something more surprising both ways. Some jump in more acute intelligence than just more pedestrian coloring in of already drawn biographical lines. Hamlet's lines and Oxford's lines should move in a more dangerously entangling helix.

So I was pushed braver by my two muses. Being the gruffly creative doctor and the elusively stinging actress. At a witching hour alone I envisioned far from my prior pages' lines. Newly *The Which* will flash the Shakespearean theatrical innovation of introspection back into its cultural origin. Being the ancient English morality plays that Oxford surely knew as a boy before Elizabeth's reign began.

The Which will now swerve unexpectedly deep. Revealing to its ignorant 21st-century American audience that Shakespeare's unprecedented internally expressed soliloquizing actually directly grew from the abstract expression of character types in feudal morality plays.

Edward de Vere was the son of John deVere, who financially maintained an acting troupe, the Earl of Oxford's Men. Oxford's Men toured England before there was any designed permanent theater anywhere. Sometimes the actors of Oxford's Men on tour were accompanied in travel by their protecting patron the 16th Earl and his curious boy Edward. Young Edward would have played with the popular clown Will Somer, who some suggest as the source for Yorick in *Hamlet*. Edward the man as Earl of Oxford himself funded two troupes, at personally ruinous expense. So Edward knew actors well all his life.

Medieval morality plays remained a popular seasonal balance to the communal medieval miracle plays, which were also continuous into Tudor times. Edward thus as a young observer of morality plays well knew the effect on an audience of their stylized chorus. The chorus "voice" expressing to the audience turning fate in real time. And so it was that Edward de Vere evolved that ancient voicing into Shakespearean soliloquy's internally articulated shifts. Shakespearean soliloquy's unique perspective introspectively torques intense moment within moment, just as does the chorus voice of morality plays.

And Oxford the mature author further sophisticated his characters' personal expression by drawing upon the new style of personally introspective essays of his contemporary Michel de Montaigne. Oxford read Montaigne in French during his sojourn in Paris in 1575. But those essays were not translated into English until 1603 by Oxford's friend John Florio. Florio as a professional writer for a time was subsidized by Oxford and lived in his household. Indeed some Oxfordians propose Florio's brunette wife as the dark lady of the sonnets. Though Anne Vavasour, Elizabeth's raven-haired lady-in-waiting whom Oxford twice impregnated, is my Mermaid Tavern bar bet. That first translation of Montaigne's intelligent introspection arrived in England dedicated to Oxford about two decades after the innovative Shakespearean introspective soliloquy form had already long flowered onstage.

So it was that I decided to write a surprise morality play scene into *The Which of Shakespeare's Why*—Shakespeare himself often placed one plot within or under another. Then I paused and blinked sadness. Realizing this insight could have been my excellent doctoral thesis. If I hadn't impatiently turned away from one promising future's door as usual. On to this waywardness.

As with the ghost of Hamlet's father there is much of conscience involved in *The Which*. Dr. Arbuthnot's prescription to jump outside tired set forms moved me to adapt the anciently popular morality play known as *The Castle of Perseverance*. In this medieval spectacle predating early modern theater the Four Daughters of God pass recommended judgment of eternal fate on the doings of a particular deceased person on trial before them and their father God. Having examined the moral facts of his or her lifetime.

I thus interjected into *The Which* this morality play chorus to conduct a godly trial of Oxford's fate in literary history.

Not arbitrarily. No, because a fair judgment by future time is actually what Oxford had Hamlet plead with Horatio to seek after his literal death. This makes forceful dramatic sense. As does using four perfectly formed Rockettes from Radio City Music Hall as the Four Daughters of God chorus since they are actually chorus girls. And anyway Iz would not rest until Rockettes were hired for something at Radio City.

This new creative plan is thus sensible. If you drink alone in a hotel room day after day. Holding a contingent large payment for still unwritten work made to you by a scheming violently ill-tempered She-Devil. Anyway, in my out-of-box Daughters sequence now poor Oxford, deep-buried forgotten so long ago, can soliloquize as himself. As unique Edward de Vere himself, called by his drinking pals Ye Willy—in modern translation, Dickhead. So Oxford now goes on trial for his soul in literary eternity. Before the Four Daughters of God judges whose diverse natures and divergent scrutinies in sum weigh all character.

I sent Lance and the whole troupe this scene's draft script three days ago. As has often happened with my creative writing efforts, nobody said nothing. So now is come the time to see if I wrote too far out for an audience that at this moment perhaps comfortably assumes that Harvey Weinstein's *Shakespeare in Love* is itself the Keatsian equation of ideal beauty (that being young Gwyneth Paltrow) to truth (that being box office gross). At least the shocking unsheathed sparkly-panty Rockettes as the Daughters of God will help focus audience interest. You have to strategize in the writing game.

*

*   *

Seeing that the first Daughter of God brushed off my hello, Lance steps over. "Ladies, this is the playwright Arch Bottom."

She's still looking analytically at me, this must be the Ph.D. Frowning just little enough to avoid a line at 40. "He just said his name is Harry."

I say, "Stage name."

"Arch is better."

Lance having broken the ice says, "Harry, I mean Arch, we have here your four perfect Daughters." They are each holding a script printout. Lance stagily slowly waves his index finger sequentially, "Truth, Righteousness, Mercy, and Peace."

I say, "Who's which?"

Guess who: "We know."

Lance: "Good. All set to read from top. Naomi, you're Truth, right? Go."

My newest not-friend says, "Lance, I have an unfair number of lines. The writer should spread them evenly."

Okay, so now is presented a half-naked snarling bitch I would not etcetera. You can't make this stuff up. Naomi is the name of the over-dressed under-sexed bank executive who had all my cartons of books put out onto a Brooklyn sidewalk. Distressed loans is her field of specialty. With a side hustle in icepick murders.

I say, "Well, Naomi . . ."

"Truth."

"Is your part a reading comprehension problem?"

"Lance, I can't work with this asshole."

"Now, now." Lance's trademark palm-down wide arm wave ending upside amid an actually charming Errol Flynn-type smile. Lance is a guy who seems to have a stylized moustache but actually is clean shaven. "All you ladies have the script, just read your lines if they aren't memorized yet. Your particular part's name is actually your allegorical measure as a judge. So, as Harry—Arch—wrote your respective lines, your name shows where you are coming from. You speak in character of your moral viewpoint.

"In context all of you are sizing up the pathetic mess of a human being who was the 17th Earl of Oxford. Who also was the existentially frustrated greatest dramatist ever. But as you four chat among yourselves during his trial it's a bit like sorority girls. Hashing over the character and doings of the college's quarterback."

I add for perspective. "This scene is riffing on a famous morality play that Oxford surely knew well from boyhood. So each of God's Daughters will advise to God a final fate for Oxford as the man on trial by them. Together you Daughters are both prosecuting and defending Oxford's final fate to be recognized as author of Shakespeare's works. Or not."

Looking to Lance smiling blandly, I add, "But Naomi, if it's too much for you I could shift your lines over to Righteousness."

There must be a backstory between Truth and Righteousness. Truth, quickly: "That's all right. I'll be fine."

"So in this scene as it proceeds, our audience recognizes the vibe of classic Shakespearean play-within-a -play dramatic tension. In flickering brevity an audience member will subtly learn a lot more to support her conclusion whether the 17th Earl of Oxford really was the writer of Shakespeare. And so it was not Joseph Fiennes the less talented younger brother of Rafe and fee employee of Harvey Weinstein."

Some Daughter of God in response: "Izzy said there would be a dance number."

Lance, Mr. Cool: "Loretta, I've spoken with Mr. Mocha about that misunderstanding. Morality plays are not his field, he was thinking we would be using a medieval *miracle* play. Which, and Loretta you are so right, did have as much singing and dancing as a Broadway musical today."

Loretta must be Peace. "Well. Okay. The money's great anyway."

*

*   *

The stage is lightless.

Oxford/Lance sits alone at center, studying his upturned ink-stained white palms atop Hamlet-black jeans thighs. Alone as he has remained for centuries past.

The Four Daughters lithely file in behind his back, in chorus line, far too sublime to undulate a hip. The convent gym's red fire exit lighting dimly glints their you know what where.

Truth: "You know who we are?"

Oxford, without looking up: "I knew who you were before I made you others."

Truth: "We are still here in your mind."

Oxford: "It's pretty late to recommend my fate to your dad God, girls."

Mercy: "He's not here."

Oxford: "I'll just bet."

Righteousness: "You never cared about God anyway."

Oxford: "I'm a Renaissance mentality. Unless the medieval God is present in individual psychology it's not my thing."

Truth: "Well, okay, Mister English Renaissance hipster, then here we go. For God is part of both early modern and modern psychology. And that's why we're sent back here by Dad to judge you."

Mercy: "God is mercy, as you well know. We saw how profusely you annotated your lovingly accessorized personal Geneva bible. Underscorings echoed throughout your works."

Oxford: "God's mercy is merciless."

Righteousness: "Don't get Shakespearean with us, Milord. We're here because of you personally and not what you hid behind."

Oxford: "Well, good. I'm tired of being hidden."

Truth: "We must bring forth prosecution evidence that has come to our attention recently."

Mercy: "It's never too late, Edward, to revise cruel fate's memory."

Oxford: "Sure. And I have London Bridge to sell you."

Truth: "Some guy already bought it and took it to Arizona. Which was beyond our immortal comprehension."

Oxford: "Maybe he'd like to build a de Vere theater near it now?"

Righteousness: "Actually, that's why we came back to haunt you. If revealed as Shakespeare you would be box office poison with the world's culturally prim. A sexy hound replacement for the sweety pie-face swan of Avon!"

Oxford: "A swan whose life facts conveniently for Stratfordians are blank as a child's new coloring book. Except his rap sheet as a crook."

Righteousness: "Point taken, my Lord Oxenford, as you prefer to be called since it's so feudal funky. We four may be stunningly gorgeous and suggestively half-naked. But for sure we're no dummies. Actually, having no authority figure male, now that God is let's say gotten quiet in old age, is really energizing us Daughters as free agents."

Mercy: "But Milord, lordy lordy. Pardon my French but what a rap sheet you yourself have."

Righteousness: "It's a problem for us. Have you read Berkeley Professor Alan Nelson's sort of biography *Monstrous Adversary?* We suspect it may be a Stratfordian message for general readers curious about you. Help us out please."

Oxford: "Well first help me. Truth, has this professor ever published a single page of his own literary fiction?"

Truth: "No. Professor Nelson's creative record is as utterly blank as any proof that Will Shaxper ever physically wrote one word on paper except pathetic signatures."

Mercy: "Milord, all of us have read both sides of the Shakespeare authorship arguments. It was good to have eternity to get down the list. So I in particular suggested you deserve an opportunity to reply to Professor Nelson's *Monstrous Adversary.*"

Righteousness: "In opposition, Milord, your own fanboys and fangirls say *Monstrous Adversary* is arbitrarily exclusionary in its biographical scope of address. They find *Monstrous Adversary,* though written four hundred years culturally removed as to mentality and mores, seems judgmental on early 21st-century values."

Oxford: "Zut alors! No need to apologize for my French. Yes, I skipped the repetitions after a while. Six hundred pages of me being a lazy alcoholic bum. Nelson in outrage just about my adventurous spelling. Though in fact Oxfordians have found some matching orthography from my letters in the authentic printed texts of the

Shakespeare canon. But it's not just the little spelling stuff as you girls saw ..."

Truth: "We are Goddesses."

Oxford: "And how. Pardon my English. But actually this Nelson fellow pillories me as far worse than a personal mediocrity, right?"

Righteousness: "Well, yes, Lord Oxenford. *Monstrous Adversary* portrays you as beneath further mention in a properly policed and disciplined English Department."

Oxford: "It's not just the Berkeley guy, girls. Goddesses. I do read a lot now that I'm unemployed. Even in the latest Stratfordian books, after a century of published Oxfordian books, I rarely get even scholarly reference footnotes."

Truth: "Well, let's be specific on the prosecution's brief. Professor Nelson's *Monstrous Adversary* did not accept a usual scope of a 21st-century research biography. He wrote from only such of your own documents as now survive. That is unusual for alert seasoned judges like us girls. Goddesses.

"For instance, Professor Nelson's writing doesn't discuss the Crown's likely contemporaneous destruction of all documents other than dreary financial ones he found. It is well known the Elizabethan Crown hid very many secrets and agendas and manipulations. We would have liked to see some further scholarly inquiry lest historical truth might have been distorted by Elizabethan contemporaries pruning Oxford's documentary trail."

Righteousness is not quite so very pretty as her sister Mercy, inside or out. Righteousness interjects, "But still. A full biographical treatment, even like the mild-mannered factual information recitations in Margo Anderson's *Shakespeare by Another Name*, would come pretty shocking as a replacement of the public's beloved simple cipher image William Shakespeare. Because today so many envision Harvey Weinstein's sexually respectful sunny-hearted movie *Shakespeare in Love* as the full biographical book on Shakespeare. So they think they know this history: puppy cute Will raced facilely through his different play-writing gigs as if they were just expense reports."

Truth: "Which, come to think of it, stretched accounting was actually the Hollywood main plot line of *Shakespeare in Love*. By the way, have any of you Girls been pawed by Weinstein? We don't want to set up grounds for a judicial prejudice appeal here."

Mercy has a good head on those hard square shoulders. She says, "Milord, you seem from this sort of biography so incorrect a badass unrepentant entitled male that today's English lit students would need a trigger warning about your character. Especially heavily indebted students. Since you yourself are a poster child for lifelong insolvency at prey of creditors after an expensive education."

Oxford: "Lots of the very best creative writers have had badass personalities off the page. I lived in heady times, after all. Some new severed heads showed up on the pikes over London Bridge's entrance every week. There was a whole lot of nervous drinking, nervous quarreling, and nervous secret sex. Vivid personalities were written by the vivid times."

Truth: "High times like practice fencing in a courtyard with an also drunk tailor's apprentice? Whom you killed. Professor Nelson is outraged at the social inequity you were not beheaded. To a modern progressive mind demonstrating a hypocritical hierarchical exploitative social structure driven by economic inequality. And that's before women and minorities issues."

Oxford: "Come, now. I was still a teenager. That was just an accidental cut on his thigh that unluckily hit an artery. Regular fencing practice was mainline in the British culture in my century, most men carried a knife or rapier. I didn't even know the other guy but he was supposed to be very good with a rapier so in a bar chat I asked for a lesson. He had a new Italian style and surprisingly danced close up to me. Anyway, the Crown's inquest jury found it was self-defense. I do feel bad about his death.

"But Nelson seems to have just assumed I meant to kill that poor guy for no reason at all other than me being such an asshole. Me as wastrel useless asshole aristocrat is the relentless theme in *Monstrous Adversary*."

Mercy: "We know that duel slaying stayed in you, Milord. As did your own groin wound from a revenge stabbing over twice impregnating a lady-in-waiting to the Queen. We've all seen the end of *Hamlet* like a zillion times. We do know the poisoned sword duel was not in your precedent material. It came from your life material."

Oxford: "Goddesses, I admit right up front here that when young I had judgment and emotional control issues. Continuing into my middle thirties. But, you see, don't you, it was those lurid episodes that truly made me capable in later life of imagining so many different convincingly vivid personalities?"

Oxford steps to the footlights, looks back over his shoulder at the Daughters' four-fold line of beauty. "Shouldn't Peace be helping me out a little here? I did write my final form works at peace, distilling my life's chaos of events done and suffered into wise vision."

Peace: "Sorry, your Grace. We girls had a long talk before visiting you. There are more prosecution issues God should consider if he does get interested in who wrote Shakespeare."

The audience surely can tell these goddess sisters really hash over human frailty in all its variety. Righteousness says, sounding troubled, "Mercy, we need to run down some more of Professor

Nelson's specific charges. I have a list tucked in under my panties."

Oxford: "The Stratfordians are everywhere."

Righteousness wants to get to the rapier point. "Truth, sweetheart, could we read these in unison?" Truth then looks over Righteousness's shoulder as they start down jointly reading aloud the offense charge sheet of the 17th Earl of Oxford in *Monstrous Adversary*.

Oxford has not shifted in his chair. He knows just what is coming his way. Four centuries has allowed a long time to catch up on bad press.

"We've got you charged on narcissism. Professor Nelson doesn't like your wardrobe outfits."

Oxford: "Four hundred years ago meant an Elizabethan world of socially entitled men in jewel-tone velvet tights, kitten heels, and taffeta blouses prancing signature-cut beards among gilded everything. I did wear some Italian clothes when I returned from living there. Though most that I bought in Italy were stolen by Danish pirates on my way home, who landed me on the Dover beach naked.

"Which event, you wise literary Goddesses, and note again Professor Nelson here again ignoring an inconvenient biographical fact, I wrote into *Hamlet* without any precedent in source texts. That is art from life. Academic critics just are not life. I was gadzooks in tights and puffy shorts. Hard to understand in this world of chinos and Dockers."

Mercy: "Well. Well, well, actually. But next. The professor also is not liking your general attitude toward Elizabethan Crown authority. He charges you with contempt."

Oxford: "So why didn't the Crown chop off my head if I was such a troublemaker?"

Truth: "My good Lord Oxenford, that was a frequent suggestion at Court. But the Queen always protected you for reasons that do not interest Professor Nelson's view in his book."

Righteousness: "Next, Milord. Professor Nelson disapproves of what he deems your betrayals of Catholic recusants who conferred with you."

Oxford: "Oh come now. This is the problem with English Departments. Full of people who are themselves virgin of personally feeling history's force in their own lived moments. Betrayals were the stuff of life in Tudor England. Betrayal to the scary Crown was as common as panty hose for men and no underwear for women.

"I was not raised a Catholic. But I was raised a feudalist. Obviously most of my plays have a retrograde feudal sentimentality. I loved imagining elite royal courts. And just as obviously so did my public. We were all living in unsettled times. Our society generally nervous as early modern time rapidly evolved from late feudal. So naturally glamorously imagined indefinite past time felt warm to Londoners. They were already becoming frazzled by modernity."

Righteousness: "Specifically, Professor Nelson says you betrayed Catholic relatives to the Queen's Protestant cops. Apparently just because you were such an inveterate asshole."

Oxford looks at each Daughter, which is very pleasant so he lingers, thinking. Because what he has to respond to this charge is not pleasant at all. "Well, a fundamental part of feudal life was the Catholic rite.

"The Tudors destroyed the Roman Catholic Church in wanton greed to seize its and Catholic families' wealth for their personal enrichment. The substitution of a stripped down replica church headed by the fascistic Crown was stunningly hypocritical.

"My ancient extended family included fine people who resisted the deep travesty that syphilitic brain-traumaed psychopath Henry VIII forced upon all of British society.

"Forced so very viciously bloodily. All that misery over some bits of dogma just wholly made up centuries after Jesus disappeared. Which had been then further manipulated for another millennium. Then really travestied by pathetically needy Henry Tudor, who was only King because his normal brother died young.

"My Uncle Henry Howard, Earl of Surrey, encouraged me to write poetry while he was my boyhood literary tutor. It was Surrey himself who invented sonnets. Being poems in blank verse in short forms ending with a rhymed couplet. In my own sonnets, observant judging Goddesses, you note I followed my revered tutor Uncle Surrey by adopting the form and meter he originated and taught me as a teenager.

"Well, the Earl of Surrey's head was cut off by King Henry because he stayed a Catholic. But that was really not done due to religion. The obvious motive was to seize my uncle's great wealth in traitor's forfeit to Henry's greedy wasteful Crown. And Surrey's father Thomas Howard, Earl of Norfolk, only escaped beheading when King Henry died just days before the execution date. But then Norfolk remained in Tower limbo until the Catholic Bloody Mary pardoned him and restored some property. A sick Tudor chaos.

"Norfolk's successor, who was my first cousin and childhood best friend, made a misstep conversing at his estate with hotheads of the stubbornly Catholic north of England. He was taken to the Tower, slated for execution as a Catholic traitor. And of course, as usual, what the nearly broke Crown really wanted was seizure of what was left of the Dukedom's remaining wealth after prior pillage.

"When William Cecil bribed me into marrying his pawn Anne

for a huge dowry I did so expressly including as the deal that the life of my best friend young Norfolk would be spared. Fool that I was. The dowry was never paid at all. And Norfolk was quickly executed on Cecil's order despite my protests all over Elizabeth's Court.

"I was terrible at judging political matters. They mortally swirled fast all around me at the center of the Court. I certainly did not live quietly in drab mass production clothing well salaried for life on a sunny university campus.

"As a young man my personality swung vividly back and forth. Unpredictably. My best part was artistic, the worst arrogant. The dumbest political.

"As a child born and raised in feudalism I admired the ancient order of Catholicism just for its ancient culture. In that mix of my own naïveté and romanticism I was lured into inebriated unwise conversations with more distant Catholic blood relatives and their friends who sympathized with European Catholic attempts to assassinate Elizabeth. But personally I adored Elizabeth's verve on the throne, and loved her personally. You know from my plays how affectionately I wrote women of strong character.

"So at a real-life point of seeing her danger from these particular Catholic plotters I went to the Queen and denounced them as traitors. The betrayal was theirs, not mine. I had no part in their plotting.

"I as a moody eccentric was an easy target for these traitors to desperately counter-denounce. That's where one of them unfortunately used the catchy term 'monstrous adversary' about me that Professor Nelson made his book's title, and refrain it seems to me. That real traitor I revealed said I was so demented I would rather drink his blood than wine as overmuch as I liked wine. Said I was myself a stooge agent of Spain. His co-conspirator also called me a queer for boys.

"Motives were multiple in every person touching these claims. The Queen artfully, wisely in her often indecisive way, just let the cross-accusations cool down into name calling. The traitors' desperate smears about Spain and pedophilia were made once and never repeated. All were let free under close watch by Crown spies throughout the rest of Elizabeth's reign. One of the traitors moved to France and worked on plots against the English. The Crown promptly poisoned him.

"So. Was I really an overdressed drunken pederast betrayer of fellow Catholic agents of Spanish power? Read just this book and it looks simple to conclude that I Oxford was just no good.

"But think more. How could I have been so lowly surrounded by affectionate elites of Elizabethan society? *The Tempest* was written to debut at my daughter Susan's 1604 wedding to the Earl of Montgomery, a celebration which performed only my plays, four of them. Montgomery and his brother the Earl of Pembroke, chancellor of James I's Crown, were my lifelong friends. And my eldest daughter married to the Earl of Stanley, by surviving letter rumored to be a secret playwright, was another personal friend of mine. The mother of Montgomery and Pembroke, the Dowager Countess, was my old friend who sponsored my daughters' marriages. This Herbert family as documented in cold fact joined in paying absolutely all the stupendous cost to publish my collected plays known as the First Folio in 1623."

Oxford's voice has grown exasperated. "Realistically could I have been such a miserable person and yet held such respect as these apex elite persons all gave to me? Including two big festivals of only my plays in the year of my sudden death."

Mercy: "Milord, point taken. Calm yourself, please. We do see you were too emotional to stay alive much longer after age 38 in the dangerous Elizabethan Court. We realize Elizabeth was your true friend in banishing you with a necessary pension your creditors could not seize. So you were consequently free to write what she liked and respected. It was good to have the Queen as your wise lifelong friend."

Truth: "Bitch in general that she was. As everybody mumbled to their trusties."

Now Oxford is smiling ruefully: "I couldn't always see her underlying good will. You Daughters come back now from a medieval religious theater that dwindled after the beginning of Elizabeth's reign. Your morality plays were about wisdom seen by light of examples of character. I carried the spirit of those ancient morality plays forward within my own plays' kaleidoscopic new dramatic visions.

"But because religion was a literally lethal subject all my lifetime, I wrote only secularly. So now it is irony to realize you Daughters from Christian religion see my own life in turn as a play woven of moralities."

Righteousness: "That's what theater is for. You yourself suffered from far too many dreams in the dangerous shifting Elizabethan world. But it made you a complex creator like no other."

Truth: "That is such cozy sentiment, girls. But if you'll pardon my Spanish, this is still an Inquisition. And our dad, I mean, God Almighty, may be listening in from some cloud.

"So Milord, we do have to proceed with addressing more charges against you in *Monstrous Adversary*. It seems that you were a lazy jerk who shamelessly begged to borrow money all his life. How plead you, your Grace?"

Oxford: "Well. Consider sums in sum. Because all that middle-class sneering about my indigence is a matter for an Economics Department not the English Department. My lifelong insolvency began with the confiscatory seizure of Earldom wealth from my grandfather the 15th Earl by the perennially broke Henry VII. And then again from my father the 16th Earl under grossly spendthrift Henry VIII. By the time of his son dead-at-16 King Edward, the upstart Tudor establishment had spent itself back down to again basically flat broke.

"And was then foreseeing an invasion war with Spain and maybe France. Which it could not afford to defend. Not after having wasted all its seized wealth. And after so many elite family Catholic and Protestant murders over three decades, the Tudor Crown administration was disorderly as well as insolvent.

"Following the disaster for England of Henry VIII, vulnerable Queen Elizabeth protected herself with a gang of tough savvy operators. Who were not even nobles until she created their titles and power by waves of her hand. Henry VIII and his hard men had already usurped for themselves all the wealth of the Catholic Church and targeted Catholic feudal nobles. So Elizabeth's next generation of mafia dons went after the remaining wealth of legitimate noble families accumulated over centuries. And also rounded on their own predatory kind, so they went after the very new wealth of some of Henry VIII's made men. It's not worth going into the new hypocritically specious legal justifications for those seizures.

"You know, since you know everything, that Britain throughout the 16th century still had no substantial economy other than domestic agriculture. Therefore pillage of the rich was the only means to new wealth.

"In this context, Daughters, I plead that the Elizabethan Age's innovated wardship system, legally cynically cut from whole cloth, created my prison of lifelong insolvency. Under it, if a noble died leaving an heir under age 21, by stunningly unjustified legal fiction all the heir's inherited wealth passed into the control of the Crown. Rhetorically that was for safekeeping but just as with killing Catholics the real purpose was looting others' wealth. Control of an under-21 heir's properties was then sold, or just given as a party favor, to one of Elizabeth's inner circle. That lucky ducky then proceeded to divert both land ownership and income. The Crown reaped tax upon tax and often penalties, because since agricultural wealth was illiquid the new taxes often became delinquent.

"All this was specifically laid on young helpless me as rich prey between ages 12 and 21. I had no protector. My supposed protectors were the very thieves of my inheritance."

Mercy: "Milord, in today's modern world all knowledge of these life facts you lived among is basically unknown. So the same as if your personal psychology never existed."

Oxford: "Well, Walt Whitman had it right. The nervous Queen created aggressive 'wolfish Earls,' and as an imprisoned Ward of State I was their lamb.

"This was the world I obliquely referenced in *Hamlet*. For plausible deniability I chose an old European source play to build on because it has a dad murdered for his kingdom. *Hamlet* was a long time coming from deep observation of Elizabethan reality, not ancient Danish.

"So Professor Nelson, yes, I was contemptuous of these predations on my birthright. Withal by the time I reached 20 I was deeply, recklessly angry. I never could grasp money arithmetic, to a degree some professor in the Berkley Math Department could call numislexia.

"Also I had severe mood swings that one of Professor Nelson's colleagues down the hall in the Psychology Department certainly could call bipolar. I rebelled foolishly. I spent money lavishly before they could take more of my assets away. Or murder me young like my friends Kit Marlowe, same age as me, and poor Tom Kidd. Being already maneuvered into debt I could never repay, defiantly I borrowed more. When I couldn't borrow more I sold properties. No one in my life stepped in to wisely counsel me. My isolation was unique.

"So you see, girls, pardon, when young I lived deeply feeling fate's present threat. As you can tell from the anger and sadness apparent even in some of my comedies. I wanted to join my military commander uncle and cousin the Fighting Veres, Horace and Francis de Vere. As an insider joke at Court I called them *Hamlet* characters Horatio and Francisco. Today Stratfordians disregard this very obvious joke as a key to my true identity. They sheeplike are not curious why soldiers in a Danish castle have Italian names, with no Italian among the characters or ever in ancient Denmark.

"But did Nelson really say I was forever lazy?"

Righteousness, who takes more partisan views than her sister Daughters: "Well, yes. Actually his charge amounts to rotten lazy, Milord. Professor Nelson writes that he is certain you did not write a word of all the plays, sonnets, and long poems. He seems to theorize that, being just a jerk to the core, your Lordship simply frittered your whole life away uselessly drinking."

Daughter Mercy interjects urgently, "But Milord, we girls, Goddesses, do see the context of your secret pension. Your pro-Tudor English history plays were becoming very popular in public theaters during the decades of menace of Spanish or possibly French invasion of England. So your history plays were good value for money.

"And we see now that the social plays respected feudal noble order. The upstart illegitimate Tudors, with so much disorder in their reign, benefited by being cloaked in your plays' glamorizing romantic glow around feudal entitlement.

"Also of course anyone can understand that hiding your identity protected the Queen and the Crown from surprises your disorderly personality might produce. So from the Crown standpoint what's not to like in burying you alive on a pension, behind which is a death threat?"

Oxford stands and strolls a few steps, then spins on his heel the way Lance loves to do. He lingers a glance across all four of the Rockets in their glimmering panties and tightly tailored crimson Beefeater jackets. "Well, Daughters of God trying me in the Castle of Perseverance, I salute your open and inquiring minds. It is a refreshing change after all these years.

Righteousness: "But Milord, there is one remaining very serious matter. Professor Nelson has also seen you as a misogynist bad guy."

Oxford: "Unbelievable. After my dozens of warmly sympathetic portrayals of woman characters? Even after all my heroine leading ladies? My six plays starring daughters who courageously reject paternalistic control?

"Anyway, nowadays don't all professors call all dead white writers misogynists?"

Truth: "Well, yes, a misogyny calling out of helpless dead writers from another cultural world helps for popularity grades that the indebted teenage students now decide to give their teachers before annual salary committee reviews. But still. In the Professor's opinion you should have been nicer to the fifteen-year-old girl whose domineering father tricked and trapped you into marrying against your will while under his aggressive and duplicitous power. And who it seemed when married became pregnant by another man since you had publicly sworn never to have sex with her. And who with her scheming father Burghley did publicly pressure you to simply accept the apparent bastard baby, meaning ruination of your plan for escape from forced marriage by nonconsummation annulment."

Mercy is getting worked up. "Very very awkward public scandal, everybody in London said. Anne claimed distraught that you did bonk her. There was some delicious rumor of her tricking sex from drunk you, Milord. With her in disguise as another woman at one of those wildly boozy Elizabethan Court dance parties."

Oxford ruefully smiling again: "Which I used as 'the bed trick' in actually three of my plays. Three. My life was my material."

Righteousness: "We know. But those plays' obvious reference to Anne and your scandal story doings became lost as Elizabethan contemporaries died and theater became banned for a next generation. So to modern Stratford scholars 'the bed trick' became just a commercial gimmick."

Oxford: "So much is lost when correspondence to life is lost. How could the world come to think the works of Shakespeare came from some ignoramus's virgin imagination?"

Mercy, looking where the strap on her wrist would be if she ever had need of a timepiece: "We need to wrap up, God's attention span is not what it used to be. Speaking of virgin, anger and embarrassment all around as to Anne's unexpected pregnancy would be natural.

"That is not misogyny in balance with your whole canon's warm empathy and sympathy with female characters and situation. Ophelia in *Hamlet* is indeed badly treated in his existential distress by Hamlet. Which includes his outraged anger at entrapment in general by her father Burghley. But then, showing signs of the author's mature reconsideration of the plight of the underlying real person Anne herself, at the play conclusion Hamlet finally leaps into Ophelia's grave overcome by remorse. Distraught at the death of the

Anne figure. You as Hamlet anguished over what unfortunately passed during life between Anne and you at your worst."

Oxford: "Thank you, Mercy. As you girls, Girls, know, for the last decade of my life I was happily married to the brilliantly educated aristocrat Elizabeth Trentham. Lilibee was a soul mate who shared my bohemian personality. She was chosen by Queen Elizabeth herself to be my mate. We are reported in multiple documents to have gone pub crawling together. Often to the Saint George, considering the too-loud roar at the Mermaid.

"And further on Nelson and his 400-year displaced misogyny call-out. I did have checkered relations with just a couple of women, remarkable considering what was on offer to the Earl of Oxford at a time when women could not earn a living. I was the tipsy seduced prey, I was not the cold predator of that Vavasour girl who got pregnant twice, leaving me crippled by her outraged uncle in a street ambush. That laughing teenage sorceress came after me unbearably hot. Quite a number. Soon after me she married another Earl, mother of my infamous bastard baby and all.

"Lady Elizabeth and I had a fine son whom we named Henry after our old friend Henry Wriothesley, Earl of Southampton. Our two Henrys became like uncle and nephew. Indeed they sadly died together uselessly fighting the Spaniards in the Netherlands. Before then my son in his twenties helped his aunts Susan and Elizabeth to gather all the material for the Folio. Some of which his talented Uncle Stanley edited before publication.

"Egad! This teacher fellow grim Nelson really does need a comic role in a new play of mine. Can't we do something about that?"

Chorus of the Four Daughters of God all together, "We are trying now, Milord."

*

*   *

[Dateline July 5, 11:00 GMT, Claridge's Hotel, London, Room 901]

[Expensive doorbell rings]

"Right on time."

"I know you are busy, sir."

"No sir for me. We're all Californians in my room."

"I'm grateful for your interest. Mr. Chairman."

"Jack, William. I have enjoyed our businesslike talks. But what's with the sombrero?"

"Perhaps, sir, Jack, I have seen too many movies. It's to foil the security cameras."

"I like it but on the street here in London . . ."

"It's a crushable model. I can roll it up and put it under my anorak."

"What a dude lid. I could use that with the ladies. How about I buy it too?"

"The hallway security camera, Sir Jack."

[Probably a laugh of sorts] "Will, buddy, SkyHi Microchips was built from my problem solving. You could put a guest towel on your head and use the stairs. Ditch it at the lobby entrance."

"Two thousand quid."

"Okay. What's a quid?"

"Not much to you. Let me show you the page now. It says exactly what I read to you over the phone."

[Sound of suitcase zipper opening. Silence.]

"Oh jee-eez!! My buds on the Folger Library board are going to go ravers. We can carve the text over the door of the performance annex I'm shelling out for. Just below my name."

"It's so right that the Folger now will house your and its triumph."

"More than you know, guy. My assistant, and that's all she is, found this kind of prediction on the Folger website—I have a photographic memory by the way—'If the current consensus on the authorship of the plays and poems is ever overturned, it will be because new and extraordinary evidence is discovered. The Folger Shakespeare Library is the most likely place for such an unlikely discovery.'

"That Folger outfit is Mister Brass Balls, right? What a crew, just like my SkyHi team of killers."

[Sound of suitcase zipper further opening.]

"I know you are busy, Sir Jack. The ten million is here?"

"I am well known for efficiency, Will. You bet. All in used unmarked bills like you said. That's a nice looking suitcase, stud red wheels and Save the Whales decal. Want to sell that too? Five thousand quid do that trade?"

"Well. I see how your company grew so fast, you seize opportunity like a tiger. It's tempting. But the cash is so heavy I need my suitcase. I couldn't very well carry it down the stairs in a towel."

"Yeah. Yeah. Sensible guy, bud. Look, I'm bumping up against a shady lady waiting at a table downstairs now. Let's shove the bucks in, shake, and be good."

"All good, dude."

*

*   *

I thought the pretty far-out morality play sequence, the Four Daughters of God judgment in the Castle of Perseverance, went well. So did Lance. As we stood chatting about it Daughter Truth exited the little girls' locker room. Apparently for her change to streetwear one of her sisters spray painted black velvet where perfect jeans would be on a perfect woman.

I'm naturally a polite guy. "Hi Naomi. Good rehearsal."

"What the fuck was *that* about?"

Her Ph.D. is probably in mechanical engineering. But Lance gave me a thumbs up as she glimmered away. And then I clicked a cab to take me straight back uptown to my torture chamber in the looming Tower of Waldorf. I still must write the really explosive part, the part that breaks open the final text of *The Tempest* and concludes on Horatio's openly weeping epilogue. With Valerie stalking out beside him as a kind of even more over-dressed Queen Elizabeth. Giving the world her gift of knowing the real Shakespeare identity as did Elizabeth.

When I spun in from the hotel's entrance door an attendant wearing gold triple braiding at his shoulders greeted me. As does a hawk a sparrow.

"Oh, good, Mr. Bottom. A young lady left a package for you to get personally when you returned. She didn't want it sent upstairs."

"Okay. Who was she?"

"She said to tell you this is from Lulubelle."

"I don't . . . sunrise blonde?"

"Oh no. Very . . . very, with black pigtails coiled on top her head."

"I see. Little tiny beauty mark to the side of her eye just where you'd kiss her goodbye?"

"I would not do that. But yes! You aren't likely to forget Lulubelle."

"Not easily." So that was Miriam in poor Desdemona's wig from the props depository. Or else Miriam just coiled some of her pet black mambo vipers up there over the fatal charm gaze.

On entering Suite 6A I went to the kitchen to knife open the insistently plastic envelope. That was good. Because soon as I did a dead fish of some kind slithered out on the counter. It had been gutted but otherwise looked calm. Given up. Delivered as food for thought. No? As I recalled *The Godfather* the Mafia's fish there was medium size. This is a little one. Actually suggesting penis size within my spectrum. Not food for thought.

I upended the envelope, a book in a Ziploc bag fell out. Fluorescent light in the kitchen picked up a glossy white medallion on the cover. "A *New York Times Book Review* Notable Book of the Year."

This was *Contested Will: Who Wrote Shakespeare?* by Professor James Shapiro. Two days before I had flipped through Miriam's previous enigmatic gift in our Central Park encounter, Professor Shapiro's *A Year in the Life of William Shakespeare: 1599.* I read fast in fear of some dreadful hard fact revelation that would ruin *The Which*'s dramatic case. But no bomb did explode. *A Year in the Life* basically inserted images of Shaxper into generic historic wallpaper, painting shadowy but geniousy Will amidst visualized historical scenarios. Reading, I recalled Peter Sellers in *Being There* and Tom Hanks in *Forest Gump*. Like Professor Greenblatt in *Will in the World*, Professor Shapiro's *A Year in the Life* simply ignored the existence of Oxford.

Contested Will was published five years later, in 2010. Somebody has read this gift paperback now in my hand. Somebody who wears illegal perfume and moistens her claws with aloe and bends down page corners very often. Some lovely fairy creature who delivered it to me in an envelope together with a poor dead small fish.

Stretched out on the Waldorf's bier of a sofa I scan fast and furrowed to page 35. Then pull out my phone. No answer from Lulubelle Corleone. I scroll and ring Lance.

"Lance?"

"All day. How's the *Tempest* thing coming?"

"It's not. I need time. No interruption. So don't come here."

"Sure, Harry. You're doing great. You'll find the right stuff. No hurry, we've got three weeks to get the last scene down."

"Have you seen Miriam?"

"No. No, when that girl's not in a scene rehearsal she goes off with the twinkly fairies. Being one."

"Oh." I have been working on eliminating my idiotic habit of punctuating confusion with "okay." "Oh" being less expensive.

And now I am alone to compose more in stony lonely Castle Waldorfinore, the Tower of Waldorf, until further notice. This is dead serious pressure time. I get my quart bottle of Grey Goose from the kitchen freezer. And call room service.

The hotel, maybe during its recent ownership by Chinese thugs, went for all black ninja-style pantsuits for its room service people. The 60-ish maid standing before me now is broad enough for three ninjas. Smiling I reach up the icy Grey Goose and she takes it.

"You can, please, take this away. It's not the hotel's. Take it home. My gift."

"Oh." I like her prim tone immediately. "My Lord Jesus Christ does not want me to drink alcohol."

"Mine doesn't either. Except at high mass." I'm looking at her inscribed name pinned over her clavicle. "Mary."

She likes me too, a fellow religious nut teetotaler. Smiling timidly: "Mary isn't my real name. It's sort of a stage name just for here."

Now we're really in good vibes. "Well, my real name is not Mr.

Bottom. But let's keep our Waldorf names since we sure are here. You can just pour the vodka all down the sink now."

And she did. And then we bade good afternoon within our cunning false identities.

*
*   *

You want alone, you got it, Harry. You want fear in silence, Harry, you got it. I could expect from skimming those first 35 pages Professor Shapiro will ridicule my *The Which of Shakespeare's Why*. He is an intensely devout Stratfordian. And he is a dangerously good writer.

So I Google Shapiro. It's bad. Dozens of press reviews loved *Contested Will*. Whatever the Theater Library Association may be in substance, they announced a prize. Some freelance guy writing in what by 2010 was the remnant of *Esquire* called *Contested Will* "the definitive treatment of the Oxfordian theory." Which quote unfortunately some aggressive Stratfordian spiked into Wikipedia's open access text.

I read on and it's worse. His *A Year in the life of William Shakespeare: 1599*, out in 2005, got two prizes, named the Samuel Johnson and the Theater Book, which I suppose would stack in a shouting barroom argument. And worse. In 2015 he published *The Year of Lear: Shakespeare in 1606*. It got two more awards though named after guys I never heard of. Maybe, just asking, literary awards are about the awarders' tax deductible egos and maybe reviewers pile on to safe bets? I, Harry the dropout, can only guess from very afar how literary wheels turn and grease wheels.

The man Shapiro does not rest. I see he just brought out a book covering how Americans regarded Shakespeare's works in different political epochs of our history. Absolutely he will get another award for that, maybe presented by the ghost of Abraham Lincoln from Buddhist bardo, like Hamlet's dad reappearing from Catholic purgatory. But, pardon, that odd Lincoln and Shakespeare and death crack is from another story I know already. That you soon will too.

Wikipedia-curious, I linked onward to a *New Yorker* piece by this Columbia professor about his correspondence with Supreme Court Justice John Stevens. Who wrote to Shapiro after moot court trials of the competing authorship claims. Stevens wrote that after further reading he was convinced the 17th Earl of Oxford was the true author, and so Will Shaxper of Stratford was some kind of false front. Justice Stevens asked Professor Shapiro how he could so utterly confidently completely dismiss even the possibility of Oxford's authorship.

I know from my brush with becoming a lawyer that senior judges have an experienced capacity when weighing circumstantial evidence. And so that sometimes a plethora of circumstantial facts equals proof positive.

Justice Stevens's letter like his prior law review article did not get into factual disputations. Or some more angled subjects of Oxfordian analysis. It did focus on the age difference of Oxford and Shaxper, and the logical probabilities of their respective chronological ages when Shakespeare works appeared. For instance Oxford's intimate observation of Queen Elizabeth's private personality as shown in the psychologically coded and linguistically erudite book-length poem *Venus and Adonis*, published in 1592 under Shakespeare's name when Will Shaxper was under 30 years of age and of record in London for perhaps only 18 months.

Oxford then was 43, and had for almost two decades been an inner-circle courtier to Elizabeth. *Venus* when printed was dedicated to the teenage Earl of Southampton. But after a century of intensive Stratfordian research no evidence exists that this most elite of Court noblemen ever even met Shaxper the rumored former butcher's apprentice from a distant market town. To the contrary there is solid documentary fact as to Oxford and Southampton bearing upon the *Venus* dedication. Because the Earl of Oxford long strenuously urged the young Earl of Southampton to marry his daughter.

Anyway, in his *New Yorker* article Professor Shapiro says cool as cold he chose to sharply cut off Justice Stevens's reach-out to him. Because the old guy was just another ignorant dreamer projecting what he himself wanted to believe. Professor Shapiro has written that Oxfordians do so because of lack of a career academic's specific knowledge of the Elizabethan/Jacobean period. Shapiro thus reported in the *New Yorker* that his return letter to Justice Stevens actually rebuked him for this romanticism about Oxford. Shapiro quotes himself forthrightly saying that any such curiosity actually could be dangerous to social order in America.

One might imagine the Justice's white eyebrows rising without smile below. Shapiro wrote, "Like it or not, your public expression of interest in the Oxford question has, to my mind at least, disturbing political implications." The lifelong teacher then warns the Justice of the Supreme Court of a theory that that Oxfordian advocacy could encourage further fringe political adversary conspiracy theories. The Professor then cut off Stevens from further correspondence, saying he will not discuss authorship with Shakespeare doubters because "nobody ever changes their mind."

Academic theory. Academic quarrel. But in Elizabethan real life real time the apparently lifelong manic-depressive Edward de Vere, even though hereditary Earl of Oxford, had great cause to fear that Crown hard men would haul him off to the Tower some night for questioning among their bloodstained torture machinery. Under Tudors that happened often to the ancient nobility. If so the black-hooded interrogator could start in on the terrified hyper-sensitive Oxford by saying in effect the very same censorious words that stern Professor Shapiro of Columbia used to rebuke Supreme Court Justice Stevens. "Like it or not, your public expression of interest in . . . ."

In . . . what? Plenty. Shakespeare's works were interested in the personal fallibility of Kings and Queens, sometimes in regicide. Had some auras of outlawed Catholic sympathy. And most dangerously for the author were populated by some characters whose personalities rhymed with those of leading figures in the Court. Thus in prudence Shakespeare's plays, which often featured lost or displaced rightful rulers, were themselves prudently "bearded" by the author as set in Europe not Britain and in some vague time of antiquity.

So what would you do if you were Edward de Vere? You would heed your friend the Queen, and agree that some non-controversial nominee can hold place as author of your stuff. Thus allowing you to please the Queen and keep her 1588 necessary pension while insulated from latent political danger. A trusted employee passes your plays not already in anonymous circulation to your own acting troupe evolved from the 1580s. Evolved to other sponsorship and names but populated by much the same professionals long known to Oxford.

This discreet private system avoiding identity linkage to Oxford worked well throughout the 1590s. Living on the Queen's generous secret pension, Oxford chose for his exile from Court life a house very near to the theaters. Oxford lived in peaceful seclusion for over

a dozen years. The central Oxfordian belief is that the Earl continued to revise early play drafts and write new ones.

William Shakespeare is the pen name for Oxford that the Crown
first approves in 1592. It was authorized for printing as author of
the sexy poem *Venus and Adonis*, which in substance is dangerously
allusive to the Queen's sexual behavior. William Shakespeare as a
name is plausibly close to that of the man William Shaksper, just
recently arrived in London and a non-controversial theatrical fringe
figure. The highly irregular dedication of *Venus* by a low caste commoner to the legally barriered young Earl of Southampton offers
this poem as "first fruit of my invention." Oxfordians understand the
word "invention" to refer to the new pen name, and of course "first
fruit" to refer to *Venus* as the first work Oxford published under the
shield of that pen name.

Some Oxfordians suggest perhaps Shaxper's equity ownership
share in the Lord Chamberlain's Men was arranged by the controlling Crown for his service as a front diverting from Oxford's
identity as author. And think perhaps some Crown cash passed to
him in his silent "beard" deal. Because in fact within about five years
of arrival in London poor Shaxper soon bought an expensive two-
dozen room house in Stratford and speculated in land, commodities, and moneylending. Anyway a share in the Lord Chamberlain's
Men enhanced Shaxper's credibility as implicitly author of the similarly named Shakespeare work.

And, famously despite massive scholarly research for two centuries, no record exists of any payment ever to Shaxper for any writing anything at all, or even any acting. Stratford was three days' ride
from London each way and Shaxper was notably out of sight there
when Shakespeare plays debuted in London. There is no trace of

any literary activity of Shaxper after he left London in 1604, the year Oxford died, until his death in 1616.

There must have been some cause for Shaxper himself to never claim of any record all his life to be the author Shakespeare. And though he filed over a dozen litigations, none were over any literary matter despite several pirated playscript printings.

What a scavenger hunt. This lack of hard proof that Shaxper was a writer of anything is very disappointing for Stratfordians. And too Oxfordians also proceed very frustrated, because their man also lacks one contemporaneous document of dispositive proof.

Futile for all Shakespeareans so blocked. Something needs to turn up further.

Part Five

Half dozing at the Park Avenue window after that exhausting Daughters of God rehearsal. My thumb is stuck at page 35 of Miriam's gift with dead little fish *Contested Will*. I have just sampled famous Professor Shapiro's confident and dismissive Stratfordian ardor. And too Miriam's actressy huggermugger has upset my mood. I have the . . . willies.

I do want to be personally intellectually honest. That is the redeeming reward of my previous failure as a scholar. And too I can't stop thinking of this: a fish the size of my penis arrived in an envelope with *Contested Will*. Mute paired gifts from Miriam Mystery who now is only sleeping with my director and covert employer, so no thanks to a chat over a drink.

Finally I take a deep held breath, firing squad target style. And then read *Contested Will* fast for two hours straight through. I register that Shapiro is humorlessly assertive in the very slim parts of his book that are not generic historic recitals. He writes that 400 years' lapse places modern mentalities at a basically impossible remove from understanding Shakespeare. So he thinks that "modern" people cannot actually now perceive and feel reality as it existed for those living in the "early modern" period of the 16th-century English Renaissance. The professor presents his credentials as a scholar of this cultural transition period, during which late feudal society was at the same time eroding and evolving. He is frank to disdain dreamy ignorance of non-specialists in that period. Period.

The base assumption in Professor Shapiro's books is consistent. He has concluded that Shaxper was a uniquely gifted intuitive writer. And so as such had no need for any biographical base in his writing. And so needed only basic education, despite the erudite content and style of writing he produced. From such a genius men-tality Shakespeare's magic mind wrote itself; that is how I anyway sum up this genius credo.

In another strongly put simple assertion, Professor Shapiro says Shaxper as a writer is actually typical of his time and place. His says that none of the theater writing of Shakespeare's period embodied personal biographical reference or personal emotion of the author. Neither in Elizabethan playwrights' present time nor as recalled in composition.

This is a bright line Shapiro draws on his blackboard. As a deeply invested Stratfordian he completely disregards Oxford. Will not even begin to discuss the literally several hundred play and poetry text resonances to Oxford's profuse biographical documen-tation compiled by Oxfordian scholars and published to small read-ership numbers.

I find in *Contested Will* no debate-type rebuttal of the Oxford case. He writes there were 6,000 or so plays presented during Elizabeth's epoch, and reports about 600 were printed somehow. In this panoply he perceives playwrights to have just been efficiently meeting current constant audience demand for new material. Sounds to me rather like American television writers in the 20th- or 21st-century. He tells his readers that autobiographical intro-spection was eschewed in the Elizabethan playwriting profession.

With a bit less assertive vigor Professor Shapiro also sees Shakespeare's sonnets as fundamentally abstract exercises rather than constructively biographical narrative. His lawyerly one-sided brief again simply completely ignores the Oxfordians' case that ties scores of sonnet-specific topics and references to specific documented events in Oxford's life and personality. I remember from law school what this partially blind kind of advocacy is called in court: special pleading

Oxfordians can point out that Shapiro traverses an intellectually slippery slope. In historical perspective Elizabethan theater actually only began well after 1560. This new playwrighting for new large audiences continued to be explosively innovative all through the latter half of the 16th century. By the Professor's guess there were about 100 Elizabethan playwrights and from them came thousands of plays, of which about 600 were printed. I saw no statement in *Contested Will* that there were fixed explicit creative "laws of theater" over this half century. Since theater was evolving so quickly and expressed so variously, then how come to say flatly no playwright in that decades-long torrent of creations ever composed with his own biographical experiences in mind?

And Oxfordians could point out a fundamental self-contradiction in Professor Shapiro's core conjecture. Being irrelevance to play content of any Elizabethan playwright's life experience. *Contested Will* affirms the Stratfordian fundamental premise that Shaxper as a writer was a unique genius among all literary ages. But consequently then, why could not that same uniquely talented innovative genius not have subtly written personally in his own independent style? Because he was such a genius, he go could go "out of the box" of the common run of all other more simply commerce-driven playwrights? Jump ahead of time to come in a century when playwrighting became more overtly personal in expression.

Contested Will briefly examines the first proponent of the 17th Earl of Oxford as being the actual Shakespeare. The candidacy of Oxford initiated via *Shakespeare Identified*, a 1920 biography of Oxford by Mister (no advanced degree) Thomas Looney—

Stratfordians love the name. But in binary choice Oxford's biography is today generally recognized as the only realistic alternative to Shaxper's candidacy.

But I was surprised the discussion in *Contested Will* of Oxford and Looney ("loany") is as cavalier as it is brief. Much of Professor Shapiro's focus in his slim book describes various failed alternate theories of authorship that arose before modern research capabilities developed. Finally he comes to Oxford. Looney's lack of academic pedigree—he is a lowly grade school teacher—is stressed. Professor Shapiro also introduces murky biographical (of all things) background for Looney's possible deeply ulterior political motive in proposing Oxford. This all at the margin I find rather too much suggested over too little importance. Protesting too much, one could say. Ducking the central debate one could say. As usual for reason some Oxfordians say.

Anyway the Oxford origin detective story is engaging for Oxfordians. Looney reported in 1920 that using a modern police department's problem-solving matrix of patterns for intellectual discipline, he read a lot of biographical fact about realistically possible authors. And it became obvious in conclusion that the well-known life story and personality anecdotes as to the 17th Earl of Oxford produce a strong overlay match-up for primary checklist factual attributes within the works of Shakespeare. Which are also entirely absent in what little is factually known of Will Shaxper, other than his extensive strictly non-literary business record.

*

*   *

If this authorship debate sounds tedious, it is not. The object of the subject is the greatest writer the English language has produced. Respect is due for both diametrically opposed and exclusionary candidates.

So pen in hand, I made question marks beside some Stratfordian zingers in *Contested Will*. Here's one: its breezy bit about Shakespeare's *The Tempest* appearing for the first time after early 1604 when that execrable wastrel Oxford died. A famous shipwreck occurred off Bermuda after his death and this is said plain proof that Oxford could not have written *The Tempest*.

This actually is a bit silly. The History Department simply could have pointed out to the English Department that shipwrecks were a constant event throughout the last quarter of the 16th century. And Bermuda centered a trade route. And indeed Oxfordians already have reported that star-crossed Oxford was an investor himself in a commercial ship that sank en route to Bermuda. And *also* Oxford disastrously lost too much impetuously borrowed money in ill-starred ship ventures seeking a Northwest Passage to China. Remember *The Merchant of Venice?* And too call in *Hamlet* where Hamlet tells Polonius/Lord Burghley in real life he is "only mad north by northwest."

Staying with *The Tempest*, Oxfordians also have brought to light that Oxford's son-in-law and literary friend and possibly writing colleague Lord Stanley had an estranged brother named Ferdinand. Lord Stanley's enemy brother Ferdinand was governor of the Isle of Man, offshore which lies an uninhabited small island. So simply there we have the enemy brother Ferdinando of *The Tempest*.

More ties to *The Tempest?* Contemporary letters show that Oxford and Lord Stanley, who was highly educated at Oxford and Gray's Inn law school and had also lived in Italy and France, were both interested in the occult and magic acts. There we have Prospero. A magician is the very essence of a playwright on his island of creativity. Oxford's library was known to contain exotica of occultism.

Despite all the above documented fact, *Contested Will*, which is a quick read for laymen and press reviewers, simply insists that one post-1604 Bermuda wreck definitely proves Oxford did not write *The Tempest* because Oxford died in 1604. Full stop. Well, would a doctoral dissertation committee simply nod with these elements in view?

Professor Shapiro tries also to explain how it is so that in all of Britain with its profuse surviving contemporaneous period correspondence not one single person so much as mentioned that the great William Shakespeare had died in 1616. *Contested Will* seems to offer that Shaxper worked so hard he had no time to make friends. And, dying a dozen years after leaving London to live in Stratford full time, he was somehow forgotten. Even though, Oxfordians point out, Shakespeare plays then remained in London performance. Even though it was an era of formal testimonials to popular writers. For example Ben Jonson and Francis Bacon received dozens of printed memorials.

And I made a question mark at a thoughtful Shapiro observation as to the troubling lack of evidence of any payment ever to Shaxper for writing anything at all, Professor Shapiro suggests this could be explained by Shaxper's ownership of a share in the Lord Chamberlain Men's acting troupe, which brought some but not all Shakespeare plays to performance. Professor Shapiro suggests that Shaxper must have settled accounts as playwright internally with the Chamberlain's and then also its successor troupe on some now lost basis.

Thus suggesting why there are no payment records for even one sold performed play of about 20. And none for the two popularly sold long poems *Venus* and *Lucrece*. But London theatre from 1575 through Shaxper's death in 1616 was serious big business. Modern-type account books were kept and survive; though fire loss must be a possibility. London's dominant theatrical producer Phillip Henslowe maintained extant meticulous records of actor and playwright payments throughout the 1580s and 1590s. In these clear financial records there is no Shaxper or Shakespeare mention at all, among thousands of entries as to playwrights and actors Not all Shakespeare plays were performed by the Globe, some were by Henslowe's theater. And many were produced first at the Court. For which Crown accounting might have evidenced payment to Shakespeare as a playwright, but none such has been found after close search of archives.

Yet Shaxper supposedly retired wealthy in a decade from London playwright success. I found no reference in my research to Elizabethan playwrights getting rich on a few plays, even Ben Jonson had money scrapes late in life. But Shaxper's record is different from hand-to-mouth typical playwrights. From a start in poverty, within just six years of probable arrival in London about 1592 (the year of first publication with the name William Shakespeare) he bought a two-dozen-room landed mansion house in Stratford, bought more land, bought speculative tax collection rights, and later speculatively bought large stores of grain during famine time, for which he was fined by Stratford government. Shaxper had a lending line of business using capital from some source.

Against all these surviving Shaxper financial records, numbering well over 50, it does seem odd there is no extant scrap of record of any payment whatsoever to Shaxper as writer. Since he was supposedly the prolific career author of 20 plays and two long poems that today could be called bestsellers. One might envision bags of coins divided informally, but year after year for over a decade and among evolving troupes and as to different performance venues logically should have produced even indirect extant evidence. And as an Elizabethan real life comparison there is Philip Henslowe's surviving very detailed payee and precise amount accounting books for the same decade from 1592 for a large competing theater to the Globe. Or perhaps every bit of Shaxper's theatrical payments financial records from every source for a dozen years were lost in a fire or otherwise sometime, but this is not addressed in *Contested Will* or seen by me referenced in other research.

But it seem the slim volume *Contested Will* is not interested in lack of records or other awkward historical questions. In dimming daylight I have to bend close to see Professor Shapiro's concluding pages. With obvious sincerity Professor Shapiro urges readers to just sensitively parse Shakespeare texts internally. He strongly insists that is the only way to appreciate their genius.

He observes it is natural for both Stratfordians and Oxfordians to share some degree of our "modern" interest in the markedly different "early modern" author's presence in text.

But finally Professor Shapiro recommends that a general reader not go "astray." Because from scholarly reading he has concluded that in the Elizabethan Age "individuality, motivation, and behavior" mysteriously were not like those categories of thought as they are in our modern age.

Professor Shapiro then says to him personally it is "disheartening" if readers seek identification of a writer other than William Shaxper. Because such curiosity diminishes "the very thing that makes him exceptional: his imagination." Warning that simply to doubt Shaxper's extreme creative genius is a "stark and consequential choice." The concluding statement expresses the

Professor's hope that readers of Shakespeare will not go "astray" from concentration on the Shakespeare texts. Because that "makes a difference as to how we imagine the world in which Shakespeare lived and worked."

Which sure enough it does. Soon so will say Trenton Shakespeare Festival at its opening night.

I have just spent most of a day trying to understand *Contested Will*. I shrug my stiff neck in the Chinese faux gilt faux Louis XV armchair. Somehow the whole Shaksper as Shakespeare rhetoric complex reminds me of medieval Christian religious credo. Both saying the same basically. A miracle occurred. And that miracle was far too long ago to really understand now. It must be simply believed. Thus the interior life of the author of Shakespeare is beyond the mental grasp of mankind today. We moderns are all now like that jackass head Nick Bottom in *Midsummer Night*. That's the character who cannot give an explanation of what he saw dreaming but just happily believes it happened. Bottom. The name Lance gave me as my own thin beard in his sometimes odd sense of humor.

The origin of this kind of magical thought was in desert lands millennia ago, among experts in both hallucination and herd management. But today we moderns know the past is never really past. So. So why cannot past minds be perceived understandably within ours now? For always rationality has existed overarching irrationality. The English Department should ask the Psychology Department down the hall.

The marked up, dog-eared and from Miriam's touch nicely perfumed but rather bitter *Contested Will* falls from my hand to floor. I am tired from reading worried what I will find. But now do feel relieved. In my crash reading of these leading Shaksper stalwarts Professors Greenblatt, Nelson, and Shapiro I have found no fact to hide in writing *The Which*. Nothing to pretend I did not know exists. There really seems to be no contemporaneous documentary proof that Shaxper wrote Shakespeare. If so these bestselling partisans would have red-lettered it in caps.

Now my own task looms. Rather than *astray* Professor Shapiro could have used the alternative word: rogue.

*

*   *

I hate this room and do I need a drink. Mother Mary bring back the vodka quart that it shall comforteth unto me. But somehow after Shapiro's book ends and is closed I cannot move on from my fake gilt fake historical chair. It is not getting any lighter out there in Park Avenue's hard-edged valley of the night shadow. Nor am I.

"Astray."

Astray.

Well. Got it.

I am tense in foreboding. I know I'm about to be personally iron-fisted by the Authorities for daring to write *The Which*. And everybody will look right through Lance's silly thin beard worn as Arch Bottom to ridicule the nobody Harry Haines whose Google already is just sad.

My own future in theater will be stickered by crime-scene-yellow warning tape. By the kind of "literary review" after which in Queen Elizabeth I's time writers did not come back out of the Tower of London alive. Or did, ears lopped off and branded, maybe a writing hand edited off. Professor Shapiro, media darling as an

Authority, warns that to err from orthodox Stratfordism will bring "stark and consequential" response in the reign of Queen Elizabeth II. What part of binary choice do you not understand, Bottom, says the bloodstained Tower Inquisitor.

This moment now I'm looking out my quite temporary window down to the far side of Park at 51st, where Ethan Hawke stalked along filming his controversial modern vision of *Hamlet*. With "matters standing now unknown" about Hamlet's "wounded name," to borrow from Hamlet's last pleading lines, the Shakespeare authorship conflicts have generated a quarreling muddle in world libraries. Even here in the Waldorf suite a hundred contradictory book bodies lie chaotically heaped up high on the neutrally beige carpet.

But history is never done with the past, any more than it will leave alone the present. Some day some way some thing will come to light that today was unseen, unthought, unexpected. Like the crucifix's unexpected shadow that began my journey to compose *The Which*. Some snippet on crumbly letter paper. Some scribbled note on a player's prompt script. Some something elevating the whole world admiring Shakespeare out of present pretty sad fratricidal disputes.

And . . . And . . .

Beyond this Bottom's mind cannot see. My eyes are blinky-strained from reading *Contested Will* straight through, every page.

Now another phrase pops to mind from my university time, this one recalled from law school. I realize *Contested Will* is like a trial lawyer's brief of special pleading. Special pleading is an argument that proceeds before a judge deliberately deleting major facts that are inconvenient to the advocate's asserted conclusion.

Will in the World's specious paralogism just shook hands with *Contested Will's* special pleading. *Monstrous Adversary* claps them both on a shoulder with a snigger.

My head aches now from all this thought. So Harry Haines this ever-flowing deep spring of regrets is now piercingly sorry he gave his quart of Grey Goose to Mother Mary. I need a drink and I need another. But cannot phone down to have Mary bring new vodka. Oh no, not to then see her sad look of a 16th-century Madonna pityingly foreshadowing my painful fate.

There is beer in the kitchen fridge. I do not actually like fizzing bread but it now appeals in this sensory desert. To be sort of neat I pick *Contested Will* up off the floor at my feet. I creakily stand in three stages. Starting across the dark room for the kitchen and a cold one.

And am knocked cold.

*

*   *

It was a short flight. The back of my head landed just after my bottom touched down.

I didn't try to get up. I didn't even cuss. There was nobody to blame but Harvey Weinstein for making the ultra-Stratfordian big box office movie *Shakespeare in Love,* and also whoever it was behind the ultra-Oxfordian low box office film *Anonymous.* And me. For putting one of those DVD disc plastic boxes on top of the other at a sloppy moment. And now walking fast beerward over them in a dim room.

I've struggled too much today. I feel like a nap as long as I look like I'm sleeping anyway. And my head throbs. *Contested Will* is still gripped in my right hand, I raise my skull to make it a pillow. But that volume really is a slim thing. My strained neck wants more pillow so, being in the middle of the dumped chaos of Lance's library suitcase, on my back I reach across the carpet and grab the nearest book to add to my pillow.

Park Avenue never gives up punishing day entirely. My unlit Waldorf room wells from indirect suffusion of the glowing line of sealed towers outside. I see the cover of the book that came to hand. It is important to know with whom one is sleeping. Especially if that may be an exotic encounter.

Oh yes, this next in hand is very fitting to join Shapiro's hardminded book under my head, which you as reader may worry is just now become concussed. *Shakespeare's Lost Kingdom, The True History of Shakespeare and Elizabeth,* is the work of an Eton- and Oxford-educated Englishman, Charles Beauclerk. Who is some sort of descendant of the de Vere family. I quickly read it soon after I came into seclusion here. Now I smile to think what uncomfortable pillowmates these two books will be. Cheek to jowl under my cracked skull.

I place Beauclerk's thick *Shakespeare's Lost Kingdom* on top of Shapiro's book. And now Beauclerk's book opens in recall under my closed eyes. For reading it actually was a bit like hearing Shakespeare talk about his world personally. And of course that indeed is *The Which*'s main tenor.

I did leave Princeton with a master's in English literature after a baccalaureate in same. So to me it jumped out that Beauclerk's upper-class English origin matters a lot in his thinking. This book is distinctly different from Shapiro's American predicate of functionality and assertion of credential, its American pressing linear direction.

Beauclerk seems somehow more instinctively comfortable with the fluid personal and social dynamics of extreme social privilege amid ongoing devolution. And indeed, in plain historical fact, that summarizes Shakespeare's actual year to year-to-year Elizabethan epoch world.

Beauclerk is a detailed, focused historian. This Englishman's generic history wallpaper is minimal. Instead *Lost Kingdom* carefully matches specific Shakespeare texts to much that is known in plain historical fact about the 17th Earl of Oxford. Whom Beauclerk emphatically believes was both Shakespeare and . . . more.

Beauclerk's scholarly biography-based approach is similar to the Oxfordian non-academic American Margo Anderson's soberly and precisely detailed *Shakespeare by Another Name*, published in 2010. The same year as was Shapiro's *Contested Will*. All three of these disputatious books appeared in the same year. That particular voilà is a rather Shakespearean coincidence in the dark comedy category.

Lost Kingdom tries to convey a view of "live" personal relationships among Oxford and various historically known personalities of the unstable and fascistic Elizabethan Court. This articulate study portrays Oxford as a covertly constantly evolving writer. Placing him in focused context with some of his specific late 16th-century contemporaries. This study envisions Oxford and those contemporaries all moving their related lives on personal arcs of four decades. And from deep within this dense shifting sublimated dynamic, so says Beauclerk, came the transmuted spectrum of works known as Shakespeare.

Beauclerk's writing in *Lost Kingdom* does have a similarity to Shapiro's in *Contested Will*. Both read as smooth, confident, lawyerly but entirely one-sided advocacy briefs. Here the English-man in overview keys his brief reader into basic themes of Shake-speare's writing. Synthesizing those themes as returning in the nearly 30 plays again and again, though always costumed differently. Beauclerk summarizes persistent, insistent themes of the writer known as Shakespeare as follows:

Identity. Hidden, mistaken, revealed, always changing a tale dramatically. The author's mind often molds crisis situations of wrongful separation and exile.

Truth. Manipulated, abused, revelation ultimately respected.

Feudal right. Existentially ordained but challenged and often betrayed. Social rank itself is so fascinating to the author that the plays' casts of characters are all royals or nobles . . . plus a few highly colorful commoner slobs for comic relief. In 1901 a scholar observed that Shakespeare cannot imagine even a shipwreck on an atoll with-out a resident King there.

Intense, often confused, sexual roles. Sexy situations for brothers and sisters. Boys pose as girls and girls as boys. Hamlet's obsession with his carnal mother. Lear's daughters' unwomanly aggressions toward their father. Iago's deadly jealous crush on big strong Oth-ello. Cuckolds seared by jealousy. Very often hormonal urgency drives heedless lovers.

Haunting female archetypes. The same two recognizable women are characterized in many varying modes and guises. Poor roman-tic, virtuous, rejected, and abused wife Anne Cecil. And dangerously volatile, unknowable, powerful Elizabeth Tudor.

Beauclerk thus far provides a well-put orthodox Oxfordian view of the man Shakespeare and his works. Typically seeing the plays and poems as richly coded between fantasy and his own expe-rience. But yet these works are so full of common humanity that even today they are not really difficult to understand well enough. Because unlocking their codes comes via factual biography as master key. Oxfordians basically ask of Stratfordians, how far can any reasonable reader go on a journey to best understanding of Shakespeare's works if having, actually just arbitrarily, decreed a principle of only wearing one shoe on this quest?

Now with the two books cushioning my perhaps bleeding head I am drifting off to a nap. With a smile. Thinking of their two authors' mutual disdain to be in bed together, and on top of them some nobody clown of a creative writer named Bottom. It's a good thing these guys Shapiro and Beauclerk do not wear practiced rapiers at the belt of their puffy shorts over gem-colored pantyhose and platform shoes. Because Shapiro's *Contested Will* luxuriates in jeering mockery of Beauclerk's supplemental theory about Oxford. Which is derisively nicknamed by Shapiro as the Prince Tudor Theory.

I'm sleepy, maybe you too. So I will just announce the Prince Tudor Theory now in a nutshell ... nutshell, the way Hamlet put it as to a world profoundly condensed. Or some kind of nut's shell as you can perhaps guess who in the Columbia English Department could put it. Beauclerk suggests that:

THE 17TH EARL OF OXFORD WAS THE ILLEGITIMATE SECRET SON OF QUEEN ELIZABETH. OXFORD WAS BORN OF HER RAPE AS A 14-YEAR OLD BY HER IMMEDIATELY EXECUTED FOSTER FATHER ADMIRAL THOMAS SEYMOUR.

Just breathe slowly some while.

*

* *

God match me with a good dancer.

Much Ado About Nothing

Horatio, I'll take the thousand pounds.

Hamlet

There is a universally known historical context of this Prince Tudor Theory. It is the troubled Tudor effort to continue the very recent upstart royal male line. That of course was of bloodily driving importance all through the reign of Henry VIII.

Crown agents thus would not have been inclined to kill young Elizabeth's male infant in case he might become crucial in the Tudors' next generation lineage. So under PTT, with a disguised later given age, her baby was forced upon the 16th Earl of Oxford, John de Vere, as a secret foster child,

Of copiously documented record John de Vere the 16th Earl was a disorderly eccentric. And was being bullied and predated financially by the Crown. As part of the Prince Tudor Theory the vulnerable secret he knew was later mitigated by wet work Crown agents. Personally unstable but famously robust John de Vere died suddenly at the age of 41.

Under PTT, John's already very estranged wife was threatened not to reveal the foster setup ever, but was also given financial means to instantly marry her underclass lover. Who happened to be a groom in the employ of reputed serial poisoner Robert Dudley. Dudley at the time was Queen Elizabeth's intense lover. Some had trouble remembering she had suddenly made up the title Earl of Leicester and simply gave Bobby a castle of royal scale where she visited in their romance. And despite no reason of family connection or otherwise at all, Elizabeth just also gave Bobby Dudley control over a large portion of the boy Edward de Vere's lands. Which Dudley looted for years. He then renovated his new gift castle at enormous expense.

The Crown brought 12-year-old orphan Edward de Vere from his home in the Earldom's Norman Hedingham Castle in Essex to be educated and monitored in the London household of Queen Elizabeth's power behind the throne lawyer William Cecil, soon promoted to be Lord Burghley. Cecil/Burghley would have legal control over the boy Edward and his wealth for nine years, shared jealously with Dudley/Leicester.

Edward's paid off "mother" never visited him once. Of course Edward heard the rumor of poisoning of his loved "father," the robustly virile theater-loving 16th Earl. Analysts of the relationship of Hamlet and his mother Gertrude have long found it confusingly confused between the characters in different moments. Hamlet is obsessed with his dead father. But he is also obsessed in a deeply wounded way by the sex-driven betrayal of his mother, and her lack of care for him in his distress. Queen Elizabeth, looking at you.

There is linear psychological sense under PTT. Consider *Hamlet*. Understand that Oxford wrote old Hamlet as hapless John de Vere. Gertrude as the sex-crazed Queen. Claudius as Dudley, like a King in his huge gift castle with Elizabeth at his side. Ophelia as 15-year-old Anne Cecil forced upon Oxford by Crown power. And of course Hamlet as the author Edward de Vere. Who in real life was cynically bankrupted for life as prey of Dudley, his legal warden Lord Burghley (Polonius in character), and arbitrary new confiscatory Tudor tax laws serving the predatory Crown's pressing financial needs.

Many generations have wondered why Hamlet is so brooding and resentful. What's wrong with Hamlet? But knowing the keys of biographical correlation, is that at all hard for a modern like you to understand basically? Is Hamlet/Oxford's' experience of inward-ness" in Shapiro's academic jargon really, as *Contested Will* put it, actually "invisible" to you?

Beauclerk delves into the documented unstable relations between Queen Elizabeth and Edward de Vere. Elizabeth being either 14 or 16 years his senior . . . depending, of course. Edward's surviving letters seem to have been severely pruned for posterity to leave only matters relating to relief from his imposed debts and request for some income grant, all frustrated. And his perennially quashed attempts to serve the Crown militarily in de Vere family tradition. Recall the entirely gratuitous *Hamlet* closing line of Hora-tio (proposed as named for Oxford's uncle the general Horace de Vere, since there were no Italians in supposed Denmark) that Ham-let would have become a glorious soldier. Hamlet partly answered the perennial question as to what is wrong with him himself, in a line often not performed or underplayed: "I lack advancement."

But even the business and debt scraps of evidence extant show an unusual relationship to Queen Elizabeth. In those letters Edward's view of the personality of the Queen is intense and stranded, and evolves volatilely. Both Edward and Elizabeth had the broad rep-utation at Court of being, as Hamlet put it, "what a piece of work."

As Court observer correspondence extensively documents, all through his 20s Edward de Vere, bearer of a 600-year lineage title, boisterously acted out as the beau ideal romantic feudal knight. Elizabeth surrounded herself with a Court of beautiful and hand-some young people. Frequent traveling dance parties and elite entertainments were exuberant. Edward was so foremost among favorites in the courtiers' complicated athletic dance steps he was called upon by Elizabeth for command performances, sometimes to music he composed.

Athletic courtiers still dangerously jousted at lavish pageants in honor of ladies, and in Elizabeth's Court that meant Elizabeth. Edward twice won major pageant jousting contests. Very bright Elizabeth could converse in Latin and French with him. De Vere was a famously fluent and witty multilinguist and published translator. Elizabeth's own sense of humor tended to irreverent mockery, and various observers report Edward could be very sharp-tongued at Court. Both drank freely. The Queen nicknamed Edward her "Turk," meaning basically "whattaguy." They quarreled openly due to their similar qualities, as strong mothers sometimes do with head-strong children and as some lovers do.

So Elizabeth had much in common with Oxford. They shared impetuosity, vanity, selfishness, and moodiness. Elizabeth habitually doted on handsome athletic much younger men, and that Edward de Vere was in very real spades. And so, Charles Beauclerk's contextual reasoning concludes, they had sex since that is what sexy people do. Mary Queen of Scotts did write to her cousin Elizabeth, in a chatty note before she knew her head was soon going to be chopped off, that rumor was Edward had publicly refused to sleep with his rejected new wife of arranged marriage so he could get a nonconsummation annulment and marry Elizabeth.

Now you have had your quiet moment. *Shakespeare's Lost Kingdom* sees no evidence either way that Elizabeth knew she was sleeping with her son. Professor Shapiro himself observes vaguely in *Contested Will* that 400-year-old ways of thinking can be opaque today. And anyway author Beauclerk, aristocratic descendant of the de Vere family, is not particularly interested in parsing old elite sex as such. Sexual impulse control historically was a big problem within Elizabeth's Court. Since everybody was always justifiably tense about everything in the world around them. And high and low in society died around age 40, so young pulses beat fast and hot.

Thus Beauclerk is neutral on whether Elizabeth knew or cared she was sleeping with a handsome brilliant young devil also her own love child. Also married to her favorite lady-in-waiting Anne who also is the doted-on daughter of her chief advisor William Cecil then ennobled as Lord Burghley.

Those matters all would be just medium-spicy Tudor soap opera.

Mainline Stratfordians and Oxfordians have agreed that several of Shakespeare's privately intended sonnets seem to be addressed to the teenage 3rd Earl of Southampton. To whom Shakespeare dedicated the 1592 long poem *Venus and Adonis* and within a year the also commercially popular *Lucrece*. But how could Will Shaxper, an under-educated nobody commoner, just very recently in 1592 arrived in London poor from a distant tiny town of 1,000, possibly have come to know the young Earl of Southampton? Southampton was then actually living as a ward within the household control of Lord Burghley, and so hierarchically barriered at the top of strictly policed Elizabethan aristocracy.

Realistically, why would someone like the very common young unknown Will Shaxper dare to send dedications of sexually infused public long poems, and also about 20 private sonnets, to an Earl of the realm presumptuously urging him to get married? After two full centuries of rigorous professional research there is no jot of evidence or inference that Shaxper and the Earl of Southampton ever even met once.

This is an ultimate binary question. Who was the writer of the mysterious and very intimate sonnets?

Stratfordians avoid it like plague. Oxfordians in turn assert strongly that obviously the 40-ish Edward, 17th Earl of Oxford, was dedicator of both the long poems and the early sonnets urging young Southampton to marry. Because demonstrably Oxford very well knew Henry Wriothesley, 3rd Earl of Southampton. Documents plainly show that both Oxford and his father-in-law Lord Burghley had long urged reportedly rather effeminate young Southampton to marry Oxford's sort-of daughter and Burghley's granddaughter, Elizabeth de Vere.

Now comes some more intensely spicy Tudor soap opera background: Oxford had previously disavowed this daughter as a bastard since he had publicly sworn not to sleep with Anne, thus seeking a non-consummation annulment from forced marriage. Though in classic telenovela tradition Oxford years later somehow recovered memory that he did just once bonk Anne drunk at Queen Elizabeth's late 1574 Hampton Court blowout dance party before he sailed away in March 1575 to live in Europe. So four miserable years later Edward and Anne reconciled telenovela style. Of course, sort of, after all that anguish.

Okay. One further step at a time. Some apparently later sequence "Shakespeare" sonnets clearly are addressed to a young man by a middle-aged man. To some mainline readers of both the Stratfordian and the Oxfordian persuasion it does seem the aging poet somehow jumped psychological track from urging procreational marriage. And went over to his own gay flirting with the same "fair youth." In this framework Oxfordians fill in the sonnets' blank names biographically as Oxford and young Southampton.

Naturally, ubiquitous Crown spies knew about Oxford's private sonnets. As well as his previously anonymously issued early form plays from the 1570s on, which tended to move from private Court performance to large public theaters. The always volatile populace likes all these history and romantic plays. So Elizabeth and the Crown advisors are dismayed hearing in the late 1580s of this dangerous relationship turn of Oxford and young Southampton. Which risked their execution as homosexuals in a climate of increasing grim Puritan censures and punishments.

Thus one easily guesses preemptive Crown action cracking down on both the aging roué Oxford and sexually ambiguous young Southampton. So it would be that the loose cannon Oxford consequently was threateningly forbidden by the Crown to ever publish in his own name. And then too, as is well documented, Oxford was emphatically dropped from personal public engagement with the Queen at Court. His requests to join the Privy Council and Order of the Garter as a senior nobleman were denied repeatedly. Requests for Crown grace lucrative financial favors repeatedly denied. Requests for military service denied. Debt relief denied. That was the situation approaching 1590 and Oxford close to 40 years of age.

Oxford's renegade's social exile from Court had begun far back in the 1570s when Oxford journeyed to Europe without permission and was immediately angrily recalled by the Crown. He left again in 1575 with the Queen's permission. That permission to travel may well have arisen from Oxford's usefulness as a quasi-spy on European Catholic powers due to his very unusual foreign language skills and social rank at highest social level in French and Italian kingdoms. In a bit over a year Oxford came home after a wildly profligate spree in Italy.

Though still spending freely to support professional author friends and an acting troupe, Oxford by the late 1580s was defaulting massive compounding debt owed both to the Crown and personally to powerful greedy Lord Burghley.

By then Oxford also previously for four years had scandalously renounced his wife, Lord Burghley's doted-on only daughter Anne. He was an explosively witty man, drinking freely and sometimes fantasizing on sensitive political topics. Dangerous figures at Court came to dislike him. Thick spy report dossiers delivered to the top of the Crown had piled up.

About then there was another widely gossiped episode. Where but for the Queen's exasperated intervention Oxford, senior Prince of England, would have dueled with poet Sir Phillip Sydney over a mere tennis court booking time quarrel. In front of gaping French spies. The commoner Sydney, in another telenovela twist, previously had been thwarted in his proposal to maiden Anne due to Lord Burghley's ambition to establish noble lineage by her marriage to the very reluctant but forced Earl of Oxford. Oxford rejected unwanted teenage wife Anne to her great distress. Sydney was a famous war hero and Oxford had been rejected from military service. Sydney, tall and courteous, was a respected private writer and Oxford—frustratingly for him—not. So across that tennis court at the Greenwich palace there was dark matter in play

Oxford's reputation and enemy troubles get darker as he aged. The Earl not once but twice impregnated one of Elizabeth's ladies-in-waiting. For that second time Oxford and the young woman and her infant were briefly jailed in the Tower by the furious Queen. Then more public gossip fodder circulated. Oxford was permanently crippled by a groin wound in a wild ambush street fight with that deflowered maiden's outraged uncle. Montague/Capulet violence comes to mind. Though like many Shakespeare maidens the lady involved had quite a will and mind of her own. And nerve plenty, since that single mom fired by the Queen was soon happily married to another Earl.

But for Oxford all gets darker still. Staying alive became evermore dangerous for him. Ubiquitous Crown spies reported that at dinner parties he repeatedly drunkenly imagined royal succession scenario possibilities. Keeping company with recusant Catholics who were also secret foreign agents. French spies are documented reporting back to HQ in Paris that it seemed Oxford could be rolled as a Catholic sympathizer. Which could have meant his death as a traitor. The crown was merciless as to Catholic takeover plot involvement.

There was even more. Oxford up to his late 30s was definitely a Shakespearean-type hell raiser. Think of one man who wrote the characters of both Falstaff and Prince Hal. And who possibly did know that he was the hidden, denied Prince Tudor. Multiple documents show that Oxford sometimes dangerously embellished his flowing signature with little royal—not the proper ducal—crown dots.

Bonded as they were, in what might even be seen as maternal patience and forbearance as years went on, Queen Elizabeth steadily protected Oxford from foreseeable Crown agent crackdowns. After the perpetual bankrupt had been thoroughly ostracized among other courtiers the Queen in 1588 voluntarily provided him with a very comfortable annual pension of £1,000, that is a small fortune—just under $500,000 American today. It was granted unreachable by creditors of Oxford's colossal permanent indebtedness, though it was revocable at the Queen's discretion any calendar quarter. Remarkably, the notoriously tightwad Elizabeth continued her annual payments of this small fortune for no stated purpose for 14 years unbroken until her own death.

And the Queen herself also arranged a marriage for controversially wayward Oxford with an intellectually accomplished and thoroughly sane mature woman from her impressive corps of fetching ladies-in-waiting. That marriage did click well. The two aristocratic intellectual kindred bohemian spirits, Lord Edward de Vere and Lady Elizabeth Trentham clearly liked each other.

Documents report mister and missus even went to taverns together. But often to the Saint George and not to the Mermaid, perhaps because as Yogi Berra would say it was so crowded nobody went there anymore. They had a son and named him Henry outside de Vere naming tradition. When grown up, Henry de Vere formed a close friendship with youngish uncle-age Henry Wriothesley, Earl of Southampton. The two Henrys together went to the Netherlands to join a military campaign against Spanish occupiers. Where they both died tragically pointlessly.

All taken together Oxford, in permanent but financially well subsidized and domestically stable internal exile from further Court life, thus was set free to secretly write and revise for nearly the last two decades of his life. In intense matured focus. Like a writerly evolved Prince Hal become King.

As Hamlet shouts to Horatio in one of his very few emotionally positive lines, "I'll take the thousand pounds." "Horatio" being Oxford's jokey nickname for his beloved Uncle Horace de Vere. And just so, Milord, say Oxfordians, that was a very good deal you accepted from the Queen as she saved your trouble-inclined neck.

Okay, it's been quiet a while. Charles Beauclerk, freelance intellectual, urges that the world consider a further possibility. In London's Dulwich Gallery there is a mysterious portrait of Elizabeth standing on a huge map of just Oxfordshire in a shapeless robe thick at the middle, her face full. Her finger pointing in the direction of Southamptonshire.

Beauclerk goes on to boldly assert that there may well have been a second unacknowledged Prince Tudor, that being the Earl of Southampton. Fathered by the Queen's lover the Earl of Oxford. And thus, in a newly interesting soap opera twist, the close personal intimacy of the sonnets addressed to a younger man would not root in eros. The loving sonnets would speak from a narcissistic poet's heart, as an aging father seeing his perpetuated self in the young man. Speaking in wistful self-love.

And under PTT theory, in this hidden relation Queen Elizabeth had good reason to commute Southampton's death sentence for participating in the Essex Rebellion, though all others were quickly executed. Oxford was very energetic in seeking the pardon. PTT also notes that the day Oxford died Crown agents sealed and searched his home and that of Southampton and colleagues. Southampton and his friends were jailed overnight in the Tower. But released next day. No explanation for this event has survived. Beauclerk might say that the Crown spies found no evidence of a possible Prince Tudor claim to the throne in this aftermath of Elizabeth's death. So okay for Southampton.

Mainline Oxfordians themselves are mostly silent about Beauclerk's multiple royal bastard theories. Though certainly family trees of centuries of royal houses of Europe produced profusely many bastard offspring. Subterfuge was in the aristocracy game.

I'm not sure about either of Beauclerk's PTTs. Actually I myself am really doubtful. Magical thinking is not easy for me. I don't understand the Stratfordian cult wishful contra-factual insistence around the Shaxper icon, try as I do.

But I have seen the big Dulwich painting myself. What was the Queen thinking in commissioning it? It does not flatter her at all as usual. In a shapeless bedroom type robe without makeup she's suddenly fat or pregnant. The Queen's facial expression is distant from the viewer's eye as if gazing to another time. One explanation is my own, reluctantly. I came up with this, that having no Tudor successor in sight by her age, then Elizabeth had the painting of her pregnant pointing toward Southampton as a possible trump card for his succession if the succession matter arose for him. Unless she changed her mind in the future. And apparently she did. For the future brought a kind of dementia upon Elizabeth in which while slowly dying the Queen forbade any discussion in Britain of her successor ... on pain of execution as a traitor. And so, the Queen dying bats in belfry, the Southampton-as-Tudor trump card was never played. It just went to storage. Of no interest to Stratfordians, as so much Oxfordian scholarship is of no interest to their narrow insistence.

My head now aches. I close eyes for restful dark. I decide it is probably better for *The Which* to stick with the Oxfordian fixed menu, already full for "the uninformed." Rather than go à la carte further into Beauclerk's intellectually exotic dishes.

I suppose. But what do I suppose Shakespeare himself would do with the Double Tudor Prince Theory? He would not be too busy to even consider. One can guess in his usual mode he would pull plausible deniability into a plot framework of some old European play or novel. Of course setting the cover in neverland nowhere. And in deceptively gorgeous dialogue let fly his own personal very deeply obsessive themes of denied legacy, hidden identity, exile, wrongful treatment . . . and ultimate dreamy happy revelation. The expression always slanted and always still dangerous among enemies and inimical social forces. Oxford sailed very close to the Crown wind sometimes. But was protected by his very cleverness. He would hide cleverly writing *The Which* today. Wasn't that actually what the Delphic actress warned me to do in our heartbreak talk at the foot of the Central Park Shakespeare statue?

Contested Will and *Will in the World* keep the existential circumstance of Shakespeare simple. The orthodoxly envisioned young Shaxper simply rapidly flows out an immensity of wonderfully inspired paper. Quietly steadily competent craftmanship like one of those anonymous workaholic lawyers out there across Park Avenue. And then, friendlessly unnoticed by all the world at The End, despite all the fame of William Shakespeare the author, Professor Shapiro's super-genius Will Shaxper silently ascends a high-towering staircase. Straight into Literary Heaven. Did anyone ever say you get the Shakespeare you deserve?

*

* *

I am awake in my Tower cell staring up to ceiling. Cell, cell phone. There is M in contacts.

Of course she does not pick up, being off with the fairies. "Miriam, thank you for the fish. It was delicious. I could tell you caught it yourself.

"I'm going to go talk to the Shakespeare statue in the Park an hour from now. At nine o'clock. I . . . hope you will come. And we can talk. Maybe come dressed as Lulubelle? I know you didn't like being my Ophelia. But you know I . . . you do . . . I . . . . Please come. Nine o'clock. Miriam, I hurt."

The ceiling is as responsive.

225 • Part Five

Next it's Room Service, very responsive. I tell them to send a bag of eight airplane bottles of vodka to the front doorman to hold for me. Do not send Mary to deliver. Where I'm going a big bottle would get me busted.

And so I come out of the elevator wearing my Hamlet doublet over a murdered rapper T-shirt I should have sent to housekeeping laundry. The usual lobby man has my envelope. I commence putting the bottles in doublet pockets. Three in the jeans back pocket which I have to remember sitting.

The doorman looks great in his gold braid uniform. And knows it, you almost can see a line of ribbon medals for good conduct if not valor. As I'm deploying the little bottles, "Mister Bottom you know there is quite a bit of . . . would it be fur . . . on your jacket?"

"Doublet, it's called a doublet. And my cat is called Star. Or she was last I heard."

"And your friend named Lulubelle, will we be seeing her here again?"

Looking at the golden revolving door fast a-spin, after three beats Lance's style, I am looking away saying, "Not sure I ever saw her." This is not corny if said with a bitter edge. I do do a good Humphrey Bogart.

Spun out onto empty dimmed Park Avenue I head up toward my interview with Shakespeare. Crossing 53rd I see the little house-wide slot of Paley Park is empty. And turn into its sanctuary, unscrewing a bottle cap as I walk. The back wall waterfall sound is soothing. My first little vodka goes down about as fast as the water falls. The second bottle follows but in slower motion. What a mess.

Who is weirder to be Shakespeare? It can only be one of two men in all history's span. Willie Shaxper a rough small business-man with untutored explosively spectacular easy literary genius? Or

Eddie Oxford, Queen Elizabeth's secret love child by teen rape, who knocked his mom up with another secret love child, but who bipolar jerk that he was labored hard and many years long in secret exile to achieve difficult spectacular literary genius? The waterfall seems to be speaking. As incoherently as comfortingly.

This is a good space Mr. William Paley gave to Manhattan. As founder of the mighty CBS network he perceived people's need to be enlivened by mental energy. There ensued thousands on thousands of filmed programs of all kinds, from tragic through hilarious. So many creations over nearing a century that all played together would sound just like Paley's waterfall here.

I've got to slow down, but open a third bottle because this is near insight. Each CBS show in the myriad was written by a paid specific person or persons. The most excellent to the most inane. But in a television show's moment nobody among hundreds of millions of people viewing cared to know the name of the hack script writer. And then very soon after the moment, the next generation had no time for the shows themselves.

The waterfall will not stop. And that does not matter.

Professor Shapiro reports there were about 6,000 plays performed in England from the time of Elizabeth's coronation until a century later. Of which 600 are known to have been printed.

But who today has seen any performance from the germane period 1570 to 1616 except by Shakespeare? Maybe at most a Marlowe or a Jonson. But the former is emptily mean-spirited and the latter basically just cute.

Otherwise, from all those thousands of smart writers who got their stuff performed for audiences, there remains only Shakespeare to reside deep in our hearts.

Indeed there was and is magic in whoever was the Shakespeare author. Questioning about that magic is spelled *The Which of Shakespeare's Why.*

*

*   *

I am walking up Madison. If you call floating walking. And at 58th Street am stopped like a shoulder tap by a shop window. Sermonetta sells fine Italian gloves, of the kind Eddie Oxford bought in Venice for his maybe mom maybe lover the Virgin Queen Elizabeth. But coming home Dutch pirates in the Channel captured him and took everything, beaching him naked under a shirt at a Dover cliff, exactly as happened in *Hamlet.* That episode is not in any source play Shakespeare drew upon, and there were no Elizabethan newspapers.

Professor Shapiro of course immediately jumps up in his classroom insistently tut-tutting. For that incident could have been heard about in chat of the jolly Will Shaxper buddies bellied up at the goode olde Mermaide Taverne. The same way Shaxper just orally sponged up his obscure European geography, protocol of Italian noble courts, replete botany, precise law, sophisticated medicine, untranslated Italian and French books, and elite field sports. The Mermaid bar must have been roaring unlike any bar ever.

I am staring at an elbow-long cherry red pair of gloves centered in the window. A woman's graceful form seems to wave. The right hand opens palm up and reminds me that Will Shaxper's illiterate bankrupt dad made gloves. I've read the late 17th-century gossip that teenage Will, brief years of rural rote lesson schooling over, was made to slaughter animals for his dad's shop's skins. That would be before prolonged Warwickshire economic depression and plague ended demand for new gloves. That being about 1592 when Will jumped town to escape a strained knocked-up-shotgun marriage, leaving destitute three kids who remained illiterate all their lives. Whose food debt from then he would refuse to pay even years later and grown wealthy.

These thin soft Sermonetta gloves are witchy. Now the right hand gracefully turns its own palm up and open. And I recall Feste's famous line in *Twelfth Night*: "A sentence is but a thin glove to a good wit. How quickly the wrong side can be turned outward."

Stratfordians thronged at their end of the Mentale Mermaide Taverne long bar gleefully shout: "See, Harry, you see right there Shaxper the glove maker's son did have life experiences, this one sentence proves it! Gloves he knew. Case closed."

But immediately an Oxfordian presses in from the bar's other end of the perpetual professorial argumentative scrum in the Mentale Mermaide. So it is I am told that upon Oxford's looting by pirates on his way home from Europe, which incident he interjected gratuitously outside source predecessors into *Hamlet*, fancy gloves he bought in Venice as a gift for the Queen were lost. But Court records show he procured a replacement and did present them to her in a 1576 Christmas gift exchange. An extant contemporary letter noted Elizabeth wore them often, saying she especially liked their unique scent. She is wearing fancy Italian-style gloves in that suggestive Dulwich portrait beloved of the PTT set. The Oxfordian to my ear: "Gloves Oxford knew. Real as it gets. Fact kissing fact. That's what we Oxfordians do."

I go in to buy them for Miriam. The young woman clerk has the same lovely form, the gloves will fit. I suppose in some other life this lithe beauty across the counter would fit too. She's dark as Calabria prefers not a temperamental blonde. I can tell she likes my Hamlet doublet but won't say so, just the gypsy eyes do. She's reading me silent as I stand. Probably guessed my cat's name from the fur on me. A Henry James kind of gal, with whom you can wordlessly exchange chapters of knowing. She's here in the moment selling gloves temp. Doubtless another drifted humanities major. But now as I do, from my flaw getting fatal, I turn away right back out into uncaring wide world.

I cross over 58th to Fifth. It's only 20 to nine. The Pulitzer Fountain's tourist pigeons have all flown to hotel roosts. The whole of Grand Army Plaza is pretty empty, not a Stratfordian or Oxfordian in sight. I've been clicking through Google. The whole of Central Park ahead of me out there turns out to be a patchwork temple of Shakespeare worship going on for over 150 years. It's not just that 1870 towering Mall statue dominant in his SM tight leather.

Additionally in 1880, when plans were made for erecting the 3,500-year-old 70-foot granite Cleopatra's Needle obelisk behind the Metropolitan Museum, it seemed a good idea to put in its foundation the complete works of Shakespeare. Sealed inside a time capsule so The Future would not assume we just watched CBS reruns in America.

And too since the 1960s the open-air free-admission Delacorte Theater has produced Shakespeare plays attended by over three million people. The feudal setting of most of Shakespeare's imagining is enhanced by a looming Elsinorish stone folly castle also built during the 1870s Bardolatry fad.

And too westward over near Central Park West came the four-acre Shakespeare Garden. Lovingly planted with all 200 or so flowers and bushes named in his plays and poems, complete with some quotes on bronze plaques.

So, even putting the massively powerful and restrictive Stratfordian educational industrial complex aside, one does not lightly mess with Shakespeare in tough but surprisingly sentimental New York.

I'm killing a little time and it's killing me back I suppose. So sitting on the Pulitzer Fountain's ridge, where Zelda and a probably reluctant but besotted in love Scott once upon a 1920s time decided to take a drunken swim, I open and reflectively sip down another little bottle. Vodka taken slowly enough is not alcoholic. Being a male animal I like the way young women walk along 59th Street and sometimes scamper as the traffic lights go yellow. Shoot me.

Of course I am hoping one will appear and be Miriam on the way to see me and really talk beside the Shakespeare statue. Frankly. So she'll probably tell me she just came from good sex with either Lance or Lester or both, or her Ophelia understudy. It is not good to get mixed up with actresses. All the actors say so, so shoot them too. Miriam would have Henry James fleeing away down a street fast as portly allows. I myself even dodge semi-employed humanities majors with gypsy eyes.

*

*   *

The paving around Shakespeare's dim statue is still a Miriam-free zone.

Did you ever notice how after four vodkas statues start to wiggle a little? Are not so existentially rigid and actually offendingly self-assured?

Of course I've Googled. This bronze statue patinaed since installation in 1872 is superior in every way that a Shakespeare fan could hope. Eight-foot-tall guy looking down super-intelligently from a high granite plinth. Hollywood handsome with a size XL forehead dome. No shabby cloth doublet, not for a genius. All Prada-quality leather, from cape and doublet to jeans that must have taken a half hour to wriggle onto soccer player legs. You can tell he's real big hung and always stiff as bronze.

It's best, vodka knows, to quickly take the offensive arguing with statues. I walk up close and turn my phone's flashlight to Shakespeare's over-confident face. The sculptor probably called it his mien.

"You know, I have seen a drawing of the bust you paid to have installed in your little poky Stratford little poky church. Where you got buried without anybody in all of Britain and Europe noticing you died. Though you are now fairy-taled as the famous literary superstud of the Elizabethan Age." I play the cold white beam across the grave graven mien. "Dude you have had some amazing work done on your looks.

"The guy who you paid to carve your actual original funerary bust had no reason to lie, you were a well known businessman in a very small town. He shows you grimly clutching a big full sack of wool or grain. Because in the period people's little graveside monuments often recorded their economic and social identity. You were actually a commodities dealer with side hustles some sleazy.

"But long after your bust portrait went up on the church wall, well after the ignorant genius Will as Saint Shakespeare cult had got rolling, some fan boy country parson and fan boy actor decided to have a mason turn the inventory sack into a satin pillow with a paper on it and stick a clownishly big writing plume in the hard fist you used on debtor deadbeats. Just the thing for writing on a pillow.

"However, your real time original grave bust was sketched by a famous historian. It still exists printed in books anybody can see today. You are scowling unattractively. So the dreamy silly local parson, who was of course professionally adept with just absolutely made-up stuff, had some local mason plaster over a new alternative face. Neutral, very neutral. Mark Twain said your face on the frontispiece of the collected works volume looks like a pig's bladder but is obviously a mask. And so is this silly fan's banal dream of you as smirky pie-face.

"Anyway, here in New York your sculptor was commissioned to give the 19th-century Shakespeare cult—the bardolators people called them—what they expected. That sculptor did, he did more. He gave them Superman before Superman."

Now I'm looking up at this face looking down at me. Me who Shakespeare would cast as some clown, I suppose, not a Hamlet. The look up there in my iPhone beam is steely as bronze gets. It says, "I am what I was sculpted to be."

It's hard to wrong-foot a statue but I try. "You know, since you know everything, your connection to the assassination of Abraham Lincoln is pretty ironic. Funds to pay for your fantasy creation here were raised in a special Manhattan performance of your play *Julius Caesar*. Featuring John Wilkes Booth, but with his dad and brother really starring, so young John just got to be Brutus. Then within months of that *Julius Caesar* performance John the flawed black sheep son contemptibly shot the very great Abraham Lincoln from behind in a theater box. And jumped to the stage inanely shouting some Brutus line from *Caesar* about killing tyrants. Breaking his leg, lifetime loser that he was.

"Well, voilà irony. Your fanboy sculptor John Quincy Adams Ward was commissioned at the same time to make both you and the

Lincoln figure for his Washington memorial. You could have made one of your biting comedies of that crossover of fate."

There is no Miriam. Nobody. Just me and all my thoughts this past month writing *The Which*. I turn off my iPhone light. My thoughts too grow darker.

"Actually you are a Stratfordian aren't you? Rigidly superior contemptuous attitude. Sold on and selling a perfect figurehead though lacking any record as even being literate much less a very prolific creative author. Questions of troubling biography just airily disregarded if not mocking the Oxfordian scholar ad hominem."
aHamlet and sHamlet and so th

I'm showing stress as well as vodka, aren't I?

That's a footstep coming behind me. Tentative, as if sneaking up. Miriam's listening with her secret ear for character. Mine.

*
*   *

Miriam will hear my Hamlet as she never has. And then we actors will speak as we never have.

Without turning to face her I raise an arm out straight, slowly holding the little bottle high. Like Lance back at our beginning when he had his inspiration wearing old Hamlet's cape in the mother superior's office, and stuck out his cellphone to call. Here now I contemplate the empty bottle glinting like our prop-chest Yorick's skull.

Now having let the pose build for my audience of one sweetheart, I let my heart flow.

"I want *everything!* Beauclerk may be wrong. But so what? To dream is the mind's best life. Dreams make art of the body's brief time. Was Shakespeare not a man? Shakespeare's own physical life flows like light fused within all his imaginations. Gilds their beams brighter the more deeply seen.

"So *yes!* I can understand Oxford was the secret child of raped teenage Queen Elizabeth.

"*Yes!* I can understand that years later Oxford, knowing his parentage or not, slept with his sexually hysterical mother Elizabeth the Virgin Queen. Which produced another secret baby also fostered to an Earl's family. And that baby became the Earl of Southampton who so obsessed Oxford.

"*Yes!* At last I can understand Shakespeare's obsessive pathos of a denied rightful kingdom. Am able at last to explain the latent anger in all Shakespeare's ironic comedy.

"And . . ."

"**Freeze! Drop the weapon.** Raise your other arm. And for God's sake *shut up.*" The Outer Borough voice is heavy and hairy.

"Who are you?"

"Police. You confess to defacing the statue and it goes easiah."

"I didn't deface it. I poured a libation of vodka at its feet. On them accidentally."

"Ah fuck! You nuts ought to get light-up badges."

"No. You don't understand. I'm an actor. I was practicing with the Shakespeare statue."

"Don't move." A strong flashlight is on me, a spotlight actually. The beam wavers as a buzzer sounds and the cop pushes a button to answer.

"Yeah, G. Got another 7. Fuckin convention of them out tonight in duh full moon. This one's foaming at the mouth. Yeah, back me up. 10-4."

"I was just saying lines from a play I'm writing."

"Ain't we all. Keep the arms up, weirdo."

Headlights come in fast off the Mall. It's one of those midget cars a cheap watch maker talked a desperate car company into producing. Since immediate deaths driving them on a highway ruined demand, New York City swung a bargain deal to use them as pedestrian area patrol cars.

The backup cop car stops 30 feet from me, lit by the cop's flashlight beam. My life of quiet failures has not involved police encounters. So no young woman cop encounters. They do look pretty cool with all the macho stuff on their hips. This one jumps out of the car athletically. It flashes she knows judo stuff. Her chest is a bit flat but you can't have everything. And it might be an NYPD issue armored sports bra thing, I am considering . . .

The new one, completely unfeminine, "Keep the arms up."

"I didn't do anything."

The guy cop behind me. "He's a 7. Check what he did to the feet."

She walks over to look, not a bit of sway. Except her wicked looking baton.

"Nothing. It's just wet on the shoes. Too high to pee on them. No smell."

I say to her, "Officer I just poured a little vodka out like I was having a drink with Shakespeare."

From behind me heavy hairy old Brooklyn: "Ah *fuck!* It nevah ends."

She's 15 feet away. Looking at me like a scientist to a lab rat. "Why do you think Shakespeare would like to have a drink with you?"

Heavy hairy: "Deb, attempted defacement. There's a bulge in his hip pocket. See if it's a spray can."

"Arms stay up, buddy." She comes around me and pats the hard bulge hard. My three full airplane bottles clink a little. She calls to the flashlight, "He's clean Harry. Just a zero here."

And to me, "What's your name?"

"Harry."

"Don't play, guy. Really."

"Really. But not when I have a role as an actor. Or writer."

"You do Shakespeare?"

Radio of the cop behind me crackles loud. "G on." Listens two beats. "Oh for sweet fuck's sake." Listens. "I'm on the way. 10-4." To Deb, "Another zonker at fuckin wacko Trump's fuckin rink. Farewell, Deb. See you strollin through dah Park some fuckin midnight real soon."

Now Deb and I and Shakespeare are in the dark together and very apart. I have nowhere but the Waldorf to go, Miriam of course has not come in my hour of need. I say, "Actually I'm playing Hamlet now."

"So we gathered."

"Really. For the Trenton Shakespeare Festival."

"Trenton, *New Jersey?*"

"Yes. But not quite. We don't have any money to get started. But I'm writing something that will fix that."

I can feel her eyes on me. It doesn't feel coppy. "You do stand-up too?"

"Not intentionally. But I can sing and dance if it comes to that."

Not a coppy laugh. "Well, I like Shakespeare. I get in a lot up at the Belvedere since I'm on Park patrol."

"I was talking to Shakespeare's statue about revealing who he really was."

Silence.

"I just read 20 books in a month about the mystery."

"I didn't know Shakespeare did mysteries."

"So you do stand-up?"

"I do cop, Harry. And sane."

"Well I do sane too, Deb. It's a long story for now. But knowing about the guy behind Will Shaxper, who was just his beard, makes all the plays more profound."

Silence.

I add, "If you know what to look for."

Not copy: "Shakespeare's great enough. Real great in this world. Why screw it up with *Inside Edition* on CBS stuff?"

Now my turn for silence. Almost everybody thinks that way. And I'm basically a hack in this for the money. So how sure can I be of pleading my case?

The cop voice tone has left the Park as she says, "I don't want a lot of tittle-tattle between me and Shakespeare's genius words. I just like to feel the guy's big intellect come straight in. Like you know what."

I do know what. This is the new kind of frankness I've found in young women, not just actresses. Though it's getting hard to remember getting hard.

So I do frank and sane. After looking over next to Shakespeare, where New York City some day might add a statue of Professor Shapiro riding shotgun for the dream here. He would be also clad all in biker leather, Shapiro's minatory forefinger raised and perpetually LED-illuminated

In my real sane tone: "Yeah Deb. That's been troubling me. But it's my writing job to do. With it I'm trying to save my acting troupe from disappearing like a closed play."

"So people can take or leave your crap ideas. Free country. That's cool."

I cannot see her face to like it. But I do. "Ah. I like to talk to you. Would you like to have tea with me at the Waldorf some time?"

Old kind of frankness. "My husband would not like that at all."

Silence.

"Good luck, cowboy."

Soon Deb's high-concept Swatch cop car will drive up along the western side of the Park's Inner Loop. She will pass by the Shakespeare Garden. Home to 220 tagged plants specifically named in Shakespeare's works. Deb will not be troubled by any CBS *Inside Edition* tittle-tattle about how the 17th Earl of Oxford grew up as a ward inside an estate property with the most extensive horticultural garden in England. So no slowdown to consider that teenage Oxford's also resident tutor wrote the outstanding botanical treatise of the Elizabethan era. Why should Deb care to know that Shaxper's family was fined by Stratford for turning their house's front yard into just their dung heap, a flower on it doubtful.

None of this matters to Deb cruising past the Shakespeare Garden looking for suspicious doing under cover of dark.

They're just plays, anyway.

*

*   *

Four days later I finished the concluding scene of *The Which of Shakespeare's Why*. Scholars see signs that Shakespeare wrote some characters with particular Elizabethan actors in mind. Of course. For instance Harry Haines could be looking back on Ethan Hawke. And Lance Gulliver on Mark Rylance.

So when I wrote my character Horatio's revelatory fulfilment of Hamlet's dying plea for recognition, I envisioned Iz Mocha. Horatio's lines to be spoken in easy old man-of-the-world irony, the trademark tone of Iz the theatrical agent.

My final scenario has Horatio and Hamlet's murdered dad play out together to resolve Hamlet's plea as to "things standing thus unknown." Speaking out from the stage's precipitous edge in front of the fallen curtain. Speaking in frankness far beyond the play's walls. Piercing the theater's fourth wall straight out to Deb in row Q, armed in her Shakespeare assumption as in her police uniform.

I like this Which's epilogue, the idea came from Puck's final address in Midsummer. Both are fair in frankness. Because any cop can see that from beginning to end Oxford's life, like his soul twin Hamlet's life, was under deadly threat of one kind or another. Shakespeare's play Hamlet started with one covered up murder. And ended with another, the victim gasping for a cop's truth.

So the Hamlets and Horatio feel their author's pain. Are it. To be seen by the seeing.

I emailed my draft just to Lance for his comment. That most easy rider of directors told me he liked it. Particularly my suggested master key, borrowing from Charles Beauclerk, as to Shakespeare's noted inability to portray parent and child in a normal relationship. Or portray a contented husband and wife.

This hallmark of many of the plays and sonnets makes immediate sense if you know that the author in his own life, until his last few years, actually experienced nothing normal as to close family relations. Oxford and thus Shakespeare just did not know how to portray normality.

And so too the pervasive distress over identity in most of Shakespeare's works makes resonating sense. Over and over a principal character's identity is lost. It is confused. It is hidden. It is exchanged. It is redeemed like a dream sequence. All that is newly understandable soon as realized coming from a displaced, alienated writer too highly intelligent to be obvious.

Lance green-lighted my last act and epilogue of *The Which*. But then paused me. He added that I am going to have to alter somewhat for something big breaking from an Omniconal hot discovery. And so told me not to email *The Which's* concluding moment scenes to our cast until we have talked through how to express it.

This awaited news will break in two days at an afternoon Omniconal interview and press conference, to be held onstage at Radio City Music Hall. Telling me this Lance paused long enough for four thoughts. I need to be there. But the press must not know I am *The Which's* author. First must come the blockbuster Omniconal revelation in its own spotlight day. Then two weeks later our surprise play showcasing it will debut.

So Lance said, after another pause, just come in disguise. Laughing, added, "Come in drag if you want. Shakespeare would have written your role that way. Otherwise Valerie and her sidekick might recognize you in the audience and get awkward."

Two months writing in an empty room. I do need a laugh now that I have finished Horatio's report to the unsatisfied of four centuries. I call Room Service and ask that Mary come up. For special laundry I have. True enough.

"Joyous peace and plenty of our Lord, Mary. It's good to see you again."

"Yes, Mr. Bottom. The staff heard about your bag of little bottles. I'm sorry."

"Thank you. It's hard for me to stay on the straight and narrow. But I have been preying."

"Oh good. I'll pray for you."

"And you can do something else to help me. I have to go to a kind of party in two days dressed as a woman. And one of your dresses would fit me. Could I please borrow one? I was thinking of navy. No flowers anyway. Could we do that as friends?"

"I cannot have sex with you, Mr. Bottom. I am a married woman. But thank you for thinking of me."

Typical sex nut religious nut. As she radared, I do like her. And I have instantly radared to myself that for this holy Mary the devilish Waldorf-rich boy with his drunken orgy potential radiates fascinating temptation. But this is serious career business for me, and serious risk for her biblical-scale conscience.

"And I thank you, Mary. But you don't have to take your dress off. I just meant for you to lend me one for a day. Also, could you buy me a wig? I was thinking black below the shoulder to hide my neck muscles."

The sex maniac is looking at my neck muscles like I said my cock.

"Mary?"

"Oh. Oh. But don't get a shiny barrette. Please."

"You're in charge Mary. Get me the rest of the outfit you want to see me in. How about I give you a thousand dollars cash now, and you keep the change. Okay?"

She adores sexiness. "I am a married woman. And I certainly could not take a lot of money from . . . *you*." Last word soft.

"Mary I would have to go out and shop myself. Shoes alone cost hundreds. The money is about the same I would spend without you.

The rest is just fair payment for your business-like assistance in my business affair."

"What affair?"

Hopeless. "I have to appear incognito to see a theater show. About Shakespeare."

Shakespeare did it. "Oh."

It's easy for me to be not sexy. "So we're all set, Mary?"

Not her. "Okay. I'll take the money to help your affair." She's looking at me now woman to woman. "What bra cup do you want?"

"Whatever you have."

"Thank you. Okay. I'll give you my black lace one. Some girls need fillers for C but I don't. I'll get you silicone."

"You are what a woman should be, Mary."

"Please don't."

"I understand. Thank you, my lady."

*

*   *

I pull my downloaded Omniconal pass from my lilac-perfumed handbag. Feeling like a football center in kitten heels but know I do look enough like a refrigerator-body matron. Mary was more creative with the wig swirls than I wanted. But I held the line on crimson lipstick. I used her Waldorf work color, a grayish-brownish shade, strategically designed to quell ardor of male guests.

The famous CBS series interview will be televised and streamed worldwide from center stage of the 6,000-seat Radio City Music Hall auditorium. With just press and some Omniconal staff invited for this press release the entrance lobby is as empty as it is vast. So there is no way I can avoid walking past Iz Mocha standing at the inner door. Iz has been undressing women with his x-ray vision for 70 years.

"Hi Harry."

"Lo Iz."

Has he seen myriad scenes in the private lives of performing artists? Iz just says, "When do I get my lines for the end?"

"Day. Or so." Tight-lipped, I'm suddenly conscious how lipstick focuses a viewer's eye on the way a woman's mouth more expressively changes shape when colored. Damned if I'm going to be sexy with the predatory old tiger Iz Mocha.

And here she comes up to us. It's the Daughter of God, Truth. The Rockette Ph.D. but probably in applied engineering studies. Keats was right, truth is beauty and beauty truth. An arm's length away from her I hear Hamlet's very last words in the Folio: oh, oh, oh.

Iz says, "Harry, I think you met my granddaughter Nadine at your Daughters of God rehearsal."

"He said his name was Arch."

"I said Harry first."

She blows cheeks out a little in annoyance, still gorgeous. "Grandaddy, I have to go backstage. Good luck with this . . . donkey dick." Did Nadine the Ph.D. pun on my beard last name she knows as Bottom, a hick who was made into an ass in *Midsummer Night's Dream*? Or do new-woman-type Ph.D.s just talk salty as old sailors? Anyway, she's insensitive. I put a lot of effort into this outfit.

Passing on from Iz I see against the lobby wall a tall silver Art Moderne sculpture so peculiar I go over to read its name. Bulging highly defined in all major muscle groups, it is labeled Eve. I feel better, though not for the sculptor.

And there in the auditorium, far apart from the scrum of reporters, amid a group of better-dressed people who must be from Omniconal HQ, stands Valerie. Scanning the crowd. I need to stay away from her since she scorned my existence at first sight. As Arch Bottom I have been paid $250,000 in advance to write *The Which*. Because Lance in his directorial unstated way gave Valerie to know I really am a moonlighting major playwright. Hiding income from my ex as we do in theater people's haunted forest of exes.

Valerie is here to witness Omniconal's stupendous announcement. But getting trapped among a pack of reporters also following Omniconal's regulatory threat stories would not be cool for the CEO.

And that's why she's also in drag today but as a man. Shakespeare would love us as a couple. Iz is not the only guy in the world who can look through clothes. Under that navy double-breasted blazer is Valerie's impressive bosom I recall well, we are both firm Cs. She does look great in a white shirt and black tie. The British blondishly restated hair tight in a man bun, no makeup or jewelry. But of course this creature is still mean as a snake. So I skitter mouse-style down an empty aisle to the other side of the immense dim hall. Sit coyly angled looking for Lance.

Lights up. The Omniconal interviewee is Clive I didn't catch it. The CBS host Barry Whatsit is I suppose famous if you watch TV. From his suave silver-templed serene baritone he has to be.

They sit facing close in front of a gigantic projection screen looming now like Chekhov's gun. Clive thanks Barry for giving Omniconal the opportunity to first announce the result of its technological breakthrough in world cultural history. A product of the benefit of inductive-deductive modern science that has been improving life from the 16th century to this moment.

This also handsome also silver-templed Clive could do TV talks himself if Valerie were ever to fire him in some spasm of violent ill will. Smoothly he goes on: "And Barry, speaking of the 16th-century and modern information technology, as you know Omniconal's motto "Just Saying" gives modern life a much richer personal content.

"Our Omniconal technology expresses mankind's fundamental curiosity about life possibilities that underlies history's finest achievements. Our thousands of employees include some of the finest engineering intellects in the world. We're not on any side at all in global civilization's amazing complexes. Except that we serve to bring curiosity and spontaneity into everyday life. We—"

SVP at CBS Barry definitely does not do infomercials. Cutting in, "Well good Clive. Our viewers will know the Omniconal story up to now. But let's turn to what you are 'Just Saying' for the first time today."

"Thank you, Barry. We have come here to announce that using its highest algorithmically addressed database science Omniconal has just solved the deepest mystery in literary history. From this moment forward no little child in the world will have to turn to her sixth grade teacher and say, "Excuse me Mrs. Wilson, could the genius plays of Shakespeare really have been written by this pukey little businessman who lived in pukey little Stratford?

"Now the answer will be, 'No, Susy. The little nobody puke did not really write Shakespeare. Thanks to public-spirited Omniconal research the world now knows that Edward de Vere, hereditary 17th Earl of Oxford, Viscount Bolbec and Great Chamberlain of England, was the sadly hidden author of all the works of Shakespeare."

Clive looks toward the audience over the top of non-existent reading glasses. "From there, folks, it's quite a story. Not a word will be changed in texts of Shakespeare's plays and poems. But *everything* is changed in the way the world now can better understand them."

Barry does not do striptease either. "Well Clive, here's the moment. Exactly what is Omniconal 'Just Saying'?"

Clive stands, what a nice navy suit, and extends his arm, gold cufflinks glint, toward the quarter-acre of projection screen behind him and Barry. He's looking into a blue-over-red camera. "Our computers derived, from four centuries of records scanned for interpolation, that the most likely proof of Shakespeare authorship would be found in an indirect document. Such as a boring bureaucratic accounting note. And that even if a researcher had skimmed through such records he she or it without gender or age prejudice whatsoever would likely not have bothered to look on the back of every dreary page of dead number lines year after year."

Clive looks to Barry and then, smiling triumphantly into camera two now blue-lit, this is not his first rodeo, "Antony Johnbeuy was a clerk employee of Queen Elizabeth's Bursary of the Private Purse. We found that Johnbeuy owned, signed, and annotated a published copy of the script of *Romeo and Juliet*. So we knew he was a Shakespeare fan. And so likely would have known the time's gossip about authorship. We then arranged a reading of every document in his office during his seven years of employment in the Queen's Bursary office. We carefully had the back of every page inspected for keyword nexus programming."

Barry is an all-pro team player, you have to be at CBS, "An . . . n . . . n . . . nd . . ."

*

*   *

The big backlit screen lights up. On a red ground the white fancy letters are a foot tall. Clive reads every word Omniconal has found on a humdrum minor ledger's back side of a moldering page. Reading aloud teasingly slowly:

Item of 1,000 pounds pension from the account of Her Majesty—quarterly 250 pounds instalment paid without receipt as directed. Delivered in coin first of June to hand of his Lordship Edward Earl of Oxford. Pursuant to standing order of the Queen in payment to his Lordship for agreed past and continuing services as author of plays. Payment made upon his Lordship's sworn compliance with constant condition that all his Lordship's works shall be ascribed solely to the name William Shakespeare.

All the heads of the journalists are immediately bent down typing like crazy. Everybody else in the crowd is saying to the nearest person some variation of "Golly, this does change *everything*." CBS is streaming the program live internationally so this announcement is big, big news worldwide instantly.

Clive definitely does do Omniconal infomercials. Back to camera one blue: "And now I'd like to bring onstage the Omniconal happy team of moms and dads, of course when parenting is appropriate. These folks led our research effort to 'Just Say' for the world who really was the author of the works of Shakespeare."

The two dozen employees' embarrassed shuffling out onstage takes some minutes. I see Barry's hand go to his earphone. He pulls out a phone and reads. And reads again. Looks frowning toward his director, speaks into the phone. Listens. Listens, frowns big.

And now stands. The mic is open again, his tone that of Edward R. Murrow during the night bombing of London in WWII. "Attention, please. CBS must interrupt this program to duly report that it has just received a threat of litigation from the Folger Shakespeare Library in our nation's capitol. It claims that in violation of the National Anti-Craptalk Act of 2023 CBS has participated in the dissemination of false and misleading . . ." (Barry looks back at 30 lawyerese words on the phone screen) ". . . stuff."

"CBS management in keeping with our tradition of truly fair and balanced reporting in strict compliance with the National Anti-Craptalk Act has asked that we postpone this program. We will now read the text of a document very recently come into possession of the Folger Shakespeare Library and just now supplied to our management and legal counsel. This document also apparently comes from an overlooked accounting entry in the personal expenses of Queen Elizabeth. I read it to you now in our journalistic transparent fairness in entirety as follows:

Item of the Queen's Bursary expenses: 500 pounds delivered to hand of William Shaxper, gent., at his residence in Stratford, Warwickshire. At her Majesty's direction to demonstrate her deep appreciation of said Shaxper's past years of service as author of plays strengthening the literary and social culture of this Sceptered Isle England."

Half of the press group gasp and half laugh. The pack of Omniconal employees trapped on the big stage look into empty Radio City's dark void smiling wanly.

Now is Clive's turn for dramatic resolution. But he too smiles wanly. The Omniconal employees slowly begin to leave the scene of this head-on car crash.

One of those coolly assured young woman reporters stands in the crowd and calls to stage, "Just how can Omni . . ."

But she pauses herself. For another young woman—I recognize this is Valerie's sergeant-at-arms Clarice—has come striding across the stage to Clive. She bends with a message just for his ear. I get it in mine. Valerie surely just told Clive absofuckinglutely do not mention *The Which* now.

I'm distracted from Clarice's slinky walk away by seeing Barry's hand again at his miked ear. Listening a full minute, he forgets his mouthpiece is still open. "Absofuckinglutely not. I have my contract rights. I . . ." Listening. "Oh. Oh. Oh . . ." and the rest same as last words of Hamlet is silence.

Now another woman walks out on the stage and stands beside Barry. No kitten heels, no kitten anything about this one. She places her feet in the tai chi warrior-on-a-horse position and says solemnly to a blue light, "Good afternoon. I am corporate legal counsel to CBS. As we stream this interview it has reached a concerned citizen who is a stakeholder in the subject matter. Under the Trump Act, officially the National Anti-Craptalk Act of 2023, CBS believes it is obligated to comply by offering that stakeholder a fair and balanced expression of his own view. Subject to normal advertising programming time constraint."

This CBS lawyer is holding an iPad gingerly, like a displayed wiggling rat. She now tells the patient world await, "Mr. James James III, well known billionaire founder and CEO of the global sexual bonding and related console game-playing website Straight In, has threatened federal, state, and local legal proceedings if CBS does not now announce the existence of a contradictory Shakespeare authorship proof document which Straight In Holding Tight Company recently purchased in commercial good faith. Accordingly we now read the text of that document in modern English adaptation and place it on our website for public and scholarly access. We hope this cooperation is legally satisfactory to Mr. James as due compliance with the Trump Act.

"Accordingly," she holds up the iPad with a rat displayed on its screen, reading it in monotone,

First of June

Dearest Eddie,

I had a lot of trouble deciding but took your suggestion. Hamlet does talk too much so I just killed him. That cut gets us in at three hours. Now we need to hash it out over Lear. We don't want our plays typecast as serial killing off the hero stuff.

I am thinking maybe we shock the groundlings and go kinky. So try this. In King Lear's ancient time rich and famous people in their lifestyle were even more relaxed about sex than all this swinging stuff that goes on at Elizabeth's Court. So Cordelia, an independent-minded though hormonally driven young woman, decides she has a thing for older men and that includes her Dad. And in our trademark from the comedies we wrap with a sexy sort of marriage scene between her and Lear in bed. Lear rips off his fake beard, it was his disguise all along as a sour old badger to keep Cordelia's hands off him.

Our crowds love removed beards and ogling the sex drive of couples. So we give them both <u>plus</u> some cheerful incest to spice things up. Hardly needs a plot. Think it over.

Anyway, still on for our weekly at the usual. Let's stay discreet. It's your turn to come dressed as a prostitute female edition. I'll bring a bottle of Rhenish with some bits in it that will chime your carillon but good. A toot a l'heure!

God bless the Queen, all of them,
Wiley Willie

The lawyer clicks off the text and silently walks offstage in a posture of defeated puzzlement.

I know the feeling. Now I feel the feeling, for over at the auditorium outside aisle there goes Valerie. Stalking fast in anger toward red-lit exit. In moments all phones within her reach will become shards of abused plastic.

Part Six

So far as I can tell, the world—no, the universe—of Harry Haines is nothing but curves.

Lance was not at Radio City Music Hall. Because he was watching the livestream on a sofa with his friend Lester Laeme and his whatever Miriam V. Sorceress. The V is for Vague.

Lester is back as patron of Trenton Shakespeare Festival. Because Lester with Lance's help is back in the hormonally driven arms of Valerie.

Looking back I suppose Lance kept strategic distance from the Radio City Music Hall announcement of the Oxford discovery. He seems to have picked up an inkling of rival proofs from sensitive director-style observation of the Omniconal spying minions. Maybe from the same "Call Me Bill" spy guy who gave me the transcript dossier after he was fired for failing to spot the fraudsters in time. Call Me Bill seems to have cast himself as an objective correlative in some homemade myth of his being a good soul after all. And too, this being as always and ever a very highly transactional world, perhaps Bill wanted advice from Lance as well as me about his new career as actor not spy.

And thus I can guess Miriam picked up Lance's troubled doubt in pillow talk. And so came her kindly meant but congenitally eccentric warning to me as very vulnerable author of the very vulnerable *The Which of Shakespeare's Why*. But a gutted dead little fish? Actresses famously typically are not good clear writers. But I see now, late as usual for me, that Miriam indeed was specially graceful in the way a fine actress can be. A kind gesture to just a colleague she felt sorry for. With striking theatrical flourish worthy of you know whoever he was.

Soon as Radio City Music Hall collapsed in laughter at the diabolically sardonic now quite rich fraudsters' triple mockeries of Shakespeare authorship passions, Lance was on the phone. He learned of the billionaire Folger board leader's personal lavish funding of a major new theater construction on expanded grounds there. And being the instinctively creative director that he is, Lance heard enough to see a new resolution to the financial quandary of TSF.

Within days they were linked arm-in-arm as Three Musketeers. Being the impulsive Folger patron, Lester the impulsive TSF patron, and between them strategically cool Lance Gulliver. So TSF magically became the new Folger Theater's new resident troupe. Easy for me to imagine the scene of Lance's intermediation. Near wordless, wreathed in wry smiles, his light touch on impulsive shoulders like knighting a medieval grail search. The Prospero touch, a Shakespearean of any persuasion could call it.

Obviously for Valerie's renewed financial support, this apotheosis of the newborn foundling TSF as foster parented by the eminent Folger institution is preferable. It is noncontroversial high prestige. The Folger for a century has embodied Stratfordian orthodoxy. She and Omniconal will be wrapped within its magisterial cultural dignity. Thus simply avoiding the pugnacious The Which of Shakespeare's Why's predictably hostile reception by Stratfordian fierce highly invested grandees. Lance was a maestro to halt the curtain on The Which before it rose to trouble.

There was only one little curve in this cordial way forward. The Folger wants a famous Shakespearean actor for its first Hamlet. And too Valerie when consulted does not want Harry T. R. (the T is short for T-shirt) Haines. Her exact words that oversharing

Marjorie overheard were "Lancey, get me abs like Lester's, not flabs like that slob." So the Musketeers swerved around Harry T. R. Haines (the R. stands for Roadkill) on their way to a quick tent debut of *Hamlet*. And so too Trenton, sad little city but indeed sitting high atop a granite montane ridge, will have to wait for that hurricane that moves submerged Manhattan's wealth and culture just a bit westward to land far enough above new sea level.

Then like important stuff that happened offstage in Shakespeare, I soon found Lance had after all thoughtfully looked after me as a friend. Perhaps there was more pillow talk with his lady friend who flies with the fairies and cared to warn me however oddly.

In this buoyant atmosphere of billionaires at play with their new ego project, Lance sent to Valerie's personal accountant the final bill due to the famous playwright bearded as Arch Bottom. Being $250,000 cash in a suitcase. Nobody in Queen Valerie's accounting staff batted an eye. Arch Bottom's necessarily secret-from-his ex-wife contract was not written anyway. But it was supposed to be for $250,000 in total, which I had already received up front. Lance simply and glibly smoked through a billing for "the other half" of $500,000. A phrase surely used at the Mermaid Tavern too but for beer. Valerie's bean counter shrugged. Billionaires will be billionaires.

I do suspect Lance and Miriam also had a thoughtful glass of wine in regard to my own realistically poor chance ever to become a successful Shakespearean actor. Anyhow Lance soon took me in to see old Iz Mocha in his theatrical agency office. After sad eyes to his confidante the blank wall, Iz recommended I start another track to success. With advance request from Lance he had reached out through his many contacts in the English-speaking world's acting farm leagues.

"You sing?"

"I was in a church choir. Not molested."

"Gimme the Beatle's 'Yesterday.'"

Some curves turn toward you instead of away. This is one of my best shower songs. Iz actually nodded his head a little in time, or maybe it was time nodding him a little.

Lance, "America's got talent, Iz!"

Iz: "Yeah well by Aussie standards. They'll like the accent compared to the mess they make of opening their own mouths to talk. Harry you ever been to Australia?"

"No."

"You'll love it for the babe-a-rama. Lots of hardbody athletes who like a drink and a laugh. I got you a principal gig in *Kiss Me, Kate*. Dinner theater company traveling city to city or whatever their population centers are actually."

"Great. I need something new. Do I go and try out?"

"Nah. I spoke to them from the world center of talent. You got the gig unless you lose it. Pay's crap but Lance tells me you just made 15 years' salary in two months."

"Thank you, Iz. Very much."

"Glad to help. Friend of the arts. And you pay me $10,000 before you leave the country."

"Oh, yes." I look to Lance watching. He does like me, I just wasn't right for his casting. That's show business. Lance smiling now without word to the kid going nowhere suddenly going forward into some unexpected athletic babe-a-rama new world.

*
*   *

That's about it all from Australia.

I have to hurry now, Laurette will be back from changing out of her sandy volleyball bikini into cheerful braless T-shirt. I don't have time to describe her. But will note that notable breasts are no longer necessary for me.

I'm cast as a secondary love interest to Laurette in *Kiss Me, Kate*. We do some duets. Nobody cares if I sleep with my fellow cast member. I, indeed, do.

Lately Laurette and I have been talking this and that what-ifs over her beer of choice, Lucky Bay. They do do Shakespeare here, particularly in Sydney. Which is our next spot. Before leaving New York I filed copyright on *The Which of Shakespeare's Why*. I alone wrote it and never signed a thing. Anyway, Valerie will want nothing to do with its controversy.

I have half a million bucks in the bank and Australia has plenty of actors who can play Shakespeare from experience. But here comes the tousled tanned barefoot damsel. Before *Kiss Me, Kate*, she was an understudy in a Canberra production of *Merchant of Venice*. This was my pickup line meeting her at an actor's afterparty beers in hand.

She had just mentioned her role in *The Merchant*. I ask, "What does the name Shylock mean to you?"

Blonde long bangs over goddessy green eyes. "Right bugger."

"There's more you should know. The guy who actually wrote the play borrowed a lot of money he could not pay back to bet on a commercial voyage. Just like in the play setup. In real life it was basically a fraud organized by a confidence man named William Lock. And in 16th-century London the slang name for a shady businessman was 'shy.' So the author of *Merchant* came up with the right bugger character called Shylock in code that the London in-crowd knew from his own true story."

Laurette rarely just smiles, she grins, and a room's dark corners lighten. "Gid *out!*"

"You can be one of the few to know more, Laurette. The fraud's caper was to get money from investors including this author for the cost of an exploratory voyage to China via a nonexistent Northwest Passage. After a promotor's song and dance about ship problems, Lock got the same investors to fund a *second* try. The author who borrowed his big investments while already bankrupt wound up *doubly* ruined.

"You were a high school Ophelia I'm going to guess. So you know this. In *Hamlet*, which is written by the same hidden author as *Merchant*, Hamlet taunts Polonius, who thinks he's plain nuts. In clever code that Elizabethan insiders knew about the real author, Hamlet tells Polonius he's 'only mad north by northwest.'

"That ruined author was not named William Shakespeare, which was just his beard name. The author of all Shakespeare was Edward de Vere, the 17th Earl of Oxford. Okay?"

Laurette does not need to speak with those eyes. But generously purrs, "Perfect."

And here I go. You know where this heads next. I will be like my hero Lance Gulliver, somehow finding myself here become pretty big in a new upside-down land. I will stage and direct *The Which of Shakespeare's Why* in Australia.

On my own dime, unless I can find another impulsive plutocrat. Come what may then from global streaming and screaming.

There is this problem, though, I must consider:

Australian accent sounds for "Shakespeare" exactly to be "Shaxper."

Harry T. R. Haines

And so. Harry and all those guys did not find the true scrap of 400-year-old paper proving their man Oxford wrote the works of Shakespeare. But Omniconal using its programmed very deductive search could have been a bit more inductive.

Reading just one document more. Here it is:

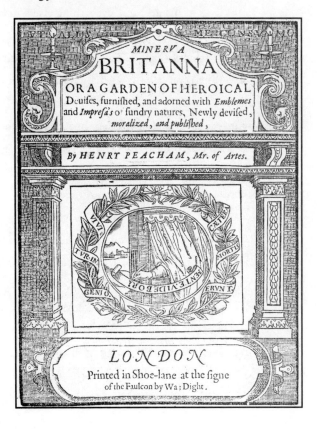

This is the cover of the "emblem book" published in 1612 by Henry Peacham. Peacham's father of same name annotated a summary of the Shakespeare canon's *Titus Andronicus* he saw played in 1574 at a palace of Lord Burghley. The Peacham family were local parson gentry and so would have known who was the author was of the anonymous play. That surely could not have been Shaxper, who was 10 years of age in 1574.

Emblem books were then a new Continental fashion of cryptic cartoons and drawings, challenging the reader's understanding of what is said. This title page drawing shows a hidden hand writing from behind a stage curtain. The two framing ribbons of Latin translate as "he [still] lives in his art" and "everything else will be of death."

The hand is writing the phrase "mente videbor," translating as "I will be appreciated in the mind." But the hand is adding another letter "i" at the end of videbor. No such word exists in Latin. Some Oxfordians see an anagram, typical of emblem book style. And that anagram of letters they unscramble to say precisely "tibi nom de Vere." Translation: "the concealed writer's name is de Vere."

The obvious sense of this emblem is as a memorial. In 1612 Shaxper was alive and well, Oxford was dead for eight years.

In 1622 this artist and writer Peacham the younger also published an exhaustive list of English poets, *The Compleat English Gentleman*. Ranked first at top of a long list is Edward, Earl of Oxford. Furthermore, the name William Shakespeare or William Shaxper appears *nowhere* in the book. This is in 1622, the year before publication of the First Folio bearing the name William Shakespeare on its cover, forwarded by Ben Jonson's carefully ambiguous near-but not-quite identification of the author as the then dead Stratford man. That First Folio coyly put on its cover a supposed portrait never seen before. There was no previous portrait.

No change of this listing (and the crucial exclusion of both "Shakespeare" and Shaxper) was made by Peacham in the *Compleat English Gentleman* editions of 1627 and 1634. In them Oxford remains top poet of England. And still despite the First Folio packaging no mention is made at all of William Shakespeare or Shaxper.

There we have it. Simple in real time among real people. In real truth the Peachams knew that Oxford's pseudonym was William Shakespeare. And out of respect for Oxford's magnificent achievement just did not play along with the Crown's political posturing using the beard Shaxper of Stratford. Peacham's 1612 emblem book puzzle cover is talking to you.

Harry must have missed the Peachams' story in his crash course reading in the Tower of Waldorf.

And this just in: futuristic Valerie overlooked programming Omniconal to read that dead language Latin.

To luminance,

Leigh Light

SOURCES

Anderson, Margo. *Shakespeare by Another Name*. Gotham Books, 2005.

Beauclerk, Charles. *Shakespeare's Lost Kingdom*. Grove Press, 2010.

Greenblatt, Stephen. *Will in the World*. Norton, 2010.

Looney, J. Thomas. *Shakespeare Identified*. Veritas Press (centenary edition), 2019.

Nelson, Alan H. *Monstrous Adversary: The Life of Edward de Vere, 17th Earl of Oxford*. Liverpool University Press, 2003.

Price, Diana. *Shakespeare's Unorthodox Biography*. Greenwood Press, 2001.

Rosenbaum, Ron. *The Shakespeare Wars: Clashing Scholars, Public Fiascos, Palace Coups*. Random House, 2008.

Shapiro, James S. *Contested Will: Who Wrote Shakespeare?* Simon and Schuster, 2016.

_____. *A Year in the Life of Shakespeare: 1599*. Harper Collins, 2009.

_____. *The Year of Lear: Shakespeare in 1606*. Simon and Schuster, 2015.

Winkler, Elizabeth. *Shakespeare Was a Woman and Other Heresies: How Doubting the Bard Became the Biggest Taboo In Literature*. Simon and Schuster, 2023.

Castle Hedingham in Essex, England, seat of the earls of Oxford for four centuries when the 11th Earl, here ascribed as author of The Tragedy of King Lear, *gave it to his three grown daughters in a misunderstanding, and thus rendered himself without a suitable residence or income.* Photo by Hoberman Collection, Getty Images.

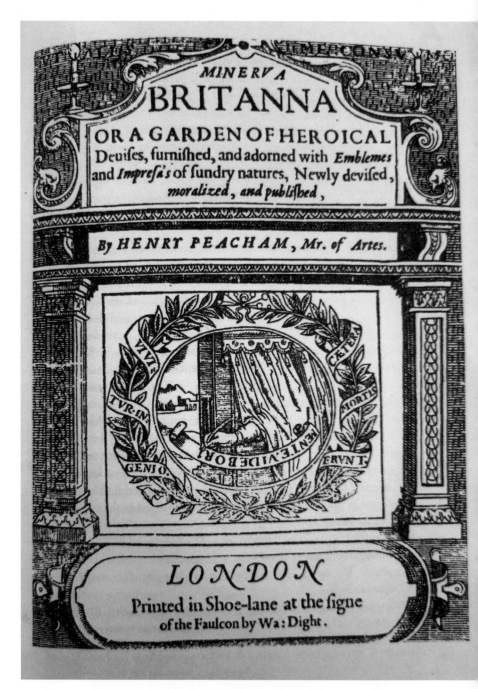

This smoking gun upside-down inscription indicated a hidden
meaning: a Latin anagram reading TIBI NOM. DE VERE or
"The Identity of this Author is De Vere"—Edward de Vere, 17th Earl
of Oxford. Published in 1612 by Henry Peacham, who would have
known that Oxford and "Shakespeare" were the same.